Who Killed Henry Smith?

by

Rose Good

January, 2010

Who Killed Henry Smith?

For information address: mickiedaltonbooks@lycos.com

First Published in 2012 in Australia

ISBN: 978-0987-1675-3-8

Published by The Mickie Dalton Foundation
Kempsey, NSW
Australia

www.mickiedaltonfoundation.com

Acknowledgements

This book would not have been possible without the support and encouragement of my husband, Ray.

Special thanks to Michael Davies who inspired me to write the novel and gave freely of his time and knowledge.

I love you both.

The Author extends her sincere thanks to the wonderful artist, Maureen Hales who painted the portrait, "Katrina" which features on the cover. As soon as I saw the portrait, I realised how perfectly it fitted my description of "Ruby Red."

Maureen's other works can be seen on her website at
www.maureenhales.com

Dedication

This book and all the hours I put into writing and developing it are dedicated to the Red Cross and all the wonderful people who maintain that invaluable organisation

Chapter 1

Matthew Hudson watched the sombre burial party from a few metres away. The faces around him reflected the usual variety of expressions: stoic calm, sadness, barely concealed grief, some openly weeping. Most of them huddled together in some attempt to find warmth on this chilly day.

One mourner stood out from the crowd. Though close to the group, she seemed remote, distant from the rest. She was quite beautiful, thought Hudson. Tall, blonde, her classic face was only partially hidden by the wide-brimmed hat she wore. Under the open light coat she had on a powder-blue silk blouse, clipped with a cameo brooch in the middle of the lace collar. Her suit was classic black and she carried a patent leather clutch purse that matched her shoes. She wore little make-up, but her ruby-red lips and nail polish provided a sharp contrast with the sombre colours everywhere else. Hudson's childhood with fashion-designer parents had given him an expert eye and he could see seriously fashionable good taste in this beautiful woman.

He dragged his eyes away from the woman that he had in his mind named 'Ruby Red' and returned to his study of the group. The service was coming to its end as the coffin was lowered amidst sobs from some of the mourners. A procession glided past the grave, each person dropping rose petals from a nearby basket as they said their farewells to Henry Smith, devoted husband, loving father, colleague and friend to so many.

Hudson went on high alert as 'Ruby Red' moved toward the open grave, opening her purse as she walked.

Was she reaching for a tissue? he wondered. He could see no signs of tears, nor of any expression in that flawless face to indicate them.

She took something from the purse. It was a small black object, perhaps a velvet pouch of the type jewellers used. She dropped the pouch into the open grave.

Hudson knew it was not unusual for people to send off the deceased with a memento of a favourite item, but it was not curiosity he felt. He was angry. That package might be critical. *Who the hell was this woman? A family member? A close friend? Henry Smith's mistress?* None of the other mourners had paid her the slightest attention beyond a few looks of masculine interest, much like Hudson's own. And none of them had reacted to the slight thud of the article as it landed on the coffin.

Hudson contemplated for a moment exerting his authority and having the grave diggers hold off on filling in the grave while he retrieved the item, but decided that would cause far more distress and attention than he could afford.

He followed her with his eyes until she disappeared from sight.

As the crowd dispersed, Detective Inspector Matthew Hudson walked to his car and drove back to the station, puzzled and slightly frustrated by the afternoon's events. Henry Smith had finally been laid to rest, but Hudson wasn't easy about the whole thing.

Who the hell was that astonishing woman?

Chapter 2

What could possibly be the motive?

Detective Inspector Matthew Hudson from the New South Wales Police State Crime Command was perusing Henry Smith's 'Missing Persons' file. It was now in the domain of the Homicide Squad.

"Henry Smith had been a well respected senior officer with the Department of Immigration and Citizenship," Hudson read aloud. As he turned the page a newspaper article caught his eye:

September 16, 2011
'IMMIGRATION HEAD DEMANDS DETENTION OVERHAUL'

A Senior Government official with the Department of Immigration and Citizenship has called for a review of detention centres.

"There is an urgent need to overhaul the government's handling of applications for asylum seekers," says Mr Henry Smith, Head of the Refugee and Humanitarian Division.

Mr Smith showed compassion towards refugees and asylum seekers and was working on bridging visas which would allow refugees to live in the community whilst their applications were being processed.

"These people are not criminals. They are people who have suffered grief and are seeking safety."

Mr Smith was outspoken in claiming that the Immigration Detention system was a mess. "The only thing the government is doing is wanting to build more detention centres and keep these people locked up for years. "This is not the answer," he said. "There are almost 7000 people in these centres." Mr Smith felt it was a waste of skills and resources to keep these people in prison. "They could contribute greatly to the Australian community," stated Mr Smith.

Well respected and controversial, thought Hudson. He noticed that the article was published a week prior to Henry Smith's disappearance.

The following week, there had been a follow up story on Henry Smith as a *'missing person.'*

Hudson looked up from the file.

Even the bald, journalistic reporting had not hidden the passionate love story that Henry Smith and socialite, Ruth Kurt-Austin Smith had shared.

"Probably married him to spite her parents at first," he muttered to himself. "It became perfect after that. Good on them both. So who the hell buggered it up by killing him?"

Hudson's phone buzzed, announcing that Maya Smith had arrived. Hudson had invited Henry's wife to view the police surveillance tapes. She had declined. Her daughter, Maya, had agreed to attend.

Hudson stepped into the foyer. Her dark eyes greeted him.

"Miss Smith. I'm Detective Inspector Hudson."

Her handshake was firm and strong.

"Please call me Maya."

Definitely the outdoor type, thought Hudson.

She was dressed in a white polo shirt, black slacks and runners, her skin flawless and tanned.

"Thank you for coming in, Maya."

He led the way to the interview room. As he opened the door, the aroma of her perfume wafted onto his senses. It took him back to happy times. Although he was too young to remember why it made him happy... being fondled and cuddled by a variety of extremely beautiful models.

"May I firstly offer my condolences, Maya."

"Thank you."

"Would you like some tea or coffee?"

"No. Thank you."

"As I mentioned on the phone, we taped your father's funeral." Hudson paused before adding. "I'd like you to identify as many people as you can."

She leaned forward, her long shiny black hair draping over the side of her face and sighed.

Hudson powered up the equipment and loaded the tape.

"I know how difficult this must be. Please take your time."

Hudson pressed the remote control and sat down with a notepad. He could detect the tension in her voice as she pointed out family, friends and some of her father's colleagues. Hudson scribbled in his pad. There were a few people she did not know. He froze the frame on 'Ruby Red.'

"Do you know this woman?"

"No, I don't," responded Maya quickly.

Hudson noticed a slight shudder.

Maya reached for her bottled water which she had retrieved from her bag and took a swig.

"Take your time."

"I don't know the woman," she repeated. "Did she attend with anyone?"

"She arrived alone," said Hudson. "And left shortly after the service."

There seemed to be nothing further to be learnt about the mysterious woman and Hudson resumed the tape.

After cross-referencing signatures from the funeral attendance book with the people that Maya had identified, Hudson finally had an extensive list of names. Apart from his interest in the mystery woman, Hudson also noticed that Mike Adams from the Coroner's office had attended the funeral.

"I'm sorry to have put you through this Maya, but we need to move fast."

"I understand." She took another mouthful of water. "Will you keep me informed of any developments?" she asked.

"Certainly." replied Hudson. "If you think of anything else, please feel free to ring me."

He stood up and handed Maya his card. He walked her to the foyer and this time her handshake was softer and gentler.

"Thank you for the information."

Hudson was guided back to the Interview room by a trail of perfume. *I will definitely have to get out more often.*

Chapter 3

It was mid morning by the time Maya parked her Mercedes sports coupe in the reserved parking spot. She leaned her head against the steering wheel, sighed deeply and thought of driving straight back out. After a few minutes, she finally composed herself. She glanced in the rear view mirror, glossed her lips and got out of the car.

She took the lift to the fifteenth floor and braced herself for the backlog of deadlines. *That's advertising,* she thought to herself. Maya was greeted by colleagues with words of sympathy and she acknowledged them with a grateful smile. Cards and flowers appeared on her desk.

The two partners of ZenKazZoo Advertising knocked and came in carrying yellow roses.

Buzz Kazi came up to Maya and held her tight.

"Thank you, Buzz," she said, reaching for a tissue.

Zenon placed the flowers into her arms and gave her a hug. "I'm so sorry, love."

"Thank you. Both of you."

The door opened soundlessly and the Administrative Assistant entered, placing three cappuccinos and raspberry muffins on the coffee table. She took the roses from Maya and, just as soundlessly left the room.

Kazi, known as 'Buzz' spoke first. "We didn't expect you in yet."

"I only came in today to pick up anything urgent."

"It's all under control," said Zenon.

"I'll be back on Monday."

"Are you sure, Maya?"

"Yes, I'm sure."

"Please give us a ring if you need to talk. We're here for you."

"Thank you. Thank you, both of you."

The partners left, just as the phone rang.

"It's Mr Adams from the Coroner's office for you," announced the Administrative Assistant. "Do you want to ......?"

"Put Mr Adams through, please." She heard the small click as the call was transferred.

"Hello Mike."

"Hello Maya. I've tried to ring your apartment."

"I've moved in with mum for a while."

"May I offer my condolences, Maya."

"Thank you, Mike. I appreciate that."

"If there's anything I can do?"

An awkward silence ensued.

"I'm sorry your promotion came at such an inopportune time, Maya, but congratulations anyway!"

"I appreciate ....."

"I've also heard on the grapevine that you've just trekked Nepal."

"Are you keeping tabs on me, Mike?" asked Maya.

"You've certainly done exceptionally well, since we ......"

"You haven't changed Mike," she interrupted. "Straight to the point, as always."

The only sound was the gentle humming of the air-conditioner as it went about its work, oblivious to any emotional trauma.

Maya broke the silence. "Seriously, Mike, I would like to thank you for the way you handled my father's identification process."

"I realise how traumatic it must have been for you and your mother."

"It was, and I'm most grateful."

"I'll help in anyway I can, Maya. You know that."

After another awkward silence, Maya said goodbye and hung up.

At the other end of the line at the Coroner's Office, Mike Adams let out a deep breath. His hand stayed gripped to the phone.

She still had that effect on him.

Chapter 4

Matthew Hudson had a sense of shadows appearing and disappearing into the darkness.

"Five minutes to midnight," he said to the silent shape on the lounge. "So, Tyson, my loyal furry friend, we come to the end of a very eventful day."

Tyson responded with a giant yawn.

"You've had a heavy day, too. Wait till I tell you about mine. Here, have a bowl of water. I'm going to indulge in my nightly glass of bourbon and it's not good for a man to drink alone. While you're having your drink, I want you to pretend you're 'Inspector Rex' and help me crack two very perplexing cases."

Tyson grunted while slurping up the cold water.

"I need some help, Tyson, and I'd like to run this past you."

Tyson gave Hudson a puzzled look then returned to slurping.

"One case is the mysterious death of Henry Smith. It's been puzzling me all day. Somewhere in the back of my mind there's a shadow moving about, trying to tell me something. I hear its whisper, but I can't quite make out what it's saying. Is it Henry Smith's ghost reaching out to me from beyond the grave, trying to help me find his killer, Inspector Tyson?"

Glad to be included in the conversation, Tyson jumped up and licked Hudson at the sound of his name.

"Our other pressing matter .... wait," Hudson interrupted himself. "Let's see if we have any chicken liverwurst in the fridge."

Two sandwiches later, Hudson continued. "If there were more dogs like you, there would be no cold cases left."

Tyson knew he was a good boy. Rewards didn't come too often after midnight. This was definitely a special moment.

"I wish I'd trained you to be a sniffer dog, Tyson. Then you could have helped with the other case I'm working on with Detective Inspector James Kerr from the Drug Squad." Tyson responded by wagging his tail at the mention of his name. There could be another reward coming. "It's a huge drug trafficking case involving cocaine importation. I got involved in this case after one of the dealers was found murdered."

He took a sip of his bourbon. "How's that nose of yours, Tyson?"

He rubbed the top of Tyson's nose. Tyson could smell the liverwurst on Hudson's hand and headed for the fridge, hoping to get lucky for a second time.

"There's nothing wrong with that snout, I see," said Hudson with a laugh. "Now, I've been on this case for over eighteen months. We're after the ring leader of this operation and we have our suspect, but no proof. We've arrested a few minnows in the case, but the big marlin at the top of the food chain keeps eluding us.

"Some of the other officers on the case call him 'the big marlin' or 'Mr Big' because of his place at the top of the feeding pyramid, but to me, Tyson, all drug peddlers are bottom feeders in the slimy ooze of the underworld."

Tyson jumped up on the lounge, placed two paws on Hudson's lap with his eyes permanently fixed on his face.

"None of them matches a noble creature, such as a dog," said Hudson, stroking Tyson's ears.

The German shepherd grunted with contentment.

"I see the head of this drug syndicate more as a slug or a snail, but I hope I'm not offending molluscs by the comparison. If you ask me, it's a pity the Department frowns on files with names like 'scumbag' and 'sewer rat' that more truly reflect the people they describe.

"But, Inspector Tyson, I did have one little triumph. Inspector Kerr and I have agreed that *'Operation Snail Trail'* would be an appropriate name for this case. I hope I can get the media to take up this theme when we snare him – and snare him we will. No more 'Mr Big' or the 'mastermind.' Those names almost make him seem human. But he is a master criminal and he keeps slipping from our grasp – so far!

"Well, that's the end of my briefing and the end of my bourbon. Thanks for your input."

Hudson patted the dog's head, and they headed outside for their nightly ritual.

Tyson searched the small yard for just the appropriate blade of grass. A full moon glistened and a slight breeze rustled the leaves of nearby trees and flowers.

Was it the stillness of the night or the scent of the spring flowers that made Hudson's heartbeat quicken? But in that split second, a thought emerged from those dark shadows in his mind.

It struck Matthew Hudson like a bolt of lightning.

* * *

Hudson couldn't wait to get into the office the following morning. It was still dark when he arrived. Hudson raced across the wet floor.

The cleaners, mops in hand, stared mournfully at him.

"Where's the fire, Sir?" asked Constable Ward as he coded Hudson into the security section.

Hudson didn't answer and raced past the night-duty officer into the interview room, lunged at the video machine and pressed 'play.'

He could have kicked himself.

Maya Smith had pointed out one of the mourners on the police surveillance tape and because he had been so preoccupied with 'Ruby Red,' he almost missed what could be a vital clue in this case.

Hudson froze the frame. He could feel the hairs at the back of his neck rise. The dark shadow had appeared.

Could this be a link to Henry Smith's murder?

Hudson didn't believe in coincidences. But, yes. There he was. 'The snail' himself.

Just then, Detective Senior Constable Jill Morellix barged in.

"I knew you were in, but couldn't find ya," she said. "That sheila, Maya Smith, rang yesterday after you left."

You can't take the 'Westie' out of that girl, thought Hudson.

Jill threw yet another coffee stained file onto the desk.

"I'm glad you've got time to watch video games, whilst the rest of us grind away," she spat through gum-chewing lips. "Would ya like a cuppa?"

Hudson recalled the first time he met Jill Morellix, his new partner. Her hair was pulled back in a severe pony tail, no makeup. She wore regulation shoes, where most of the female detectives opted for the stylish, softer version of the Department's occupational health and safety pattern.

When she shook his hand, she loudly mouthed "G'day," in what Hudson considered to be an accent straight out of the western suburbs of Sydney. Her knowledge and experience had not been through any academic achievements, but through the *'university of life'* as she often made it known.

Oh, shudder. A partnership made in hell! thought Hudson at the time.

"Bugger the coffee. Come and have a look at this, Jill," he said, ignoring the sarcastic remarks she was so well known for. "Take a look at who attended Henry Smith's funeral. Is that a co-incidence, or what?"

Jill sat down next to Hudson, crossed her legs and leaned towards him.

"It's Colin Jackson!" she screeched into his ear. "He's the fella you're investigating at Narcotics. What on earth is he doing at the funeral?"

"I've no idea."

Jill whistled. "That is too much of a coincidence."

"Keep this to yourself, for the time being, Jill. Colin Jackson is the son of one of the leading barristers in Sydney."

"How did Narcotics get onto Colin Jackson in the first place?" asked Jill.

"His name first came to our attention about twelve months ago when two arrests were made in the Eastern Suburbs for cocaine possession."

"The land of the prominent and wealthy."

"Exactly," said Hudson with a smile. "One of the dealers was employed at the Happi Frog nursery in Dural, owned by Colin Jackson. Both dealers were represented in court by Richard Jackson, SC. They each received a fine. One of the men was found shot a few days later. The other man disappeared interstate before police could question him."

"Why would a top barrister be interested in representing such low grade scum?"

"Indeed. That's when we got interested. From the reports I've read, the drug squad decided to stake out the nursery. Surveillance of Jackson showed that he regularly went overseas to South America. His company imported large quantities of garden ornaments and accessories which he distributed around the State. A drug task force was formed involving the Australian Federal Police, Customs and Border Protection Services and the NSW Police State Crime Command's Drug Force.

"Customs would contact Detective Kerr when a shipment arrived destined for the Happi Frog nursery, and the drug squad would be sent in to investigate. But, as you know, there are enormous gaps in security at the waterfront. Shipping containers move around the Sydney ports without any scrutiny. The investigation of several shipments came up zero."

"There've been a few big busts lately, though," said Jill. She took another swig of cold coffee and put the mug onto a file.

Hudson lifted the mug, extracted the file from beneath it and placed the mug on the table.

"Mainly cocaine," Jill continued. "The 'caviar' of street drugs. They're smuggling it in any way they can. Inside tins and packages of food and other imported goods. Remember the cocaine concealed in stone pavers?"

"Eighty-four million dollars worth," corroborated Hudson. "It *was* one of the largest busts ever!"

"Damn right," said Jill.

"Anyway, to finish my story," continued Hudson. "The drug team had a gut feeling that everything wasn't quite above board at the nursery, but gut feelings don't hold up in court, and Jackson continues to elude them. At times when the shipment was held up, Senior Counsel Daddy would step in with a heap of legal jargon and threats, and send the team back to the drawing board."

"Have they gone through his books and accounts?"

"We can't get into the nursery without a warrant," replied Hudson. "But we do know that his assets include an apartment block in North Sydney overlooking the Harbour, plus shares in a horse stud in the Hunter Valley which boasts some outstanding race horses. These assets appear to be out of proportion to the income expected in a nursery. We do, however, have shipping documents from the Customs Department giving a detailed description of his imports."

"I wouldn't mind having a look at those," said Jill.

Hudson's phone buzzed before he could answer.

Jill picked up the handset, listened briefly and extended the phone towards Hudson. "It's that Smith bird again."

"Hold on a moment please, Maya," said Hudson into the mouthpiece.

He handed the file to Jill with a wave-like motion. But Jill didn't take the hint to go out. She took the file from Hudson, sat down and started to read.

Hudson sighed to himself and turned his attention back to the phone. "Yes, Maya, good morning."

"Detective Inspector Hudson, I have some information for you," said Maya without any standard courtesies.

"Yes?" Hudson couldn't believe his luck. "I'd rather not talk over the phone," he said. "Could we meet?"

"I'm tied up all day," she said. "However, I could meet you after work."

"You pick the time and place and I'll meet you there."

"How about Tattersall's in the city?"

"Sounds good to me. Around seven?"

"Around seven," echoed Maya and hung up.

Hudson replaced his phone, feeling smug.

"Date for tonight?" said Jill, stroking and twisting her ponytail.

"No! Miss Smith has some information for me," said Hudson, watching the byplay with interest. "And I didn't want to miss another opportunity to perhaps question her about Jackson."

"Do you need a chaperone? I could take notes."

"When I need a chaperone, young lady, I'll have been dead for two months."

But it was too late. Jill had left, slamming the door behind her.

Chapter 5

Perhaps I should revert to my maiden name before the story gets out!

Ruth Smith poured herself a cup of tea and sat down in her favourite chair overlooking the garden. It was early spring and still quite chilly in the exclusive harbourside suburb of Vaucluse, east of Sydney. However, the flowers had started to bloom, as if to pay their last respects to the man who had so lovingly tended their garden. A tidal wave of sweet smelling jasmine cascaded over the bamboo fence entwined in drooping clusters of pale violet and blue-purple wisteria. The stunning goblet-shaped magnolia tree was in full flower, sharing the garden with the exotic bromeliads, bird of paradise and daffodils. How her beloved Henry loved to walk amongst the banksia trees in the backyard, their branches spreading upwards, topped with spectacular red, orange and yellow flowers.

As Ruth gazed out at the garden it felt strangely empty. The garden had suddenly lost its beauty.

This is a bad omen, she thought.

All those dark secrets that had plagued her family would now be played out in the public arena. There would be no rest for Henry Smith, even in death.

She heard the doorbell ring through a haze of confusion and tears. Ruth did not want to answer the door. She wanted to be alone with her grief. But something made her stand up, more of an automatic response, and make her way up the corridor to the front door.

She peered through the peephole and it took a few seconds to focus through her reddened, tear-stained eyes at her best friend, Sarah. Ruth flung open the door and fell into Sarah's arms. They sobbed, deeply and unashamedly, together. They held each other close as huge waves of emotion washed over them.

Ruth pulled back, took Sarah's hand and led her to the lounge room.

"My God, who would want to harm Henry?" said Sarah. "Everyone loved him."

Ruth burst into tears again.

Two hours and numerous cups of tea later, Ruth had finally settled, like the calm following a tumultuous storm. She reached for a framed photograph on the mantelpiece.

"Remember this?" she asked. "You, me and Henry."

"Oh, yes," replied Sarah. "The Multicultural Festival in Sydney. What year was that?"

"It was 1976."

Ruth recalled the first time she met Henry.

* * *

"Damn, Sarah, it's cold!" Ruth was dressed to party in a light skirt and blouse, killer heels and her hair loose round her shoulders.

"Honey, twenty minutes into seeing all those gorgeous men ogle you in that outfit and you won't feel the cold," retorted Sarah, dressed equally lightly in a silk dress that reflected the lights and colours of the Multicultural Festival in the Rocks.

"Well, I didn't spend a week's pay on this production not to be ogled, so I hope you're right!"

"Hey, look *Balalaikas*!" Sarah pointed out the two young men sitting on high stools playing the traditional Russian instruments.

"Now that's sexy!" Ruth said. She giggled. "Will they start that wild Russian dancing, do you think?"

"No time to wait and see," said Sarah. "Too many men, not enough time! Let's just parade around a bit, see what we can see!"

The cold was soon forgotten in the brightness, the colour and the music of many different countries as the two young women strolled along taking in the extraordinary richness and diversity of the art, the food and the culture.

They both stopped at the German stand, entranced by the festive *'Oktoberfest'* where several tables were parked, with a good crowd of people dividing their attention equally between the beer in enormous steins, and the three well-endowed young *Fräuleins* behind the bar, all seemingly made from the same mould of statuesque splendour, with long legs and astonishing chests. One of them was occupied demonstrating the art of beer-pulling to a tall, tanned young man with dark hair who was making a terrible fist of it because of the distracting neckline of his teacher.

"Oh, my God, he's simply gorgeous!" exclaimed Sarah. "I think I'm in love."

"You take your turn, Sarah, that one's mine!"

"Well, I suppose you always did go for the dark, rugged, piratical type," said Sarah. "Let's just see, eh?"

Noticing the two girls' faces turned to him, the young man grinned cheerfully and advanced on them, carrying two glasses of his attempted beer-pulling.

"Can I offer you two ladies a glass of .... er ..." He looked down at his glasses. "Foam?"

The girls were prevented from answering by the advance of the impressively under-dressed *Fräulein* carrying three steins of beer which she plonked down on the table, and removed the foam-filled glasses from him. "You may be an efficient public servant, Henry," she said, "but a barman you are NOT!"

He chuckled and gestured at the seats and the beers. "I think these are for us. Will you join me?"

Charmed by the man's good looks and easy, comfortable manner, Sarah and Ruth smiled and took their seats.

"I'm Ruth."

"And I'm Sarah. And we know you're Henry."

He grinned. "Horrible name, isn't it? Henry Smith, just about as boring as it gets."

"But you're not boring," responded Ruth. "Even if you are a public servant as *Fräulein* Booby said."

The attraction between them was obvious, and Henry's smile at her was warm.

"Immigration and Multicultural Affairs," he said. "How about you?"

"I've just applied for a position with the Family Court as a social worker."

"A very worthy occupation." He turned to Sarah. "And you?"

"I've just finished University. Don't know what I want to do, yet."

"Ladies, to your health and your future!" He picked up the heavy beer stein and took a long, deep pull at it. Sarah and Ruth did the same and exchanged secret smiles with each other as they returned their steins to the table.

Sarah needed no hint. After another long draught of beer, she stood up. "This foxy lady has a hot date with a Corvette-driving, champagne swilling, empty-headed young stud this evening, so I'll be off to get ready. You two have fun! Henry, I know I'll see you again before long!" She waved cheerfully and strode away, many male eyes following her attractive shape and dancer's walk as she headed towards Circular Quay.

Henry turned his full gaze on Ruth. "Looks like something is happening here," he said seriously.

"Yes, it is," she murmured. Ruth moved her hand to his by the beer stein until their fingers touched.

"Let me show you around the festival and then we can watch the fireworks tonight," said Henry. He took Ruth by the hand and led her towards a very colourful Spanish stand.

"Are you hungry?"

"Yes, I am."

"Are you happy for me to order?"

"*Hola, Como estas*?" Henry said in fluent Spanish. "*Quiero pedir, por favor, calamares a la romana, gambas a la plancha, mejiilones e patatas fritas. Gracias.*"

"Oh, you speak Spanish?"

"Yes, I speak Spanish and French. I was born in Argentina. We spoke Spanish at home, and I learned French and English in school.

"What did you order?"

"I hope you like seafood. I ordered fried squid, grilled prawns, mussels and chips."

"Sounds great."

They both sat at one of the round tables. Henry ordered two glasses of white wine. The food was delicious.

That night as she watched the fireworks with Henry, Ruth knew she was falling in love.

* * *

"It's been magic," said Henry, after one of their intimate dinners. "I never thought a month could go by like this."

"Nor me." Ruth took a sip of the Fumé Blanc they were drinking with their dinner. The remains of stuffed vine-leaves, potato pancakes and sauerkraut lay around the table of the Hungarian restaurant in Bondi they had both fallen in love with.

"But something's worrying you." His voice tightened up with the pressure he suddenly felt at her attitude.

She reached over and took his hand. "Just a little. One small problem."

"Parents being obstructive? I thought they liked me."

"Oh, they do, my dear Henry, they really do, despite being a non-medical Goy! They're still a bit disappointed, but they're probably comforting themselves that it will all come to an end soon, and I'll see the error of my ways."

"And will you?" Tension still showed in his tight voice.

"Not a chance! Don't be silly!"

"So what is it?"

She picked up the bottle of wine and filled both their glasses. "About a month before we met, my parents said that if I got my degree, they'd give me a present. A big one."

"And you passed with honours. So ..... what, a sports car or something?"

"Nothing so common! No, tickets to London for Sarah and me and six weeks of touring England and Europe. Sarah's been bouncing off the walls with excitement. She's never been overseas."

"So you have to go, obviously?" Henry seemed relieved. "You couldn't spoil her dream by cancelling out."

"You've no idea how much I want to, Henry. But you're right, Sarah would never forgive me."

"So when do you leave?"

"Next week. Will you wait for me?"

"Of course, I will! How could you be concerned?"

"Well, I am! So I want to make certain."

She put her glass down and reached for his hand.

"Henry Smith, I want to marry you!"

* * *

Ruth had not been interested in getting married at first. She wanted to pursue her career, have fun and travel.

Her parents had frowned on her dating a public servant. After all, Ruth Kurt-Austin had had a privileged upbringing. Marriage to a lawyer or other professional was the acceptable norm in their social circle. And Henry wasn't even Jewish!

Pressure from her father to date within the right circles escalated when she returned from her trip. Eligible bachelors from her father's circle of professionals would suddenly appear at the dinner table. Rich, shallow, one-dimensional plastic people. Their conversations limited to their investment brokers, property prices and expensive cars. Dead boring!

In the end, Ruth proposed to Henry, more to spite her snobbish parents, than to scare poor Henry out of his wits.

* * *

Sarah broke the silence. "You've been reminiscing."

"Oh, Sarah, I don't know what I'll do without Henry. He was my whole life, and yet I didn't know him at all."

What a strange thing to say, thought Sarah.

Chapter 6

It's about time I gave up the macho image and the smoky pub scene, and found a new social niche in life.

Hudson was more excited than he thought. He tried to remember the last time he dated. But of course, this wasn't a date. Was it?

Hudson looked around his bachelor pad. Black leather lounge, black onyx ashtrays scattered on grey smoky glass coffee tables. A large grey rug with two black borders and a symmetrical centre hugged the polished timber floors. The room was a sharp contrast to his parents' 'divine' pink carpets and white and gold velvet chaise sofa.

Hudson smiled to himself. He could almost picture his father feeding grapes to his mother every time she draped herself on one of the chaise sofas. *Metaphorically speaking, of course.*

A photo of his parents and their current prized poodle looked out of place amongst the photos of rugby mates and motorbikes.

Hudson turned to Tyson.

"That's your sister in that photo. I've spent many a night curled up with one of those diamond studded excuses for a watchdog."

The only objects that sparkled in Hudson's lounge room were his football trophies. He had been determined to play sport to balance out his childhood of being dragged mercilessly to fashion parades and cocktail parties, while school mates played sport and trail biked the many muddy creeks around the Northern beaches of Sydney.

He opened his wardrobe and went straight to the unopened gifts from his mother and father. Dress shirts, cashmere sweaters and designer ties of every colour. Some of the ties sported hideous, sparkling 'bling.'

Tyson had been following Hudson from room to room, hoping a walk would be forthcoming.

Hudson pulled out a dark jacket.

"What about this, Tyson?"

Tyson responded to the charcoal with a grunt.

"I wonder if I'll fit into the Armani suit my father bought me last year for a cousin's wedding," he said. "Remember Tyson, you stayed at Jill's farm in Doonside."

Tyson wagged his tail.

Hudson took out the grey cashmere suit his father had bought and recalled the conversation with his mother, Lily.

"What are you going to wear, Matthew?"

"I'll find something in the wardrobe, Mum."

"It will probably have dog hairs all over it. Why you didn't get a poodle, I'll never know. They don't shed any hairs at all."

"*I have the camel sports jacket you sent me for Christmas.*"

"*No! No! Matthew. It's not a sports jacket affair.*"

"*People wear jeans to weddings now. Mum, are you there?*"

She's probably fainted, he thought with a grin.

"*I'll put Dad on, Matthew.*"

Hudson then heard his mother telling her latest poodle what a naughty, ungrateful son she had raised.

His father, Ashley King-Hudson, certainly had style, Hudson recalled. He had bought the suit for Hudson in a dark grey cashmere with a very faint pin stripe. His father had also bought a grey silk shirt which Hudson wore out, untucked, much to his mother's horror.

Hudson recalled his mother's reaction.

"*He looks too casual.*"

"*That's the look, dear, for the young people.*"

"*But everyone is wearing black, Ashley.*"

"*They look like undertakers, dear. Matthew looks 'trendy.'*

"*You must remember 'trendy' from your modelling days, Lily.*"

"*You could at least have bought a pink shirt and tie to offset the grey. You were supposedly the expert in colour co-ordination.*"

"*The grey looks fine, Lily. Come on, the bride will arrive shortly.*"

"I'm wearing a pink carnation, Mum."

Hudson chuckled to himself as he put on the suit, minus the carnation. He fed Tyson and was out the door, arriving early at Tattersall's for a much needed drink.

He ordered a bourbon at the bar and carried it to a table against the wall. He placed his drink on a coaster. Moved the coaster. Changed his seat to face the door. Changed back. Ordered another drink.

Maya arrived, turning a few heads as she headed towards Hudson. Gone was the athletic look and in its place was a magazine cover goddess. Her hair was styled in a French roll with fine wisps around her face. She wore a black ensemble of a short black dress and matching long sleeve jacket. The only piece of jewellery was an antique Victorian sterling silver, rhinestone heart pendant on a long chain around her neck.

"I came straight from work," she announced.

From his experience of women and his mother's habits, Hudson was quite certain that Maya had changed her mind several times before choosing the appropriate outfit. He could almost hear his mother's war cry, *I have absolutely nothing to wear,* as she would fossick through her numerous wardrobes, trying outfits on, discarding them and finally, after changing six or seven times, she would ask his father the eternal question: *"Does my bum look big in this?"*

Hudson stood up as Maya reached the table.

That unforgettable perfume. "What would you like to drink?" he asked.

"Chardonnay, thanks."

Maya took off her jacket to reveal a sleeveless and backless dress, exposing her smooth velvety skin to just below the waist.

The bartender brought the glass of chardonnay for Maya and another much needed bourbon for Hudson. The admiration with which he stared at Maya before retreating made Hudson feel proud.

"It's nice to see you again, Maya."

"Likewise. Detective Inspector Hudson."

"Matthew, please."

"Matthew."

"How's your mother holding up?"

"She's not coping very well. I realise I lost a father, but mum lost her soul mate."

"It must be so difficult for both of you. Does your mother have any other family support?"

"No, she was an only child. She has a few close friends from the synagogue and the bridge club."

"What about your father's side of the family?"

"Dad came to Australia with his parents when he was ten. Both parents died before I was born."

"Where did your father come from?"

"Argentina."

The waiter returned and announced that their table was ready.

"I'm sorry," said Maya with a smile. "I've been rambling on. Let's go and eat and then we can discuss my bit of information."

Hudson followed the tanned and toned naked back. *She definitely works out,* he thought. *And from the way she walked in, she's probably a dancer, too.*

The ritual of studying the menu took some minutes before Maya ordered grilled quail with a Grand Marnier dressing while Hudson had opted for the 'catch of the day' flounder with lemon sauce. He knew they would eventually get down to business, but he wanted to prolong the evening. He was enjoying her company.

"Have you been to South America?" he asked.

"No, I haven't. But my next goal is to trek Machu Picchu."

She sighed softly before continuing. "Now that my father's gone I'm realising just how little I knew of his family. He never spoke about them, or his homeland."

She took a sip of wine. "However, he did try to teach me Spanish and French which he spoke fluently, but I wasn't interested at the time."

"I wish I could speak French," said Hudson. "It would have come in very handy when I travelled."

"Have you been to France?" she asked.

"Only with my parents, when I was younger."

"Did you visit the Louvre?"

"Yes! And yes, I did see the Mona Lisa."

They both laughed.

"The trips did give me an appreciation for art," he added.

"What are your favourite works of art?"

He could feel her enthusiasm, as she leaned towards him, listening intently.

"I'm no avid dilettante, but my favourite artist would have to be Rembrandt. I've seen a few of his paintings over the years."

Hudson realized that they had a few things in common. *Travel and art for a start. Perhaps that will give me an excuse for a date in the future.*

The waiter had brought their meals. Hudson realized he hadn't ordered the wine. The waiter smiled politely and said, "You were both so engrossed in conversation, I didn't want to interrupt."

Hudson ordered a bottle of Oyster Bay chardonnay.

"You were saying," said Maya. "Your favourite Rembrandt ....."

"I don't know if there is a favourite. But I must admit I sat for hours at the Hermitage Museum studying many of his artworks, especially the *'Return of the Prodigal Son'.*"

"You've been to Russia? I am so impressed. Do go on."

"I feel Rembrandt captures something that you don't see in any other paintings. This particular painting depicts the darkness of human existence, illuminated by the tenderness of the Father. The spiritual awareness of the outstretched hands as the ragged son takes refuge in the Father's mercy. But the most memorable thing about that painting is the hands of the Father. One hand is depicted as masculine and the other feminine."

"You *are* passionate about art," said Maya.

"Our dinner will be stone cold, if we don't get started, " said Hudson, taking a large sip of wine.

Conversation was light as they concentrated on their meals. They both skipped dessert and settled for coffee and mints.

After a short silence, Maya leaned forward and in a slightly conspiratorial tone said. "About that information ....."

Hudson put his coffee cup down.

"When I got home last night, I told Mum about the young unidentified woman at the funeral. It must have triggered something in her memory. She remembered receiving a phone call from a young lady the day before my father's funeral. The woman told Mum that she was the daughter of Ivan, one of Dad's friends."

Hudson noted from Maya's conversation that the female had been unaware of Henry's murder. She had rung to let Henry know that her own father had passed away four weeks previously.

"Did the woman leave her name?"

"My mother said she was too distraught at the time to remember the young lady's name, but said it sounded foreign."

"Was there an accent?"

"Mum never mentioned one. Anyway," continued Maya, "when my mother told her that my father had died, and that his funeral was being held the following day, the phone dropped out."

"So," said Hudson. "What does that imply to you?"

"It seems rather strange that it took so long for communication of the passing of two good friends to be circulated to the families," said Maya.

"Tell me what you know about Ivan. How does he fit into the picture?"

"My mother had never met Ivan or his family, and neither have I," she continued. "Ivan lived somewhere in the Lower Blue Mountains which is quite a hike from here. All I know is, my father and he shared a passion for chess, and he would often visit Ivan on his rostered days off."

She took a thoughtful sip of the wine, staring into the glass. "Perhaps the mystery woman was Ivan's daughter paying her last respects," she concluded.

"Does this Ivan have a surname?"

"I've never heard it," said Maya. "Perhaps you can turn up something from staff records at Immigration. My mother felt that Ivan was connected with Dad's work somehow."

"I'll certainly follow it up. If you or your mother think of anything else, please let me know."

Hudson did not want anything to ruin this evening. But he could also feel that her enthusiasm for conversation was waning.

All this talk about her father and especially the mention of the Blue Mountains where her father's body was found must be wearing her down, he thought. *Not a good time to bring up Colin Jackson. That will have to wait.*

Maya offered to pay, but Hudson claimed it was his idea, and that the information was worth the dinner.

As he walked her out to her car, Maya held out her hand. "I've had a wonderful evening, Matthew. Thank you."

As the perfume goddess drove off, Hudson felt strangely empty. It had been such a long time since he had been so excited or stimulated by a woman.

The evening had ended in a shuddering anticlimax.

Chapter 7

Nina Renowicz had only just come to terms with the loss of her father when a second wave of disaster hit her like an Exocet missile.

She hugged the cushion close to her heart for comfort as she relived every dreadful moment of the conversation with Ruth Smith:

"Hello, may I speak to Henry Smith?"

"Who is calling, please?"

"My name is Nina Renowicz. My father, Ivan was a friend of Henry's."

"Oh, yes, hello. I'm Ruth, Henry's wife. Henry often spoke of your father. How can I help you?"

"I just wanted to let Henry know that my father died four weeks ago. I'm terribly sorry that I haven't rung earlier, but my family has been grief-stricken by his sudden death."

Nina recalled the long silence. She strained to hear what she thought was a soft sob.

"I'm so sorry," said Ruth. "But I'm afraid this is a bad time for both of us. Henry has passed away and his funeral is tomorrow. The tragic story of his death has been in the newspapers."

A cold shiver passed down Nina's spine as she recalled the news headlines of a senior government official found in the Blue Mountains National Park, his body and car winched from a ravine.

With barely a whisper of deepest sympathy Nina, distraught and fighting back tears, had replaced the phone in its cradle. She closed her eyes and had tried to control the spots of white light bouncing around inside her head, before falling face down on the bed and sobbing.

It was the next morning that she had decided to pay her last respects to Henry Smith.

Chapter 8

"You okay, Sir?"

Hudson lifted his eyes from the folder on his desk which he had been looking at blankly for the last unknown period of time. The fresh-faced young constable standing in the doorway was staring at him with obvious concern.

"Conference in twenty minutes," the young man said. "Do you want me to get you a coffee or something?"

Hudson focused his eyes and his mind. Ryan Cooper, he recalled after a panicky second of struggling to remember the man's name.

Not good for leadership, forgetting your team's names, he thought.

"Er .. no, no thanks, Cooper. Just make sure everybody's there."

"Right oh," said the constable cheerfully and vanished from the doorway.

God damn, thought Hudson. *This mood must be showing. They'll be inviting me out for a beer next, trying to snap me out of it. Got to stop this.*

But he couldn't. He tried to concentrate on the dossier on his desk, but he immediately slipped back into the depression that had enveloped his soul like a cold fog since Friday. Maya was unavailable, for now, he knew that. But more depressing was finding out from colleagues that she had been dating Mike Adams previously. He was beginning to dislike Adams intensely.

He badly wanted a cigarette, but there wasn't an office in the country that permitted smoking any more. He didn't have time to walk downstairs and outside to join the pathetic bunch of nicotine addicts that were a feature of every entrance these days, never mind his refusal to be seen with them.

"Maybe if I solve this murder, she'll fall into my arms and proclaim me her hero," he muttered.

He snarled at his schoolboy infatuation and reactions, gathered up his folders and walked out to the conference room on the floor below.

The scene was eternal, almost like some medieval painting. Paper-strewn tables and rubbish bins already overflowing with old paper coffee cups. The aroma of coffee permeating the air. A number of detectives standing or sitting on tables, talking among themselves. One or two looked edgy, perhaps craving a cigarette to go with the thick brew. Occasional hoots and roars of large trucks on the main road found their way through the thick glass.

"Morning everyone," said Hudson. He walked to the front of the room by the whiteboards and waved his hand casually at the chorus of responses.

"Okay. The suspicious death of Henry Smith," he continued. "You've all had the details so far, but now you're getting the rest ...."

He was interrupted by the door opening as Mike Adams, accompanied by Doctor Neville Ting, walked in.

"Sorry," said Adams. "Heavy traffic."

Hudson nodded, but didn't stop his presentation. He turned to the whiteboards and picked up the video remote control. He pressed two buttons and a screen began to descend from the ceiling, while in the middle of the ceiling a trap door slid aside and a projector moved down.

"This was the funeral of Henry Smith over a week ago," continued Hudson. "We've identified everybody there, but for one woman. That one."

He switched on his projector and a tiny red dot appeared on the screen where the picture had paused. He moved it to the woman he thought of as 'Ruby Red.' A chorus of wolf whistles and appreciative comments broke out from the male members of the audience.

Hudson looked across at Detective Senior Constable Jill Morellix, who was shaking her head as if in pity at the juvenile male reactions.

He resumed the video. "However, while we'd like to know who she is, there's another person of interest."

He turned to the screen and waited a few moments before stopping it again. Hudson focused the red laser pointer on a well dressed man in his mid to late thirties, sporting a full-length coat, blue scarf round his neck and a black trilby hat.

"This is Colin Jackson," he said. "Quite a lot of you will already know this gentleman, if we can call him that."

He paused as murmurs of agreement ran round the room.

"He may or may not be related to this matter, but what is getting our attention is that he attended Henry Smith's funeral."

Hudson stopped the video and nodded at Mike Adams, who, he noticed was mumbling something under his breath as he walked up to join Hudson.

"Most of you know Mike Adams from the Coroner's office. He's got some interesting stuff for us."

"Thank you Inspector."

Mike Adams came to the front and busied himself taking a memory stick from around his neck and plugging it into the desk computer. He picked up the controller and set the video running while he worked his way through the files until he brought up the first picture of what would likely be a series.

Adams showed several pictures of Smith's body as they had found him, commenting as he went.

"Henry Smith's body was found at the bottom of a fifty metre ravine deep in the Blue Mountains National Park. Police received a call from local bushwalkers after they spotted a leg protruding from beneath the wreck of a car.

"As you can see from the photos, the body was in bad shape. Fortunately, conditions were dry and cool and this slowed down decomposition.

"The crime scene blokes examined and collected the physical evidence at the scene. A wallet containing a driver's licence, credit cards and cash was found on the victim. The glovebox of the car contained an electronic passport. The chip in this e-passport contained biometric information including digital fingerprints. So with all that data, we had no trouble in identifying the victim.

"In addition, Ruth Smith, the victim's wife, identified his body, together with an engraved wedding ring and the clothing he had worn the day of his disappearance.

"Forensics found no traces anywhere of drugs, disease or poison. His tox report was negative," continued Adams. "The entomologist examined the bugs on the body and determined the postmortem interval which corresponded to Smith's disappearance ten days previously.

"Initially, it was thought that the death was accidental. However, the discovery of penetrating ballistic trauma to the neck was made during the examination. Subsequently, the car, or what was left of it, was winched up for further investigation including blood spatter analysis.

"The Forensic Medicine Unit found nothing in fibres, loose objects or stains around the crime scene or in Smith's car to give us a lead.

"I will now hand you over to Doctor Ting for the autopsy report."

"Thank you, Mike."

Doctor Neville Ting was a highly respected forensic scientist. His reports, though methodical and detailed, were relatively simple and straightforward. He would impress on his staff that the value of the autopsy, no matter how skillfully performed, would be greatly diminished if the findings and correlations could not be adequately communicated to the end users of this information.

Doctor Ting placed the autopsy photos onto the wall.

"It is my opinion that the main factor involved in bringing about the death of Henry Smith was the extensive bleeding caused by a gunshot wound to the back of the neck including the suboccipital region."

Ting pointed to the first photograph. "The bullet passed through the occipital artery, the sterno-mastoid muscles and the supraclavicular nerves, which caused massive internal bleeding. However, the severed external and internal jugular vein caused the external bleeding and eventual death. I've inserted a metal rod into the entrance wound to show the path of the bullet on the radiograph."

He pointed to the second photograph. "The entrance wound to the back of the neck is shown in this photograph. As you can see, it's a small keyhole lesion. However, the exit wound is much larger, as shown in this third image."

Doctor Ting paused.

"I have also attached a report from the forensic science lab on the blood-stained shirt. Due to the large volume of blood on the shirt and blood pooled on the seat of the car, it would appear that the victim bled profusely and death would have been instantaneous."

Ting nodded at Adams to indicate that he had finished.

"Thank you, Neville," said Adams. "Are there any questions?"

Jill Morellix raised her hand.

"Yes, Jill."

"A question for Mike Adams. Was the gunshot wound at close range?"

"Yes. A very intense deposit of gunshot residue was found near the contact entrance hole," replied Adams.

"Was the bullet recovered?" asked Jill.

"What was left of the bullet was found in the car. We don't expect to get much from it."

"Doctor Ting," said Hudson. "Could the wound have been self-inflicted?"

"That theory has been eliminated. The entrance and exit angle of the bullet was examined by forensics and a full report is attached to the paperwork I have handed out."

"Was a time-frame established between the victim being shot and the car being pushed over the edge of the ravine?" asked Jill.

Ting shook his head. "An accurate time frame could not be established. However, there are details in the postmortem lividity report."

Adams added to Ting's reply. "Smith's car is currently being analysed for bloodstain spatter. We should have a full analysis within the next few days."

Adams removed the memory stick from the computer and slipped it into his suit jacket pocket, whilst Doctor Ting handed out the reports.

The group of detectives studied the photos Doctor Ting had placed on the wall. Some had sat down to read the reports.

Doctor Ting and Mike Adams strode out of the room, shaking hands with detectives as they departed.

* * *

"You might as well stay for the briefing," said Hudson, turning to Detective Inspector James Kerr. "Henry Smith's murder and the 'Snail Trail Operation' could be linked."

"I can see now why you invited my team to the meeting," replied Kerr.

"I didn't recognise Jackson at first," said Hudson. "It wasn't until Henry Smith's daughter Maya, came in to identify the people in the video that she mentioned Colin Jackson, a common enough name. But, I was too busy watching some red-lipped sheila throwing memorabilia into the grave and I missed it. It *suddenly* dawned on me; *a day later*." Hudson shook his head and they both laughed.

"Now he's up on your wall as well."

"Yes. Next to the small-time dealer we found dispatched."

Jill had brought the Henry Smith chart up to date. There were now six detectives studying the chart and taking notes.

Jill turned to Hudson. "I thought you would have asked Maya Smith about Jackson, Sir."

"The conversation I had with Maya Smith is in the report I handed out."

"It's what's *not* in the report that would be more interesting."

Hudson gave Jill a look of disdain.

Jill took the hint and didn't continue.

Hudson started up the proceedings again. "Firstly, we need to look for a motive. We can rule out robbery. His wallet with three hundred dollars was found on his body."

"Maybe it was revenge or a crime of passion?" said Jill.

"Or perhaps Henry Smith had stumbled onto something accidentally?" said Kerr.

"It certainly appears to be an execution-style shooting," said Detective Sergeant Sam Gilroy. "The gunman certainly knew what he was doing, according to Doctor Ting."

James Kerr raised his finger. "I realize we've been working together on the drug dealer's murder, Matt, but given the recent new evidence, I'm suggesting that we include both our teams in this investigation."

"Sure, we don't want to overlap or spread ourselves too thinly," said Hudson. "The resources are meagre as they are. Let's say we meet Monday mornings, here in the conference room."

Mutters and nods of agreement ran through the group.

"We need to piece together Henry Smith's last few days," continued Hudson. He turned to Jill. "I want you to go to Henry Smith's office at Immigration and check all phone calls and appointments for the week before he disappeared. Also, get statements from the four colleagues who attended the funeral. Try and ask some intimate questions, but be discreet."

Jill and discreet don't go in the same sentence, thought Hudson. *She'll go in with guns blazing. Maybe I should have asked Sam to interview the colleagues. Too late, I've already allocated the job to Jill.*

Hudson turned to Sam Gilroy. "We also need some information on Ivan, Henry's chess mate. According to his daughter, Ivan lived in the Blue Mountains and died recently. Ruth Smith believes that Ivan could have been a retired work colleague and that Henry may have planned to visit him on the day of his disappearance."

"Jill and I will probably go together," said Sam.

"Okay, I'll be visiting Ruth Smith at her home," said Hudson. "We'll meet back here tomorrow at 5:00 pm."

Chapter 9

Hudson made his way to Vaucluse and found the elegant home near Nielsen Park. The place reeked of money he thought as he rang the bell at the front door.

Ruth Smith greeted him at the door with only a brief, "Good morning," and showed him into the living room without further words. While she insisted on preparing tea and scones, Hudson looked at the surroundings.

The décor was elegant and luxurious with the warm tones of timber. Two beautiful Victorian settees with carved rosewood armrests and feet sat either side of a large coffee table. Antique back chairs with rosewood frames and covered in English silk surrounded a small French table in the corner. Elegant chiffonade curtains in ivory draped the large windows. A turn of the century French display cabinet with bevelled glass stood next to a matching, exquisitely carved bookshelf, inlaid with mother-of-pearl. Original artwork adorned the walls. The floors were polished timber, covered with a large Persian cashmere and silk rug. The whole room looked as if nobody had ever actually sat in there.

One painting caught Hudson's eye. *What a magnificent reproduction of Gustav Klimt,* he thought.

"I was just admiring the artwork," he said, as Ruth entered with an antique silver tea service. "This artist certainly expressed what dreams must look like."

"Do you know of the artist, Mr Hudson?" Her throat seemed dry, as if her voice was like the room, rarely used.

"Only by reputation."

He put two sugars in his cup. *Damn, I only needed one sugar in this small cup.* "Where did you acquire the poster?"

"The posters came from Henry's father," replied Ruth curtly.

Hudson picked up on the plural. *There's more than one!* "What line of work was Henry's father into?"

"He owned an import and export company in Balmain. The company was sold when Henry's father died. Long before I came on the scene."

Ruth took a sip of tea. "Now, what did you want to talk to me about?"

Normally a conversation about art can go on ad infinitum, Hudson knew from experience. However, he felt that this one had run its course.

"As I mentioned on the phone, we're trying to piece together Henry's movements from the time he left home, or more precisely twenty-four hours prior to that time."

Hudson watched Ruth as she sighed deeply before she spoke.

"Henry left early on Saturday morning for the Villawood Immigration Detention Centre," said Ruth.

"Did he normally work on Saturdays?"

"No. It was purely voluntary," replied Ruth. "Henry was a unique human being. Very sympathetic to the plight of refugees and asylum seekers."

Ruth stopped and dabbed her eyes with a hankerchief.

"Henry actually started the voluntary programme at the centre," she said proudly. "He would often visit the detainees with bits of furniture and timber and show the men how to repair and restore antiques. Sometimes he would just have a game of chess with the men or a game of cricket with the kids. He was also planning to attend an antique auction sale in Katoomba on Sunday. Probably to bring back more junk," she added with disdain.

She looked slightly embarrassed by the outburst.

"Sorry to call it junk, but Henry often came back from these events with broken down bookshelves, coffee tables and chairs to use for his voluntary work with the refugees."

The man was a saint, thought Hudson with an internal wave of irritation. "Was he going to Katoomba from Villawood?"

"No. Initially, he was supposed to come home for a family dinner on Saturday and leave on Sunday," replied Ruth. "So I got quite annoyed when he rang me and said he would be late. He told me that there had been a violent protest at the detention centre."

"Yes," Hudson agreed. "It was all over the news. The detainees had set fire to the medical centre, the kitchen and the computer room within the compound. The riot squad and the firefighters had to be called in."

"I didn't know how serious it was until I saw the news that night," said Ruth. "Henry rang me a few hours later. He said he was heavily involved working with the police in the process of gaining control at the centre."

Ruth took another sip of tea.

"I remember saying to Henry that I felt their behaviour was appalling. He replied that the detainees had been pushed to breaking point after it was revealed that some of their applications for permanent residency had been rejected. We had words." She started to cry.

"What time did Henry ring you?"

"About 8:00 pm. He said he wouldn't be coming home. Said he was heading straight for Katoomba and not to expect him until late Monday night. On Saturday evening we had our family dinner, without Henry. We were all glued to the television. The protest had got completely out of hand. I realised how serious the situation was, and I was sorry that I had argued with Henry. That was the last time I spoke to him."

Hudson nodded sympathetically.

Ruth dabbed her eyes with a lace handkerchief and continued.

"I didn't hear from Henry at all that weekend. I rang his mobile several times, but it went straight to messagebank. On Monday, I normally play bridge. I came home around six, had a light snack and listened to music. I went to bed around ten o'clock. I didn't realise Henry hadn't come home until the following morning."

"Just going back to the Saturday evening, Mrs Smith. Who was at your family dinner?"

"Maya and Colin. My best friend Sarah and her husband David."

Hudson looked up quizzically. "Colin? Is he a member of your family?"

"Colin Jackson is Maya's partner."

Hudson tapped his pen on his notebook. "How long have they been together?" he asked without looking up.

"On and off for about three years."

"How did Henry get on with Mr Jackson?"

"They got on very well. Henry often helped Colin with his business interests."

"In what way, Mrs Smith?"

"Colin's company imported garden and outdoor ornaments from South America and Henry helped with language translations."

"Where did they conduct this business?"

"Mainly in Henry's office. Colin would never come to dinner without his laptop and Henry didn't go anywhere without his. I'm sure their laptops and mobiles were fused to their bodies."

She smiled.

Hudson glimpsed the beauty that lay beneath her pain and sorrow.

I don't recall seeing a laptop computer or mobile on Henry Smith's inventory list, he thought.

"Did they meet socially?"

"Colin often took Henry to the races."

It's obvious chess and antiques were not Henry Smith's only interests. "Would you mind if I went through Henry's office?"

"By all means. I haven't touched anything in his study or his work shed."

"Thank you."

Ruth pointed the way to the study. It was a separate building at the back of the house, which appeared to be a converted garage. The study was huge. A hand carved ivory chessboard sat on the coffee table next to the leather recliner. A small bar fridge hummed under the bookshelf. A computer rested on an antique desk with drawers on either side. Henry's telephone book was next to the phone and a briefcase sat on the floor beside it.

Hudson opened the briefcase and found a diary. He decided he would ask Ruth's permission to take those items, knowing full well he could get a court order and confiscate anything he found of interest. But having her consent would make it all smoother.

He rummaged through the drawers and the bookshelves, but found nothing of interest. And then he noticed the second *Klimt* poster on the wall. It was probably too erotic to hang in the living room and had been banished to Henry's study. Hudson looked closely at the painting. He lifted the artwork off the wall and turned it over. A strange stamp on a brown tag adhered to the timber oak backing together with a collector's seal. He took out his mobile phone and photographed the painting before realising that the thumping sound was his own heart beating wildly.

Hudson moved toward the door to the adjoining room. It was locked. A simple lock which took no time to pick. What he thought may have been a storage area or workshop was in fact a bedroom. The wardrobe contained male clothing.

That's odd, thought Hudson.

To the side of the large wardrobe was an ensuite which contained male toiletries.

On either side of the bed stood a pair of antique painted Italian Rococo-style chest of drawers. Hudson looked through the drawers. He took all the paperwork and placed it in a plastic folder. In the bottom drawer he found a small rosewood document box. Hudson pulled out the drawer. It held two photos. A young woman. A young woman and child. There was a sadness to the old black and white photos that had yellowed over time. He took out the photo of the young woman and turned it over. Written in ink was the name Laticia Alavarez. The child was Henry. He placed the photos in the plastic folder.

Hudson walked out through the side door to the garage, behind which was a small shed. It was unlocked and he walked in. Inside to the right of the door was a very organised woodwork shop. A thick hardwood bench, complete with a vice stood against the back wall. Shelves and hooks above the bench held a variety of power tools, saws, planes and hammers. To the left of the door was a jumbled pile of broken pieces of furniture and bits of wood. On the shelf were some finished products, mainly an assortment of ornate timber boxes. The smell of gloss lacquer was quite strong, but it did not deter from the lovely aroma of the camphor laurel. Hudson picked up each item. He admired the grain, the smell and feel of each wooden piece. Document boxes in Huon pine with rosewood inlays; jewellery boxes, large and small, beautifully handcrafted in red cedar contrasted with layers of camphor laurel.

Hudson went back into the living room. He sat next to Ruth.

"Henry was quite a craftsman. Where did he learn the trade?"

"I don't know. I presume from his father."

"I know how difficult this must be for you, Mrs Smith. We don't know who killed Henry or why. We have no motive and we have very few leads. I need to know everything about him."

Tears welled up in Ruth's eyes again.

"I don't know what else I can tell you."

They were interrupted by the doorbell.

"I'm leaving anyway," said Hudson. "Would you mind if I take these items?" he asked politely.

"Not at all," she said, barely looking at the documents.

They both stood up.

Ruth opened the door to a large, bearded man wearing a black suit and a wide-brimmed hat, accompanied by a pretty woman in a well-tailored black dress.

"Good morning, Rabbi," said Ruth.

She introduced Hudson to the rabbi and his wife. Hudson followed the rituals and left as the newcomers came in. He didn't get a chance to ask about the bedroom in the study. It would have to wait.

Chapter 10

Hudson was back at Headquarters after lunching with his best friend, David Samit. He had just helped himself to a mug of coffee when Jill walked into his office.

"Anything new to report?" they asked in unison and laughed.

"I'm writing up the report on my visit to Ruth Smith."

"Well! While you've been drowning in Bollinger champagne, Mr Armani, I've managed to do some police work," quipped Jill.

What would she know about Bollinger champagne. It doesn't come in a schooner glass. Hudson smiled to himself. Jill was a good cop, despite her appalling attitude that would have her suspended if she was working for anyone else.

"We'll wait for Sam and meet in the conference room," he said, returning to his report.

Jill stood there, not moving. "I'll bet you don't know anyone west of Sydney, Sir. That would be like crossing the border for you."

"Yes I do." *They all wear 'flannies' to parties where you come from,* thought Hudson, ignoring Jill's sardonic remark. *Although, I read somewhere in the fashion magazines that the grungy flannel check shirt was making its mark on the fashion scene for women. Shock! Horror! I must ring Mum and tell her. That information should keep my mother busy with her friends for months.*

"Go!" he said with an imperious wave. "I'll see you at 5:00 pm."

Jill looked down at her notes.

"I've interviewed three of the four colleagues. One was on holidays, due back in a fortnight. The first was Joanne De Vere, who is now the Acting Senior Immigration Officer. She spoke very highly of Henry and his sensitivity to people's situations, which at times were tragic, especially the refugees'.

"Henry Smith worked hard, she told me. Far beyond the call of duty. He would do anything to speed up the detainees' applications for residency."

"Could there have been a disgruntled deportee, given his job?" said Sam.

"Write it up on the board," said Jill. "We're a little short on motives."

"I then interviewed Matt Wilke," she continued, looking at her notes. "He was more personally involved with Henry. Their wives were friends and played bridge regularly. He got a bit uppity when I asked if Henry got a bit on the side. I didn't use those words exactly."

I'd hate to think what words she did use, thought Hudson.

"Matt Wilke didn't feel Henry Smith had a mistress, or had ever been unfaithful to his wife. The last person I interviewed was Susan Harvey, Henry Smith's personal assistant. She told me that she had already been interviewed by police when Henry had gone missing, and had nothing further to add."

Until faced with Jill Morellix. This should be good. Hudson straightened up in his chair as Jill carried on.

"Ms Harvey told me she was on leave that week. She was very articulate and answered my questions in a very efficient and concise manner. However, when I started asking personal questions about Henry Smith, she froze me with an icy stare.

"I then asked if she could verify where she was during that week. Ms Harvey said something about it being a private matter, wanted to see a warrant and walked out. I wasn't game enough to follow her and create a scene."

Thank God! thought Hudson and suppressed a laugh.

"I did a routine check on Ms Susan *'Iceberg'* Harvey," continued Jill. "There's more to that chick than meets the eye. It seems she worked for the spooks at the Australian Security Intelligence Organisation in Canberra before transferring to Immigration five years ago. I couldn't get any more than that. It was classified."

"I've got a mate in ASIO," said Hudson. "We went to Uni together. I could give him a call if she becomes a person of interest. Good work, Jill."

"I've also put in a full report on Henry Smith's phone records and appointments for the week prior to his disappearance," Jill added. "I'll check them out and report anything unusual."

"While we're on the subject of phones, could you check if Henry Smith's laptop and mobile phone were found in the car?" asked Hudson.

"I don't remember seeing those items in the evidence room. I'll check on it," said Jill.

"Those items could be lying somewhere at the bottom of the ravine," said Sam.

"Indeed they could," said Hudson. "What have you got to report, Sam?"

"Can we get a coffee?" asked Sam Gilroy. "My report is quite lengthy."

They all filed out and were back in ten minutes, coffee and biscuits in hand.

"I went straight to Personnel and left Jill to attend to the gossip stuff," said Sam, ducking a broken biscuit thrown by Jill.

"James Fisher, the Personnel Officer, had been with Immigration for over forty years. He remembered Ivan. And, no! Ivan didn't work at the Department, his wife did. She was Henry Smith's assistant, Zoya Veloski. That was over twenty-five years ago."

"Well that clears up one of the puzzles," said Hudson.

"Fisher could recall details and events as if they happened yesterday. His memory was amazing. I didn't even have to ask any questions," continued Gilroy. "I asked if Veloski was Ivan's surname, but apparently Zoya retained her maiden name after she married Ivan. James couldn't recall Ivan's last name, but stated that it should be in the Immigration records."

Gilroy read from his notes. "Ivan had arrived in Australia on a visitor's visa from the Ukraine. He met Zoya at a wedding and within three months, before his visa expired, Ivan and Zoya were married. Henry Smith had been instrumental in helping Ivan remain in Australia. Zoya left the Department shortly after she got married.

"I then asked James Fisher if he could access Ivan's arrival in Australia, which James recalled as being around 1983."

They roared laughing as Sam Gilroy mimicked James Fisher with an Aussie twang:

"I remember that year very well. My daughter, Isabella, had just moved to Perth and was having her first baby. My grandson, Raymond, he's now a fully qualified doctor, you know. Has his own practice, prattle, prattle. I nearly offered him fifty cents to ring someone that gives a damn," said Sam. "Fisher finally referred me to the visa section. The clerk at the visa desk was baffled."

Sam referred to his notes for the name of the clerk.

"Here it is. The clerk's name, Jerry Niraski. Jerry cross-referenced countries of origin against the granting of citizenship. He checked dates of arrivals from particular countries, but no records could be found. Mind you, we didn't have a surname for Ivan."

"That is so weird," said Jill. "Could someone have deleted the file, or did it in fact exist?"

"I then drove out to Chippendale to the Department of Births, Deaths and Marriages," continued Sam. "They did have a record of Zoya Veloski's marriage to an Ivan Renowicz. Both Zoya Veloski Renowicz and Ivan Renowicz are deceased. They also gave me copies of the names and dates of birth of the two children that Zoya and Ivan had. Twins apparently."

"Bingo! Good work Sam. See if you can locate the children," said Hudson. "I've written up a report on my visit with Ruth Smith. The last time she spoke to Henry was on Saturday night. He was killed either late Saturday night or the early hours of Sunday."

"Where was he going?" asked Jill.

"According to his wife, he was going to an antique show in Katoomba."

"Obviously didn't make it," said Sam.

"It appears that Colin Jackson had an alibi for Saturday night," said Hudson.

Jill and Sam collected their paperwork and headed for the door.

"Jill," called Hudson.

"Yes, boss," said Jill, rushing for the door.

"Hang on, I haven't finished," he yelled. *That girl is faster than the first beer on a Friday night.* "Can you leave the Susan Harvey report with me? Thanks."

Jill came back from the doorway, threw the file on his desk and raced out.

Her football team must be playing tonight, thought Hudson. *League, poor excuse for a rugby game.*

Chapter 11

Susan Harvey needed to get to her secret box quickly. She arrived at her unit in Berowra, north of Sydney where she lived alone with her cat, Jaspa.

Before she could key in her security number, her neighbour, Jacob Burns, 'Old Stickybeak' as he was known, called out.

"That Siberian tiger of yours has been harassing my Milo."

That walking toupee. Poor excuse for a dog if you ask me. Looks like it should be sitting atop a court judge's head. "I'll give him a severe talking to, Jacob," she yelled back.

Susan hurriedly opened the door, and was met by the furry fury. She knew people did not warm to Jaspa. Even alley cats and small dogs ran away in fear. Susan had placed a large bell around Jaspa's neck to at least warn other creatures to get out of his way.

Jaspa rubbed himself against Susan's legs. She bent down and rubbed the cat's ears.

"No-one understands you. Do they Jaspa?"

The huge cat continued his ritual of purring and licking, but after five minutes, he'd had enough stroking and sharing affection and headed towards the fridge, meowing like a jungle cougar deprived of food.

Susan poured herself a coffee, leaving Jaspa to devour his gourmet meal - at least that's what it said on the can.

She headed for her bedroom to the place where she kept her secrets.

She took out the small cedar box. Tomorrow she would put it in a safe deposit box at the bank.

Those bloody coppers are just as likely to do something irrational and want to search my unit, she thought to herself.

"If they try that, I'll take out a complaint of harassment," she said to Jaspa, who was now curled up on her bed, purring with contentment.

"Now! Where's that business card of that silk that Henry gave me when that internet date started hassling me? Ah! Here it is. Richard Jackson Senior Counsel, Barrister at Law."

Chapter 12

"Renowicz! Now there's a name you don't hear every day." Sam Gilroy took a chance with the Penrith and Lower Blue Mountains directory. There were two listed numbers. He rang the first number and the phone was answered by a female.

"Mrs Renowicz?"

"Yes."

"My name is Gilroy. Detective Sergeant Gilroy and I'm after some information on Ivan Renowicz."

"That was my husband's father," said Mrs Renowicz, her voice breaking up as she tried to quieten the shrieks of children in the background.

"Can I speak to your husband, please?"

"Alex is at work. Would you like the number?"

"Yes, thank you." *That was easy.* He took down the number as the woman recited it, pressed the disconnect button and dialled.

A female voice answered. "'Rotating Plants.' Can I help you?"

"May I speak to Alexander Renowicz, please?"

"Hang on a moment."

Sam heard a few muffled words and then a male voice spoke.

"Hello, Alex speaking."

"Good morning. I'm Detective Sergeant Sam Gilroy and I'm after some information on Ivan Renowicz."

"What kind of information?"

Sam noted the intense caution in the voice.

"It's in relation to a case we're investigating. Look, Alex. I'm on my way to Penrith," he lied. "Could I drop in and see you?" *Face to face is so much more productive,* he thought.

"Sure, I'm here all day," replied Alex. "Have you got the address?"

"No. Can you give it to me, please?"

After Sam took down the address, together with some directions, he thanked Alex. "I should be there in an hour or so."

Sam had a good run from Parramatta to Emu Plains, just west of Penrith. Arriving at the small family nursery he was greeted by Alex. Sam was quite surprised by Alex's appearance. He was tall, towering over Sam by some six inches. His dark smoldering good looks were enhanced by his blue eyes. For some reason Alex appeared vaguely familiar to Sam. The two men shook hands and went into the small office.

"We're investigating the death of a government official. Your father's name has been linked as a friend of Henry Smith's," said Sam.

"Yes, Henry Smith was an old friend of my father's," replied Alex.

"How did your father die, Alex?" asked Sam.

Alex got up and walked over to a small jug, filled it with water and switched it on.

"He committed suicide."

"I'm very sorry."

"The Penrith police have all the details. Would you like some coffee?" he asked.

"Yes, thank you."

Sam thought about his own parents. He had migrated from the United States to start a new life shortly after both his parents were killed in a motor vehicle accident almost two years previously. He knew that Alex would still be going through the grieving process and decided not to ask Alex any more questions about the death of his father. He would call in to the Penrith police station for that information.

"Did you know Henry Smith?" asked Sam.

"Not well. I met him a few times when he came to visit my father," said Alex. "My father was a historian in the Ukraine, and when Henry visited they would both spend hours talking about history. They also played chess together, fanatically. If I happened to drop in while they were playing, my father would give me a *look* as if to say, *'Here's your hat, what's your hurry?'*"

They both laughed.

"Do you play chess?" asked Sam.

"No, I'm more the outdoor type," said Alex with a laugh.

Not surprising! thought Sam. "How's the plant business going? It seems pretty quiet this morning."

"We get very busy on weekends," said Alex. "Although, the most profitable side is the rotating plant business."

"What is that, exactly?"

"Well," said Alex, sounding enthusiastic for the first time. "Many large companies, clubs, shopping centres and top restaurants have indoor plants in their foyers and offices. Rather than them employing their own gardeners, I deliver plants on a regular basis. I take out the old plants and replace them with fresh ones. I then bring the old plants back for repotting and rejuvenation."

"What a great idea!" Sam exclaimed. "How many employees do you have?"

"It's just a small family business. My father used to come and help. Now I employ a part-time lady," said Alex. "My wife does the accounts from home and I have one full-time driver/salesperson-cum-gardener. You need to be multi-skilled these days, don't you?"

"You sure do," replied Sam. "When was the last time you saw Henry?"

Alex jumped at the sound of the jug as it switched off. He stood up and began mixing two mugs of coffee.

"Milk and sugar?"

"No, thank you. Black."

"I can't remember, exactly."

"Would it be weeks or months?"

"Probably months."

"Did you know he was murdered?"

"Yes. My sister, Nina, told me."

"Did you know he was murdered in this area?"

"Yes. I read it in the papers."

Sam took out his notebook and pen as Alex returned to the table and placed the mugs on small mats.

Alex sat down but seemed to shift nervously in his chair. He picked up the coffee cup and without drinking placed it back on the desk.

"Can you recall when you last saw Henry Smith?" Sam asked again.

"It was probably last Christmas. Henry would always visit us before Christmas with gifts for everyone, including my two children. He was very generous."

Sam jotted down some notes. There was not much else he could ask Alex at this stage. He asked a few more minor questions and obtained some more background, chatted socially about the plant business then thanked Alex for the coffee and set off to the Penrith police station.

Sam introduced himself to Police Sergeant Thompson and apologized for not ringing in advance. But there was no difficulty from the local station. Thompson gave Sam the Renowicz file and Sam found a quiet office where he read it, coming out briefly for a coffee. After an hour he rang Hudson.

"You could drive a bulldozer through the holes in this report!"

"Steady on, Sam! You can't get the Penrith Plods' noses out of joint. What have you found that's got you so riled up?"

"Can you request that I take the report out?" asked Sam. "I need you to look at it, especially the photographs."

"Okay, I'll put in the request. It should only take a few minutes."

Ten minutes later, Sam Gilroy left the Penrith Police Station with a copy of the Ivan Renowicz case file, together with a set of photographs and headed back to the city.

Chapter 13

Colin Jackson reached for his glass of red wine.

Aboard the *'Nymph'* moored at one of the more secluded spots in the prestigious Marina, Jackson was cooling off, lying naked on his belly with his heart thumping wildly from his workout.

The Marina and Yacht Club catered to the rich and famous. It was one of Jackson's biggest outlets.

The 'nose candy,' the vibrating mat under the velour sheet and the slow rocking of the boat caused him to release the wildest moan of ultimate pleasure.

As he sipped the wine, he switched off the vibrating mat. He had bought two of these toys. One for his secret hideaway and one for Maya.

Oh, that girl will try anything, and she insists on videoing everything. Now that would fetch big bucks, he thought, as he smiled to himself.

He needed the energy boost and mental clarity that 'snow' gave him, unlike the junkies and party animals addicted to pleasure. Finally, he got up from the mat, took a shower, put on his casual clothing, picked up his laptop computer and headed for the airport.

His timing was impeccable. His alibi perfect.

Chapter 14

The atmosphere in the squad room crackled with excitement. Telephones rang off their cradles and detectives shouted and bustled towards their urgent destinations.

Even deep in thought over the materials on his desk, Hudson sensed the increased tempo and noise coming from the station. It was no surprise when Jill shouted to him from beside the overworked photocopy machine, which was hissing ozone into the mélange of odours in the room.

"Showtime, boss!" she announced, her voice reverberating through the building. "The drug guys need us in the conference room, sort of immediately!"

"What's going on?" said Hudson, picking up his notepad and mug.

She nodded approvingly at the mug. "You're going to need that. The shit has really hit the fan!"

Hudson went to the nearest dispenser, more out of habit than from need. He placed his mug on the metal shelf and savoured the scent of the coffee as it gurgled down. Strong and black, the way he liked it first thing in the morning. No sugar, and the harsh bitter taste would sharpen his mind when it cooled down from boiling point.

Jill talked as they walked briskly down the corridor towards the meeting. "Massive load of coke hit the streets last night. Our blokes have collared the usual pile of party animals, but just the small fry. Nobody seems to know who brought this load in or how. The Narc Squad blokes are ropeable."

Hudson opened the door to the conference room and let Jill go ahead of him. She smiled at this unexpected courtesy and Hudson caught the whiff of her perfume as she passed close to him.

Hmmm, not too bad a pong, for a westie sheila, he thought to himself in amusement and then lost the idle fancy as the conference room atmosphere hit him. It was a zoo: phones ringing ceaselessly, loud conversations, some voices expressing much anger and frustration, wild arm gesticulations and a general sense of only partially suppressed violence. He and Jill moved to the side of the room and waited without speaking.

A loud bellow came from the front of the room, as Detective Inspector James Kerr in a shabby sports jacket, loosened tie and hair looking like it hadn't been combed for a week, was standing. He looked like he needed a couple of nights' sleep.

"OYE!!!" shouted Kerr. "Can we have some silence?"

Slowly the racket diminished until Kerr had the room's attention. "Okay, everybody. We've all learned that a shitload of high quality stuff hit the streets yesterday, right under our noses.

"We've been able to trace that the first wave was at the Randwick Racecourse yesterday. More cash changed hands between the dealers and their upmarket clientele in the private boxes, than between the bookies and punters in the betting ring. But overnight it worked its way to Kings Cross and Rose Bay and all those rich bastard areas. We got a few samples and this is the real *McCoy,* it's top grade, no fillers, no traces of glucose or lactose. High purity cocaine selling for up to four hundred bucks a gram."

A buzz of conversation ran through the meeting. Jill leaned towards Hudson and in a subdued tone said, "By the time I've paid my bills, I'm lucky to buy two schooners at the pub. Who buys this shit?"

Kerr waited until the whistles and hubbub died down again.

"This is really heavy, guys, and bloody dangerous because, whoever is behind this is well-connected and well-financed and we're going to have to be extra bloody careful. We'll be treading on some expensively manicured toes, you can bet your lives."

Hudson raised his hand and Kerr saw it immediately. "Something you can add to this, Matt?"

Hudson put his coffee mug down on the table and moved to the front of the room.

"Good morning, everybody," he said. The coffee had done its trick and his mind was sharp.

Turning to the whiteboard that covered the wall behind him, he wrote the words Randwick Racecourse, Saturday's date, then next to it WHO? HOW?

"This is a bad one, obviously. The analysis of the coke confirms that it's top grade, and we know it's coming in from South America. Now, I don't have anything but a good nose and this smells like someone we know. Let's be hypothetical for a moment. If it *is* Jackson we're dealing with, he's well-connected, and he's got deep pockets."

Hudson picked up the marker and drew a line from the racecourse to the Happi Frog nursery at Dural.

One of the drug squad team spoke up in some irritation.

"But, Sir! We've had that bastard under observation for months! We know that he travels to South America regularly. He exports goods from Argentina and Brazil, two of the major cocaine transit routes. We've poked our noses and scanners into every one of his shipments. Even the latest Customs technology which includes the container x-ray facility, has come up with a duck."

"You'd better translate that for Sam."

"It means a score of nought. In cricket it was originally called a *'duck's egg'* because of the *'O'* shape in the scorebook," said Bazzer seriously.

"I know what it means Bazzer," Sam said in a conspicuous American accent. They all laughed.

"But, you're right, Bazzer," said Hudson. "I don't know that anyone could have watched Jackson more than you blokes have done. But this smells of Jackson and we do know from past experience, that approximately one month after every one of his shipments, regular as clockwork, another wave of high-grade coke hits the streets. Like I said, the bastard's clever. So where do we look?"

Kerr interrupted. "If it *is* Jackson, he's either got a good laboratory somewhere or he's getting the stuff into his nursery through some other means."

"The drug operators are very sophisticated now and use the most unusual camouflage and concealment methods to import their drugs into the country," said Hudson.

"Not only that," added Kerr. "They can use digital encryption devices, high frequency transmitters, radar tracking devices and even waterproof GPS to guide them to drops from sea vessels, even submarines. With 25,000 kilometres of coastline, it's like looking for a needle in a haystack. No match for our coastal patrols."

"Don't be too hasty," said Sam. "The Australian Federal Police recently seized a cocaine shipment from Colombia worth $78 million."

"I heard that on the news," confirmed Jill. "Three hundred kilograms came in by yacht into Queensland."

"Apparently they were Spanish nationals sailing into the quiet port of Bundaberg under the guise of the Annual Port-2-Port Yacht Rally," said Sam.

"Yes! *That* operation took months of work and a lot of resources from every quarter, the AFP, Customs and Border protection and the Queensland police to nail them," said Kerr.

"But I do agree that this latest distribution smells of Jackson and we need to have a good sticky-beak at that nursery."

"So how do we do that?" asked Sam.

Kerr looked irritated. "We've tried several times, but the judge has always refused a warrant to search the place. He says all we've got are suspicions but not enough evidence to justify a warrant. We'd get our arses kicked in court if we tried to search without one."

"Can we get someone in there under cover?" asked Jill.

"It's worth a try," said Kerr, sounding more positive.

"James, what can you tell me about the staff at that nursery?" asked Hudson.

Kerr opened his notepad. "He's got three office staff. There's an old school buddy of his, Jarryd King, who is his manager and accountant."

"Any form on him?"

Kerr shook his head.

"Squeaky clean," he said and bent his head back to his notes. "Some bloke called Damien Leed working in sales and an office assistant. No dirt on either."

"Anyone else?"

"Two women working sales at the weekend. I don't know their names. Two guys in the distribution centre, Bryson Stochic and Leon ... spelt N, G. How the hell do you pronounce that?"

"Ung," said Hudson. "Any questions about their legal status?"

"Not that we know of," replied Kerr, "But we haven't done a check on them."

"Best to do it, just in case. It might provide an opening."

Kerr nodded and pointed a finger at one of his team, who immediately left the room.

"Two people in the potting shed, one of them a full-time horticulturalist, and there are also two full-time gardeners," continued Kerr. "And before you say it, Matt, we'll find out about all of these people."

"Good on yer, James. So we have to find somebody who can fit into that operation without seeming suspicious. Anyone got any ideas?"

"I think that the only way we are going to crack this case is to get one of our people employed in that nursery to see what really goes on," repeated Jill.

"Do we have any detectives who may have worked in a nursery in their youth? We need fresh information. Badly."

Hudson would have felt much better about the case if he knew that a big break was about to come his way – and from a most unusual source.

Chapter 15

"Bolt from the blue?" asked Jill, following Hudson into his office.

"Damn right," he replied. "Refill my coffee with two sugars this time, and I'll tell you how we nail this guy Jackson, once and for all."

He waited until they had sat down across from each other at his desk, fresh coffees steaming. "I've got a friend, David Samit, he's in charge of the New Apprenticeship Scheme with the Industrial Relations Department."

"Gotcha," said Jill. "They're the people who organise work experience for young unemployed people."

"Yup."

"Who have you got in mind?"

"What's that kid's name? I'm forever forgetting it. Yes, Cooper, Ryan Cooper. Invite Cooper for a drink with us tonight," said Hudson.

"Sure," replied Jill. She sounded disappointed.

Was she hoping for the undercover role? Hudson wondered.

"What's going on, Hudson?"

David Samit resumed his seat after standing up for Hudson's arrival at the busy restaurant in Darling

Harbour. "It's not card night, it's not football and they wouldn't let me bring my bike into the restaurant."

Hudson grinned, sat down across from his old friend then nodded at the waiter. "Two Victoria Bitters, please." He waited a few moments as both men gave full attention to a pair of mini-skirted young women brushing by their table.

"Jail bait," said David. "You should know, of all people! How's the detection business going?"

"Ploddingly. That's why you're here having lunch at the taxpayer's expense."

"This is official? I'm just a poorly paid civil servant! What the hell can I do to stem the full flood of crime in this city?"

"Actually, David, you might be able to help a hell of a lot." The two men sat back as the waiter arrived with their beers and waited till he'd departed again. They chinked glasses.

"Cheers," muttered David. "Okay, explain."

"If I've got it right," said Hudson, "your department helps place unemployed young people in training positions. Is that correct?"

"Why do I have a queasy feeling about this? You're going to ask me to do something highly questionable, aren't you?"

"You're not just a pretty face, Samit. You're right. I want to place a young apprentice at the Happi Frog nursery in Dural."

Samit was quiet for a few moments. "Does this person look like a young unemployed kid?"

"They call him 'baby-face.' He looks seventeen, but he's a cop and he's twenty-two."

"And what about paperwork?" Samit was wearing the poker face that Hudson had seen across the card table all too often.

"We'll create identity papers showing him as seventeen and enrolled at the local college in an appropriate subject."

"Will he be safe at the nursery?"

"No."

"Does he know that?"

"He's done undercover work before. But this one is the worst."

"Any background in the business?"

"Yes, actually. He attended an agricultural high school. He can walk the walk and talk the talk."

Samit drank half his beer in one gulp and let out a long sigh. "You're quite sure this will help the police?"

"It could kill a major drug ring."

"Christ!" Samit looked hard at Hudson. "It really is serious!"

"Deadly."

"Send me the paperwork," Samit said, picking up the menu.

"No need," replied Hudson, as he reached for the envelope from his jacket pocket.

Samit took it without a word, tucked it away and finished his beer.

"Seeing as you're paying, I'm having a steak," he grunted and put the menu back on the table.

"I'm Ryan Cooper," said the scrawny kid in the blue jeans and white tee-shirt. He tried and failed to hide his admiration of Helen Zaylen as she met him at the entrance to the nursery.

"Delighted to meet you," she said with a playful grin. "We could really use the help! We're short-staffed this week."

"Glad to help." Ryan followed her to the potting shed, enjoying watching her hips move in the close fitting skirt she had on.

That night, he rang Hudson at home.

"I tell you what, boss," he said, "that Helen Zaylen is one grouse looking sheila!"

"Cooper, you're there to look for drug equipment, not drool over the female staff."

Despite the stern words, Ryan could hear the smile in Hudson's voice.

"Yes, sir. I haven't seen anything too obvious yet. They've had me working flat out like a lizard drinking..."

"The first honest work of your life then?" interrupted Hudson, smiling to himself.

Ryan ignored it. "There's a door out of the potting shed. It's marked 'Private' and there's a seriously heavy lock on it."

"Key or combination?"

"Combination. I was able to have a quick look at it this afternoon, and I took a picture of it with my phone camera."

"Good man. Send that over."

"Stand by, Sir."

Hudson opened his phone and waited a few moments. With a small chime, a photo appeared in the tiny display screen.

"Okay, Cooper, good work. I'll pass this to our experts and we'll find out just what type it is. Call me again, this time tomorrow and we'll go from there."

"Yes, Sir. Good night."

"Good night, Cooper. And stay alert."

Hudson hung up the phone and looked again at the image of the combination lock. It certainly looked too sophisticated for a potting shed store room.

"Okay, Cooper, listen up." As instructed, Ryan had called Hudson at the same time the following night. "Tomorrow morning, go to the newsagents on Marshall Street before you start work. You know it?"

"Yes, Sir."

"One of our blokes will be there. He knows what you look like. He'll hand you a small package, about the size of a pack of cards. Put it away until you're certain you're alone and you can get time inside the store room. When you do, open that package. It's a device to open the lock. Stick one end to your ear, it's obviously an earpiece, the other one you hold against the lock at one end. Try each roller in turn and you'll hear when it's the right number. When you get in, just take pictures with your phone, don't hang around, get out again and relock the door. Got that?"

"Yes, Sir."

"Just make bloody certain you have at least ten minutes with nobody around."

"It could take a few days before anyone leaves me on my own, Sir."

"Take as long as you need. You may be a total waste of space, but some misguided fools around here think you might make a half-decent copper one day."

"I appreciate that, Sir," said Ryan, suppressing a laugh.

"I'm not one of them."

"Of course not, Sir. I'll report in every night as you ordered."

"Damn right you will."

Ryan replaced the phone, grinning from ear to ear.

* * *

It took almost two weeks before Ryan got his break.

He had been helping outdoors at the Happi Frog nursery under the guidance of the chief gardener, Archie. Archie was a sight to behold. He looked and acted like everyone's grandfather until the sales people plundered one of his treasures. Archie would erupt like a volcano, yelling after the sales people to make sure that the customer knew how to water and prune *his* plants. How to use the right potting mixture on *his* plants. Or else he would turn the hose on them.

Get a life, thought Ryan. But this was Archie's whole life.

Ryan had just finished re-potting some of the mature plants when Jenny came over and asked Ryan for some help in the potting shed.

"Are you sure you'll be okay on your own?" Jenny asked. "It's just that Helen's off for the day and I have evening classes tonight. I have to leave at three."

"I'll be fine," said Ryan, feeling a surge of excitement. "I'll finish placing the seeds into the sterilising solution. You go to your classes."

"Thanks Ryan," said Jenny. "I'll make it up to you sometime. The people in the office will lock up. So just leave when you're done." Jenny looked relieved.

Ryan watched Jenny remove her working smock, pick up her handbag from the locker and stride out of the potting shed. He felt his heart start to pound. He walked up to the mysterious door and pulled the device from his pocket. Each night he'd examined it, and he was sure he knew what to do. He unwound the coil and gently pushed the earpiece into his left ear. Clamping the sensor to the end of the lock and holding it with his left hand, he carefully rotated each roller and heard a distinct 'click' when the roller hit the right number.

It took just a minute to open the lock and he quietly hung it on the clasp, gently opened the door and looked inside. It was quite dark, but there was a light switch by the door. Light flooded the room, revealing equipment and machines that he did not recognise. Mindful of Hudson's instructions and well aware of the danger he was in, he quickly took a photo on his phone of every segment of the room. He switched off the light, put the camera in his pocket and walked out again, replaced the lock, closed it and rolled the numbers at random.

Realising he hadn't taken a breath since opening the door, he let out a long and slow gasp and went back to the seeds. It was a while before his heart stopped pounding and his breathing returned to normal. The sweat in his armpits and groin took a lot longer to dry.

Chapter 16

The screen was filled with the pictures Ryan Cooper had transmitted from his mobile phone the previous day.

Hudson, Morellix and Kerr sat in the conference room. The silence was a far cry from the usual racket of many people talking at the same time, the coffee machine was cold and the cleaners had left, so the room was unusually tidy.

"What are those contraptions?" asked Jill.

"That large vacuum sealer is usually used in packaging food," said Kerr. "Those large glass jars are desiccators or dehydrators used for preserving moisture-sensitive items. The room has two air-conditioners, an industrial vacuum cleaner and lots of high ventilation fans."

"Is it a clandestine laboratory?" asked Hudson.

"I doubt it," said Kerr. "It's more likely to be a packaging plant. However, if they are storing and packaging cocaine in that room, even if they clean and vacuum it thoroughly, there will be particles in the air-conditioning filters as well as traces in the vacuum bags."

"Is there enough evidence for a warrant to search the place?"

Before James Kerr could answer, the phone rang. Jill picked it up.

"It's for you, boss. David Samit. Says it's urgent," said Jill.

"Morning, David. How are you?"

Hudson heard David gulp, then clear his throat as he blurted out, "Ryan Cooper has disappeared!"

"What? When? How?" bellowed Hudson, jumping to his feet.

"Helen Zaylen rang me ten minutes ago," said Samit. "The workers in the potting shed found drops of blood on the floor near Ryan's locker and when they opened the locker, Ryan's bag and wallet were still in there from the previous day. One of the workers raced into the office to notify the manager, who had just received a phone call from Ryan Cooper's mother looking for him. God, I hope nothing sinister has happened to him."

"Leave it with me, David," snapped Hudson. "I'll get onto it straight away and get back to you."

"What's going on?" asked Jill as Hudson replaced the phone. "Your friend sounded frantic."

"Ryan Cooper's disappeared! Get everyone into the conference room, pronto. I'll make a phone call and be with you shortly."

He turned to Kerr. "Get your boys in too."

Hudson dialled the cafeteria to bring up the sandwiches that he had pre-ordered that morning. He then joined the Homicide and Drug Squads who had assembled like soldiers after the 'Reveille' bugle call at sunrise.

Hudson poured himself a mug of coffee, helped himself to a plate of sandwiches and sat down to eat.

The roomful of detectives looked at him in bewilderment.

"What?" said Hudson. "There's plenty, just help yourselves."

The room erupted like a volcano that had been lying dormant for years, spewing out lava with a plethora of questions and rude remarks.

"How can you think of eating at a time like this?"

"What are we going to tell his family?"

"This is great news!" said Hudson, bringing the room to an instant hush. "Ryan's okay," he continued, grinning like a Cheshire Cat. Let me explain. When David Samit got Ryan into the Happi Frog, Ryan was very limited in what he could do. I had to devise a plan to get into the place. With Ryan's disappearance we'll get that chance. We have to investigate the young lad's disappearance, don't we?"

"Hudson, you're a genius. Why didn't you tell us that before you ate all the sandwiches?" asked Sam.

"I needed a head start," Hudson said with satisfaction.

The team rallied around the food and coffee.

Hudson addressed Kerr. "We need to formulate a plan and act quickly," he said seriously.

He moved to the whiteboard. In large letters he wrote, 'Routine Check – Missing Boy' and underneath a 'to do' list.

"I need to stress that this operation has to be low key, no waves, no suspicious behaviour. This list includes all of you. I want you to read it, understand what each officer is doing, underline your responsibility, put your name next to it and make sure the task is done as smoothly and efficiently as possible. The objective is to give the forensics bloke enough time to 'suss' out the operation and take samples for analysis. Are we all clear?"

There was a chorus of 'yes, boss', somewhat muffled by mouthfuls of food.

"I'll go in with Detective Inspector Kerr," said Hudson. "I'll arrange for the nursery staff to meet with me in the administration office while the Inspector does the probing in the potting shed. By this evening we should have enough evidence to obtain a search warrant."

How will this end up? thought Hudson with excitement. *Will there be a connection between Jackson's drug dealings and Henry Smith's murder?*

Neither Hudson nor anyone could have predicted what happened next.

Chapter 17

"Good morning, chief," said Jill as she barged into Hudson's office.

"What's so good about it?" grunted Hudson.

"Look, chief," said Jill. "Things go belly up in the drug world all the time."

There was no response.

"Have you read Kerr's report, yet?"

Hudson nodded without looking up.

"Don't you just love the part where he states that the mixture of manure, fertilizers and fungicides hit his nostrils like a boxer's glove? He should have been a writer, he is so descriptive."

"All right Jill, what's your point?"

"It could have been worse, chief. The room could have been filled with garden gnomes, and the report could have read, 'Police arrest a roomful of garden gnomes'." Jill was now suppressing her laughter and not doing it well.

She's thoroughly enjoying herself at my expense, thought Hudson.

"You'll get over it," said Jill, trying to sound empathetic.

"I've got work to do," hissed Hudson. "Get out!"

"You definitely need a coffee. I'll put lots of *sweetener* into it."

She ambled out humming to herself.

Hudson picked up Kerr's report again, the nature of which should cause little surprise to his superiors. The event would go down into the police archives as an unsuccessful operation. To Hudson it was a grand stuff up. He broke out into a cold sweat as he recalled the previous day's debacle.

The drive from headquarters to the Happi Frog nursery took just over an hour, with the last fifteen minutes winding upwards past the stylishly built homes on acres of picturesque lawns and floral gardens.

James Kerr flicked on the car blinkers indicating to the Ford Ranger paddy-wagon following to pull up under the shelter of two large ghost gums on the side of the road.

Hudson and Kerr instructed the officers in the van that the Happi Frog nursery was one hundred metres down the road on the left hand side and that they were to remain in the van until signalled.

"At which time," instructed Kerr, "close the place down. No one is to enter or leave the premises. We expect to make several arrests."

Hudson, Kerr and the special technical 'Scene of Crime Officer' Michael Gibson drove off. They parked in the visitor's space and walked purposefully to the main office where they were met by Helen Zaylen.

"You're here about young Ryan."

"Yes, Miss."

"I'm Helen Zaylen." She held out her hand, giving Hudson a warm smile. Hudson took her hand which he noticed was very soft for someone who worked with plants and potting mix. He introduced James Kerr and Michael Gibson.

"Take a seat, gentlemen. Would you like some tea or coffee?"

"No, thank you, Miss," said Hudson. "Could you please assemble the staff? We need to ascertain when Ryan Cooper was last seen. By whom, what time and where."

Helen had drifted out of the office like a vapour. Hudson turned to Kerr and spoke conspiratorially, with little movement. "She doesn't seem too worried."

"Nope," said Kerr. He sneezed. "Boy, the perfume from all those flowers really gets up your nostrils. I'll be heading for the antihistamines at any moment."

"It's the other stuff that gets up your nose that we're after," whispered Hudson.

A noise behind them made them both turn. A procession of 'gardening types,' as Hudson would later describe them, shuffled their booted feet into the room. With their eyes downcast they answered 'nope' to all the questions, with the exception of Jenny, who left Ryan Cooper in the potting shed the previous afternoon.

Hudson had thanked the staff and assured them that this was just a routine line of enquiry, and he was sure the young work experience lad would turn up unharmed.

Hudson had then turned to Helen and asked if she could show them the way to the potting shed.

"Sure," she had replied, giving Hudson another infectious smile. "Follow me."

Gibson took photos of the potting shed and the blood spots on the floor. He also dusted the locker for fingerprints.

"What's behind this door?" asked Kerr, pointing to the combination lock.

"We keep our fungicides, pesticides and fertilizers in there. All the 'out of bounds' stuff," said Helen.

Kerr walked towards the door.

"It's locked," said Helen.

"Could we have a look inside?" asked Kerr.

"Would you like me to open it for you?"

Very compliant, thought Hudson.

Hudson nodded to Gibson to be ready with the camera. Kerr was poised for action with the Two-Way Radio.

Helen swung open the door, flicked on the light and stepped back, holding her hand over her nose and mouth.

They were greeted with pallets of various stinking horticultural chemicals and hundreds of bags of pelleted chicken manure. It hit their nostrils like waves of putrefied garbage in the midday sun.

Kerr had a quick, but critical look around and then joined a stunned Hudson who was already outside in the fresh air with Gibson and Helen.

Kerr radioed his team informing them that the mission had been aborted and headed back to the car, quickly followed by Gibson.

"Thank you, Miss Zaylen, for your co-operation," said Hudson in his most professional voice. "We will let you know of any further developments."

"You're welcome, Detective Inspector Hudson." Then she added "Anytime," giving Hudson not only a naughty grin, but a little 'eye flash' to go with it.

"Bullshit!" said Hudson to himself as he made his way to the car. *Someone must have given them the tip off!*

"Anyway, my report will cheer you up," said Jill, returning with two steaming brews. She dropped the file on the desk with a thump which brought Hudson back to the present. "This should take your mind off the fizzer."

"Your report?"

"Yes. Everything Henry Smith sent out into cyberspace."

"What are you talking about?"

"I took Henry Smith's computer and gave it to our forensic technicians. One of our technicians, Nikoya Taoh, scanned the computer with the *Forensic Evidence Extractor,* a small plug-in device that can decrypt passwords, analyse computers Internet activity as well as the data stored in the computer."

Jill looked smug. "It took me forever to fish out the interesting bits, though."

"I didn't know you took his computer!"

"It was the only thing of any interest in his office, apart from Susan 'Iceberg' Harvey," claimed Jill. "By the way, did you get any more information on that bird?"

"It's on my list." He opened Jill's report. "I see you've highlighted the relevant bits."

"Smithy did a lot of research into paintings. Stolen paintings, to be precise," said Jill.

"Yes?" said Hudson with renewed interest.

"Henry Smith seemed to be interested in the artist, Gustav Klimt. Whoever he was," said Jill.

"He was a very famous 19th century artist," said Hudson, rolling his eyes. "In 2006, according to press reports, one of Klimt's paintings, the *'Portrait of Adele Bloch-Bauer 1'* sold for one hundred and thirty-five million dollars. Even Klimt's posters are not available on the market below a five digit dollar price."

"Woooo!" interjected Jill. "He must have been some artist!"

"There's been some controversy surrounding his paintings recently. Many of his paintings were stolen by Nazis in WW11. Apparently some of his art turned up in an Austrian gallery," said Hudson, thinking that this information was completely wasted on Jill. "Anyway, leave the files with me, I'd like to study them further."

"Sure. I've found some other interesting stuff to follow up on," said Jill as she walked towards the door.

"What interesting stuff?"

"I'm not divulging it yet."

"Do you want me to slap some handcuffs on you?"

"You pick the time and place, and you're on," said Jill in a husky voice.

"In your dreams." He returned to the report.

Thank heavens Jill highlighted the pertinent bits, thought Hudson as he perused the lengthy print-out. Henry Smith had been Googling the World Jewish

Restitution Organisation, a group which was set up after WW11 to look for stolen art.

Henry Smith had also used the Internet for Ancestry Research and German Genealogy Links for the family name of 'Schmidtz,' in particular 'Frederick Schmidtz.'

Towards the end of the printout, Hudson focused on something of incredible interest. Retrieved from the computer was a document which stated that in the event of Henry Smith's death, he was bequeathing two paintings by Gustav Klimt to Susan Harvey.

Chapter 18

Hudson let out a big breath, pushed back in his chair with the idea that if he looked relaxed, he would feel relaxed. He found the idea of ringing ASIO quite confronting, even though Nick Beard was his best friend at University. He had visions of being asked a lot of embarrassing questions before being put through to Nick. It just wasn't done for police to ask questions without official sanctions and the correct paperwork. Hudson swallowed his last mouthful of coffee.

"What the hell," he said to himself and dialled the number. He was relieved and surprised when he was put straight through.

"Nicholas Beard," said the deep educated voice.

"Nicholas Beard, the ace spy catcher?" whispered Hudson into the phone, trying to sound mysterious.

"Who is this?" said the voice in a cross between amusement and alarm.

"Hudson of the Yard calling. Protector of the innocent and little old ladies."

"You old bastard!" said Beard. "How the hell are you, mate? It's been months. Is this a social call or do you suspect bugs in the woodwork down there?"

"Just a bit of unofficial info, Nick, on someone who worked there five odd years ago. Maybe you remember her, Susan Harvey."

"That's before my time, old mate. But I've got to tell you, she has legend status around here."

"What do you mean by legend?"

"A genius, a real trail blazer. You've heard of hackers. She was the queen of hackers. Employed by ASIO to detect flaws in security systems and retrieve information even when codes were lost. They used to say that nothing was safe on the computer with Susan around."

"Dangerous, Nick?"

"Not that I know of!" the ASIO man replied. "Most of the stories around here make her sound like a celebrity. Apparently a big loss to ASIO when she left."

"Do you know why she left?"

"The story goes that she was a workaholic, and her husband was doing the horizontal mambo with his secretary. There was a nasty divorce. Susan spat the dummy and hit the road for Sydney."

"She certainly must have left her mark to be remembered five years later," said Hudson.

"Well, there's been a revival recently. Susan went to work for the Department of Immigration, and it was her boss who was recently murdered," said Beard, his voice suddenly fading. "Good grief, you don't suspect Susan had something to do with that, do you? No, don't tell me. I don't want to know. Let's get together soon. Although, I'd be interested to know what turns up, regarding Susan."

"You'll be the first to know. We'll catch up soon," promised Hudson. He chatted further for a few moments before hanging up.

Susan Harvey, he mused. *There's definitely more to you than the unresponsive public servant you portrayed to us.*

Chapter 19

Hudson had entered the details of the *Gustav Klimt* painting into his computer and a myriad of information emerged like some electronic Medusa. Information from the atrocities committed during WW11 to the erotic positions of drawings based on Klimt art, were listed within seconds on his monitor. There was also a list of over 100,000 stolen paintings, booty taken by the Nazis. Amongst the data there appeared a logo which looked very similar to the one at the back of the painting in Henry Smith's office. It was described as an emblem the Nazis placed on paintings they had confiscated from art galleries.

If this painting is an original, it could be worth millions, thought Hudson. *Certainly could be a motive for murder.*

Hudson was so engrossed in the information that he didn't hear the phone ring. He was suddenly jolted into the present by the slamming of the door behind him.

Turning, he said, "I was just about to ring you, Sam. I need a 'good cop, bad cop' scenario for this afternoon. Are you free?"

"Sure. Who's the quarry?"

"Susan Harvey."

"Not the iceberg? That should be a challenge," said Sam. "However, I came to see you about another matter. Jill and I have just finished reviewing Ivan Renowicz's autopsy report."

"Have you found anything interesting?"

Before Sam could answer, Jill charged into the room waving a handful of photos like some Samurai warrior wielding a sword.

A course in decorum would not be wasted on that girl, thought Hudson.

"I've seen a few suicides in my time," she heralded. "I know for a fact that a suicide victim will rarely shoot themselves through clothing. And the gun is a hundred metres away from the body."

"Stop exaggerating," said Sam, interrupting her excited rambling with humour. He grabbed the photos and began placing them on the board.

"Look at the way the body is slumped. You have to agree that's a strange angle for someone who just shot himself through the chest," said Jill, working herself up into a crescendo.

The three detectives studied the photos intently.

"I'm glad you had these photos blown up Sam," said Hudson. "I can clearly see that there are *two* coffee mugs on the small table next to the recliner and there are chess pieces scattered everywhere. "Is there anything in the interview reports regarding the chess set? Was it on display permanently, or had it been set up that day?"

"There's no mention of the chess set," replied Sam.

"Were the cups tested?"

"Nothing in the report."

"I see the gun was a small calibre Luger hand gun. Had the police traced the origins of the gun?" asked Hudson.

"No. The gun was unregistered."

"Was there any investigation done at all?"

Jill handed Hudson the forensic report. "This report," she said. "It shows that the fingerprints on the gun belonged to Ivan Renowicz, as did the dried blood. That would have convinced the Coroner that it was a suicide. But there were no witnesses and neighbours did not see or hear anything unusual on the day of his death. The conclusion was that it was self-inflicted and the case was closed."

Sam flipped through the autopsy report giving Hudson and Jill a summary.

"The autopsy report shows that the shot was at contact range, angled slightly upward. The bullet entered the thoracic cavity and demolished the heart, killing him instantly. The daughter, Nina, found her father the following morning on her way to work."

"The daughter could have moved the body," said Hudson. "She could also have accidentally kicked the gun away from the victim's body, prior to the police arriving. I think I'll pay a visit to her and clarify a few things before we jump to any conclusions."

Sam placed the remaining photos onto the board. "Why would anyone set up a chessboard, make coffee and then shoot themselves? It just doesn't add up."

"Did either of you two notice anything unusual about the date of his death?" said Jill.

"You are so annoying Jill, when you smirk like that. What date?" asked Sam.

Jill walked up to the board, and with a red marker she underlined September 24.

Ivan Renowicz and Henry Smith had died on the same day.

* * *

"You drive, Sam, said Hudson. "I'll familiarize myself with Susan Harvey. Did you organize a meeting with that fellow who was on holidays, Eric Sweepe?"

"Sure did," replied Sam. "By the way, which cop am I?"

"Neither. I'm both."

As Sam approached George Street in Sydney, he put his blinker on to turn right when Hudson suddenly said, "Chuck a U-ey."

"Chuck a what?"

"You could have made a U-turn at that last intersection."

"Why didn't you say that in the first place? You Aussies have the strangest jargon."

"Good afternoon, Ms Harvey, I'm Detective Inspector Hudson and this is Detective Sergeant Gilroy."

Susan Harvey looked less than thrilled at the appearance of the two police officers. "How can I help you?" she said icily.

"We would like to ask you a few questions," said Hudson warmly.

"In regard to what?"

"You met my partner, Jill Morellix a couple of weeks ago and..."

"I gave her all the information she requested," interrupted Susan. Her stare matched her voice.

"We just need you to fill in some gaps," said Hudson. He looked down at his notes. The silence was deafening.

The iceberg fidgeted. Sam watched the drama unfolding.

"You stated that you were on leave the week after Henry Smith disappeared," said Hudson finally.

"Yes. Yes, I was."

"Could you tell us where you were that week?"

"Do I need an alibi? Because if I do, I'd rather have my lawyer present."

"No. No. Not at all," said Hudson calmly. This is only routine. Our supervisor doesn't like loose ends, he wants his t's crossed and his i's dotted. We're just following orders." Hudson turned to Sam who nodded in agreement.

Sam knew that Hudson had been trained in psychological interrogation tactics. *He'll go for the jugular shortly.*

"Just let us know where you were that week, and we're out of here."

"I flew to Bali," said Susan cautiously.

"When did you fly out?"

"I came to work on Monday. I flew out late afternoon on Tuesday," said Susan, reaching into her handbag and taking out her passport. She handed the passport to Hudson.

He studied it then passed it to Sam who jotted down some notes.

"I didn't know Henry was missing until I got back from Bali," said the woman.

"Thank you, Ms Harvey." He nodded to Sam who handed the passport back to Susan.

"Where were you on Saturday and Sunday?"

"Dinner and movies with a girl friend on Saturday. Home all day Sunday. And before you ask, this is the woman." She wrote down a name and telephone number and handed it to Hudson.

"Where did you stay in Bali?" he asked

"At the Four Seasons Resort."

"On your own?"

"Yes."

"We can check that out." Sam made a note in his book.

"I was with a male friend," she added quickly.

"Name?"

No answer.

"Come on, Ms Harvey."

"He's married."

"What about the name on his passport? He'd have had to show that at the hotel when he registered."

"I'm not giving you his name unless I have my lawyer present."

Although she worked hard at keeping her voice calm, Sam noticed that frustration and anxiety was creeping into her voice. Her demeanour had changed dramatically. She kept her head down, constantly tucking her short hair behind her ear.

"That's fine, Ms Harvey. I'm sure that won't be necessary."

I hate it when he's being nice, thought Sam. *It won't take us long to get that name from the hotel.*

Hudson didn't take his eyes off her. "We know about the paintings, Ms Harvey," he said in a monotone voice.

It took Susan Harvey only micro seconds to compose herself before fixing Hudson with an icy glare that he ignored.

"What paintings? I don't know what you're talking about."

"The penalty for blackmail is ten years."

"Blackmail?"

"We have evidence that you tried to blackmail Henry Smith." *Another exaggeration by Hudson,* thought Sam, admiring the pressure his boss was bringing.

A look of disbelief spread across her colourless face.

He got Susan Harvey to trust him, thought Sam. *Now he'll scare her to death by telling her some of the horrible stuff. Fear will usually make people talk.*

"Those paintings are worth millions," said Hudson. "It's a good motive for murder."

"Murder?" Harvey looked blankly at him.

Hudson slammed his fist on the table. "It's time to come clean, Susan or we'll take you down to the station, now."

He leaned forward. His eyes narrowed and he stared deep into her eyes without so much as a blink.

Pressing his hands together, he finally said. "What did you have on him, Susan?"

Looking severely confused and intimidated, Susan stared blankly at the wall behind Hudson before she started to speak. She swallowed hard.

Sam waited for the confession.

"I accidentally stumbled on Henry deleting files about twelve months ago. After that I hacked into everything he was doing and that's when I found out about the paintings. But I didn't murder him."

"What type of files did he delete?" asked Hudson.

"Henry Smith was a naïve idealist. A do-gooder. He was mainly responsible for identity and health checks on asylum seekers." Her voice suddenly turned hostile. "Even when those queue jumpers didn't meet the criteria, Henry found a way to let these criminals out of the detention centres and into our society."

She took a deep breath and stared at the two men in turn. "What happens now?" she asked.

"You didn't answer my question," said Hudson. "What type of files did he delete?"

"Henry was obviously deleting the files of people to whom he had granted citizenship and who by rights should have been deported. He knew he was being investigated by Internal Affairs and was trying to cover his tracks."

Why do I have a gut feeling that she's not telling all? thought Sam.

"That's all for now, Ms Harvey, said Hudson. "We'll keep in touch."

That's Hudson's style, leaving the prey dangling in suspense, thought Sam as he headed towards the door.

Eric Sweepe greeted Hudson and Gilroy in the foyer and introduced himself.

"Would you like some tea or coffee?" asked his assistant.

"Yes, thank you."

Eric Sweepe guided them into his office and closed the door, taking a seat behind his desk.

"Thank you for seeing us on such short notice, Mr Sweepe," said Hudson as the two police officers took seats across from him. Sam sat back and watched the interview again.

"I'll help in any way I can," replied Sweepe. "It's been such a tragic time for the family. I don't know how they're coping?"

"Yes, it has been tragic. You are obviously close to the family."

"Henry and I knew each other for over thirty years."

"When was the last time you saw Henry?"

"We had lunch on the Friday, and Henry mentioned that he would be going to an antique show in the Blue Mountains over the weekend. I've written everything in the diary," Sweepe said, handing Sam the diary which was opened on the day in question.

"Did Henry talk to you about any personal issues?"

There was a long silence, as Sweepe fiddled with his pen, clicking the top up and down in that most annoying fashion. But Hudson kept quiet.

"I'm very close to the family," said Sweepe, breaking the silence. "I still keep in touch with Ruth."

Another long silence ensued. This time Sam was tapping his pen on his notebook.

It's amazing, thought Hudson. *How silence seems to bother people.*

"I wouldn't do anything to hurt Ruth," said Sweepe eventually. "But something has been worrying me. Can this be off the record?"

"We'll decide that when you tell us what you've got."

The assistant came in with coffee and biscuits. Eric stopped the conversation until she had left and closed the door behind her.

"This happened a long time ago. I wouldn't even have mentioned it, only that Ruth told me that Ivan Renowicz had committed suicide on the same day that Henry was murdered."

How on earth did Ruth find out about that? thought Hudson. *There's got to be a mole in the department. Jill only uncovered that information this morning.*

"After Ruth and Henry had been married for about four years," continued Sweepe, "they split up and Henry moved in with me for almost three months. I was single at the time. I still am, the eternal bachelor."

He took a deep breath and then continued. "During their break, Henry had an affair with Zoya Veloski."

Sweepe paused.

Hudson and Sam sat like statues with folded arms.

Eric continued. "Prior to Henry's reconciliation with Ruth, Zoya had met Ivan Renowicz, a visitor from overseas. When Zoya asked Henry to help Ivan stay in Australia, Henry had granted him permanent refugee status, even though Ivan would not have met the criteria. Shortly afterwards Zoya and Ivan married and, dare I say," he whispered. "Zoya had the twins six months later."

"Did Ruth know about the affair?" asked Hudson.

"I don't think so. I've kept that secret for over twenty years."

"That's a pretty big load to carry," said Hudson.

"I did it for Ruth."

After thanking Eric for the information Hudson and Sam left in silence.

Before he reached the car Hudson turned to Sam. "While I think of it, can you check out Susan Harvey's story and her bank account details?"

"Do you think she's involved in Henry Smith's murder?"

"She's holding something back," said Hudson. "I don't think she killed him. But she could have hired a hit man."

"The mystery man in Bali?" said Sam.

Sam got behind the wheel. "Do you think the bachelor has a 'thing' for Henry's wife?"

"Nothing would surprise me," said Hudson.

Chapter 20

Night had fallen and Susan Harvey was alone. Loneliness and despair had crept into the room. It seemed smaller tonight as it caved in around her. Two black, cold wardrobes looked menacing.

Suddenly, a growling noise caused a prickling sensation of fear to pass through her body and out of her fingertips. It was coming from outside the window. She had closed the windows. Hadn't she?

What animal makes that sound, she thought to herself. She placed her hands over her ears. That's when the whole room started to shake. Or was it just the bed?

Susan gripped the side of the bed and listened. The growling noise was coming from deep inside her and it was her own body that was shaking violently. *Was there an entity in the room? Or was she dying?* She started to pray.

A sudden calmness engulfed her. The shadows started to fade. The moon smiled at her through the curtains which Susan was sure she had drawn before she went to bed.

"Damn you, Henry," she suddenly cried out, punching the pillow with her fists. Jaspa slid off the bed leaving claw marks down the bedspread as he hit the floor.

She thought of her lover.

Susan tried to pick up the cat. "I'm sorry, sugar plum."

But Jaspa would have none of that. He headed out of the room, slipped through the open window and disappeared into the dark alley where it was safer.

"Leave me, Jaspa. They all do."

She was now sobbing into the pillow.

How dare those detectives accuse me of blackmailing Henry!

Chapter 21

"Analyse the motive and we'll solve the crime!" said Jill. She put her feet up on the chair.

"We have a myriad of motives," said Hudson. "But understanding them is a different kettle of fish."

"Kettle of fish?" asked Sam.

"I keep forgetting that you're from another galaxy," said Jill. "It just means a mess up or a muddle."

"But you're right, Jill," said Hudson. "Identifying the motive is the key to understanding the crime and the criminal. We've just been given another possible motive. Henry Smith had an affair with Ivan's wife, and Ivan's twin children could have been a product of the affair."

"Jealousy?" said Jill. "Henry Smith is slowly losing his halo."

"Given the remoteness of the area where his body was found," said Sam, studying the board, "the person must have been familiar with the area."

"Why do you say person, Sam? There would have had to be another car involved, otherwise, it was a long walk out of the National Park," said Jill.

"I don't know the area," said Sam.

"The killer must have been known to Henry," continued Hudson. "There was no sign of a struggle or hostage-type injuries found on the victim. All we need now is the WHY? to lead us to the WHO?"

Jill slipped off her shoes. "How was the visit with the iceberg?"

"Her alibi for Saturday night checked out," said Sam. "However, she did withdraw ten thousand dollars the day before her trip."

"That's over the top for four days in Bali," said Jill.

"Inspector Hudson thinks she hired a hit man."

"We don't know that for sure," said Hudson.

"Didn't you ask who the bloke she stayed with was?" said Jill.

"I didn't want her to tip him off," said Hudson. "We'll find the male companion through airport surveillance or through the Bali hotel."

"How?" asked Jill. "You don't know who you're looking for!"

"She obviously travelled with him," said Hudson, tiring of the cross-examination.

"There's something fishy about Ms Iceberg," said Sam.

"You two crack me up," said Jill as she roared with laughter. "Kettle of fish, icebergs and fishy tales!"

Sam and Hudson both stared blankly at Jill.

"Forget it. Neither of you have a sense of humour."

"And we can't dismiss Jackson as a possible suspect, yet," continued Hudson totally ignoring Jill's idea of a joke. "We know that Jackson had business dealings in Argentina and Henry Smith assisted with translations."

"Henry might have threatened to expose Jackson," said Sam.

"I think there's another side to Henry Smith that hasn't been revealed yet," said Jill.

"He also had paintings in his possession, which could be worth millions and he leaves them to his assistant," said Hudson.

"She was probably blackmailing him," said Jill.

Hudson pulled out a file from underneath a mountain of paperwork. "Apart from Henry Smith Googling stolen paintings, he was also looking for information on genealogy links for the family name of Schmidtz, which could have been Smith's original name."

"That doesn't sound Spanish," said Sam.

Hudson took out another file. "We don't have a lot of information on Henry." He opened the file, had a cursory look, and handed it to Jill.

"Henry Smith arrived when he was ten, that would make it roughly 1966 when the family came to Australia. Ruth Smith also mentioned that Henry's father had an import and export business in the Balmain area. Jill, see if you can find out anything about the business in Balmain. You're pretty good at that," said Hudson, with a laugh.

"They don't call me the ferret for nothing."

Hudson walked over to the window. He looked aimlessly at the passing traffic. "We're going round in circles with this case. Pressure is mounting from above for some answers. Sam, I'd like you to check the airport cameras for the day that Susan left. See if you can get a make on the married guy. It should be easy with the new IP system they have installed."

"What's IP?"

"It stands for Internet Protocol. There's over a thousand cameras installed linked to a computer processor and web server, all in one device. The airport security staff will have access to the information instantly, without the need of searching for hours through video tapes. And it will be quicker than going to the Bali police to check out the hotel."

There's something about that woman, said Hudson to himself. "And I can't quite put my finger on it."

"Put your finger on what?" asked Sam.

"Nothing. Just thinking out loud," said Hudson.

"All you need is a traditional hand bell," said Hudson as Jill entered the room in the style of a town crier.

"You owe me big time," she said as she unrolled the proclamation. "I started with documentation from the Balmain area," she continued. "Sifting through all that microfilm took forever. Didn't find anything. Then I looked up the mother's maiden name, which I found at the back of an old photo and accidentally stumbled on a 'missing person.' Can you believe that? A cold case still active after forty years archived on microfiche!"

"What are you on about, Jill? Who went missing?"

"Believe it or not," said Jill, dragging out the suspense.

"It's like watching a turtle crossing the finishing line," interrupted Hudson.

"Patience, my dear Watson."

"It's slowing running out, Sherlock!"

"Read for yourself," said a triumphant Jill. She flicked the page towards him. Hudson grimaced as he caught the gliding sheet midstream. He read the part Jill had highlighted:

Neighbours in Balmain reported the disappearance of a woman who recently arrived from Argentina. Laticia Alavarez Smit had not been seen for almost six weeks claimed Mr and Mrs MacLivish.

Police are baffled that the husband, Frederick Smit had not reported his wife missing. Police are interviewing the husband.

"I got interested in that tidbit because the woman came from Argentina and her name was Smit," said Jill. "Pretty close to Smith, I reckoned.

"There were also several statements of domestic violence reported by Mr and Mrs MacLivish, which of course in those days would have been totally ignored."

"Yes, unfortunately," said Hudson. "In those days there was limited recognition of domestic violence as a crime. The relationship between husband and wife was one of ownership. Women were vulnerable to poor treatment."

"Here's another interesting bit. Henry Smit must have changed his name to 'Smith' somewhere along the line," continued Jill. "Probably to escape his criminal record."

"You're kidding me," said Hudson, snatching the sheet Jill was waving under his nose.

"Henry Smith spent a year at Mount Penang Juvenile Justice Centre when he was fourteen," said Jill.

"It would have been called a training school in those days. Why on earth did he end up there?"

"That information was a bit tricky to find. Read that bit," she said, pointing to a highlighted section.

Hudson read the psychological report which described Henry Smit as a troubled and socially isolated teenager who rebelled strongly to male authority. The problem below the surface became evident when he struck his male teacher.

"Is there anything else on the missing mother? Or the father?"

"I couldn't find anything else. But," added Jill, "the MacLivish's still live at the same address."

"Perhaps they could fill us in on a few details," said Hudson.

"It's worth a drive out to Balmain for lunch. Your shout," said Jill.

"I could do with a beer," said Hudson. "Great work Jill."

* * *

Hudson and Jill relaxed over a counter-lunch of shepherd's pie and an icy cold beer at the historical hotel located right in the heart of rustic Balmain in inner Sydney.

After lunch they made their way to the home of Mr and Mrs MacLivish and knocked on the door. It took only a few moments before an elderly woman opened it.

Both Hudson and Jill displayed their warrant cards and announced themselves. The woman looked puzzled but opened the door wider.

"Do come in," said Colleen MacLivish.

Hudson and Jill climbed the narrow staircase to the floor above.

"Can you manage, luv?" said Colleen to Jill, who was struggling up the narrow staircase behind Hudson.

"I'm fine," puffed Jill.

"You could do with some physical activity in your spare time," said Hudson.

"Shut up."

Hudson grinned to himself. Jill's rather primitive social graces no longer bothered him.

The living room had that musky 'old closet' smell. The furniture was very old and worn. Photos of children and grandchildren covered every available wall space.

Bill MacLivish had the race guide next to him and an old wireless which he turned off as the visitors walked in. He placed his bifocals, leaning precariously, on the arm of a large brown vinyl lounge chair and stood up to greet Hudson and Jill.

A china plate with a couple of Iced Vo Vo biscuits and their coconut remnants sat next to the teapot, still in its cosy.

"Would you like a cuppa?" asked Colleen.

"No. Thank you. We just had lunch," replied Jill.

"Thank you for seeing us," said Hudson, sitting down on the sofa where Colleen had just removed a colourful rug she was crocheting. "As Jill mentioned on the phone, we wanted some information on your neighbours, the Smith family. We didn't know if you would remember them after all this time."

"How could you forget *that* family, eh, Colleen?" said the old man with a snort.

"They weren't neighbours, as such." Colleen drew the curtains back exposing the narrow street.

Hudson grimaced as he watched a small truck trying to get around the police car parked on the very narrow street.

"They lived right there," said Colleen, pointing to a double-story Victorian terrace house across the street in polychrome brick and a filigree-style balcony.

"Some of the terraces have been renovated since then," said Bill. "They were considered slums back then. Now they're sought after, being so close to the city."

"Young professional people live in them now, so it's very quiet during the day," said Colleen. "They call them yuppies."

"More like yappers, if you ask me," retorted Bill. "Especially on weekends."

Hudson and Jill smiled at each other. Bill and Colleen obviously didn't get too many visitors. They were making the most of their audience.

"Why were they so memorable, Bill?" asked Hudson.

"When the Smits first arrived, I thought that the wife was his daughter, she was so young," said Bill.

"And very attractive," interrupted Colleen. "With her beautiful dark skin and long black hair."

"Women notice these things," said Bill, rolling his eyes. "I remember the car," he continued. "A grey Volvo."

"Trust you to remember the car," said Colleen.

"It was the only car in the whole street," said Bill, waving an impatient hand at Colleen. "They also had a ten year old boy. We couldn't remember his name when you rang."

"It was Henry," said Jill.

"That's right. They called him Heinrich sometimes," said Colleen, looking very proud of herself for remembering.

"The father was a big brute of a man. Fair skinned with a good head of grey hair and a bushy moustache," continued Bill.

"He was a sadistic man," said Colleen, clutching her cardigan as if to protect herself from an attack by a charging wildebeest. "I can't bear to think of that poor woman and what she must have gone through."

"Let me talk, Colleen," said Bill, taking charge. "We watched them move in and within two weeks he had his business up and running."

"What sort of business?" asked Jill.

"He imported paintings and antiques," said Bill. "We didn't see much of them. I worked during the day at the local Council in Balmain and Colleen was busy with our two children and the tuck shop at school."

"The young lad started school," added Colleen. "Poor fella, I wonder what became of him?"

"Henry Smith died under mysterious circumstances," said Hudson.

Colleen and Bill looked at each other.

"Oh, dear," said Colleen. "What a tragic and wretched family they were."

"Yes. And we witnessed some of that tragedy," said Bill.

"We couldn't help it. Could we, Bill? When the windows were open, you could hear every word. There was very little privacy."

"That's right," agreed Bill. "Not only did we hear them, but we saw more than we should have. In those days, people had those sheer nylon curtains."

"They were terylene, Bill."

"Yes, okay Colleen."

"You could see right through them."

"Some people had venetian blinds, Bill."

"Yes, dear. The police aren't interested in furnishings. I was just trying to make a point."

Hudson and Jill exchanged glances.

"Maybe we will have a cup of tea," said Hudson.

Colleen, happy to be of service, disappeared into the kitchen. Hudson and Jill turned their attention back to Bill.

"As I was saying," he continued. "We were watching the telly one night, when all of a sudden we heard shouting." Bill flicked his thumb towards the front window.

"Colleen and I raced to the open windows and to our horror, Smit, in full view of the window, was completely naked. He held a riding crop and was whipping away and shouting in some foreign language. We couldn't see who was at the receiving end. It was blocked from view by his huge, fat, hairy body," said Bill, with disdain. "I made Colleen go back inside."

"Was there anyone crying out?" asked Jill.

"No." Bill shook his head. "And then I saw her when Smit moved to the end of the bed."

Bill shuddered. He took a deep breath and continued. "She'd been gagged," he said in a low voice, although there was no-one near enough to overhear.

Colleen had walked in quietly with a tray. Bill waited until Colleen had poured the tea. He picked up his mug and took a sip.

"He was a giant of a man," he continued. "I closed the windows, but not before I saw the young lad sitting outside on the street with his hands over his face." His voice trailed off.

"Did you do anything about it, Bill?" asked Jill.

"No. Not at first. I watched Mrs Smit the following day. She was acting as if nothing had happened, running up and down the stairs, bringing Smit coffee and cake and serving him lunch while he pottered around in his shop."

"I told Bill, at the time," interrupted Colleen, looking most embarrassed, "that I had read something in a magazine where people sometimes played those sorts of games."

"One afternoon, a few weeks later," continued Bill. "I was home early from work and I heard a loud crash, like china being broken. I was downstairs and as I looked out onto the street Mrs Smit was trying to get out of the front door. She didn't stand a chance. Smit had grabbed her by the waist and shoved her back inside, slamming the door. He dragged her up the stairs. I then heard a distressed female voice from the top floor. I can't begin to describe to you what he did to her that afternoon.

"I told Colleen later that day, that they definitely weren't playing games." Bill's voice dropped to a whisper. "I wanted to go and rescue her, but my legs wouldn't move."

"You were in shock, luv," said Colleen, topping up his mug.

"I rang the police that afternoon, said Bill. "They asked me to come down and make a statement. I was painting quite a vivid picture to the young copper, when he suddenly stopped typing and called out to a senior officer. The senior officer leaned over the typewriter and read what had been written." Bill shook his head, and with all sincerity exclaimed. "I'm sure they've never heard or seen anything like that before."

I'm sure they have! thought Hudson. He looked over at Jill, who was trying to keep a straight face.

"I asked them if they could do something about it," continued Bill. "The senior copper replied that there was little he could do through the legal system with domestic violence. And that was the end of it."

"Tell the detectives what you did after that, luv," said Colleen.

"I'm getting to that. I decided to front the man. I went into his shop and told him what I thought. He had those steely blue eyes that seemed to pierce right through you. He hit his fist on the table and told me to mind my own business. That man scared the living crap out of me."

"And always the young boy would be sitting outside in the dark," said Colleen.

"Two years later it all stopped," said Bill. "The mother disappeared." Bill took another sip from his mug, which was instantly refilled by Colleen. "I stopped the young lad in the street one day and asked him about his mother. He kept his head down, and without even a word or so much as a gesture, walked away. I went to the police *again*. And this time they did come out. We don't know what the final outcome was, but the story in the street was that she ran away."

"Did you believe that?" asked Hudson.

"I know thousands of people go missing every year, but I don't believe for one moment that she ran away."

"What do you think happened to her?" asked Jill.

Colleen hung her head and clasped her hands together as if in prayer.

"Do you think he killed her?" asked Jill.

"Surely they would have found her body," added Hudson.

"They would never have found her body around here," said Colleen.

"Why is that?"

"As you know Balmain was quite an industrial town with shipyards and coal mines," said Bill. "And about the time she disappeared, one of the largest coal mines was being demolished right down the end of this street. The shafts - some of them went down to about two thousand feet - were flooded and sealed. That was only hearsay. You can't do anything about it now. The site was redeveloped in the 1980's with townhouses and an up market marina."

"Anyway," continued Colleen. "The young lad started high school about this time and then twelve months later, *he* disappeared. I told Bill to go to the police again."

"We were becoming regulars at the cop shop," said Bill with a smile. "However, the police did tell me that young Henry had gone to reformatory school for hitting a teacher."

"When Henry came back, he was a tall, good looking boy," said Colleen. "I felt sorry for him, though. He didn't play sport or socialize. He just helped his father in the shop on weekends." As Colleen passed the biscuits to Hudson and Jill, she added. "Oh, that man was a brute."

"The brute," mimicked Bill, "would go out every Friday night and come back in the early hours of the morning."

"Henry finished high school and went on to University. That was about the time the father got killed," said Colleen.

"Good riddance, I said to Colleen at the time," said Bill.

"How did you find out about his death?" asked Jill.

"That's a long story," said Bill. "One day I said to Colleen that the old fella's gone. I noticed that the shop had been closed for over a week. Then I saw a police car outside the house talking to the young lad. Colleen made me go over to the house of horrors to find out what was going on. Threatened me with a whip, she did," said Bill with a chortle. "That's how we found out that Mr Smit was murdered."

"There was a lot of gossip in the street," said Colleen. "One of the neighbours recognized Mr Smit's car in a newspaper article."

"I remember the article," said Bill. "It said the victim was killed execution-style and that he died from a single gunshot wound to the back of the head."

"Yes, that's right," said Colleen. "The body was found next to the car in the red light district of Kings Cross. Tell the officers what else they found in the car, Bill."

"The article also mentioned that cocaine had been found in the boot of the car and that the murder was probably drug related," said Bill. "The unit went on the market shortly after that. Sold quickly. And the lad moved away."

"Did they ever find the mother?" asked Colleen.

"No! She is still a missing person."

Jill and Hudson stood up.

"Thank you for your time," said Hudson. "You have been most helpful."

"It was the house of *Houdini*," said Jill as they walked back onto the road.

Chapter 22

Nina sat alone in her father's home.

It was the first time she had ventured in since that tragic day so long ago, it seemed. There was a mournful quietness about it, a sense of the past, a life time of memories. Memories Nina was trying to cling to.

A wave of emotion engulfed her as she looked around the room that held the history of her family. The display cabinet which held every gift she had made for her father, standing with pride amongst his souvenirs and collectables. She pictured the Staunton chess set in dark Rosewood and Boxwood which usually sat on the coffee table waiting for Henry's next visit but had been banished to a plastic bag after the crime scene cleaners had cleaned and sanitised the home.

How my father looked forward to Henry's visits and the challenge of a game of chess, she thought. But Henry came for more than a game of chess.

Nina reached for the family album. She turned each page stroking the photographs as if this would somehow bring her loved ones back to life, even for a moment. She lingered on a photograph of Henry Smith and her mother, Zoya, taken at a government ceremony in 1982; a photograph her mother had insisted be included in the family album. Henry had received a Humanitarian Award for his work and contribution to the cause of refugees and asylum seekers. In his acceptance speech he had called on Zoya to share the moment. Henry had organised a press release acknowledging that Nina's mother's story had been his inspiration. She unfolded the Immigration Department's monthly bulletin which was tucked away behind the photo in the plastic sleeve and read:

Zoya Veloski came into the world on a cold day in February in the year 1948, in the small township of Brauweiler near the city of Cologne in Germany to parents Ludmilla and Victor. Zoya's home was the site of an old 15th century stone monastery linked to a former jail by a courtyard. It had been turned into a camp for refugees. Zoya and her parents shared this camp with two thousand people, where mothers slept with their babies tucked under their jackets away from rats that came out at night to nibble at the ears and toes of sleeping infants.

Conditions were appalling. People shared army type communal toilets, where they sat side by side with no privacy. There was very little food. The International Red Cross handed out used clothing. Parents would wrap children's feet in paper and then put on socks to try and keep them warm.

British administrators were responsible for feeding all the refugees, which consisted of one meal per day. Everyone would queue up outside the camp kitchen at two o'clock in the afternoon. The main diet consisted of daily rations of half a loaf of bread and watery rice soup. Sometimes cheese and marmalade, even coffee and a daily spoon of sugar would be issued. Many children died from malnutrition and a variety of diseases such as typhoid fever and whooping cough. Zoya had survived whooping cough.

The men in the camps would often go out and search the nearby fields for food. Sometimes they would come back with carrots and parsnips, even plums. But mostly potato peels they had found in local garbage bins.

Zoya's mother, Ludmilla, had desperately wanted to return home to the Ukraine. A home that had been ravaged by war. A home where their families had been annihilated. Hitler had occupied the Ukraine for three years between 1941-1944, ordering the Ukrainians into forced labour camps. Ludmilla had been taken in the summer of 1942 to work in a munitions factory. She was only eighteen.

Nina had often asked her grandmother, Ludmilla, how she survived the horrors of the war and the camps. Nina recalled her grandmother's prophetic words.

"Nina," she would say. "If ever you are depressed, lonely or feeling hopeless, go and help someone else or do something for someone else."

Nina felt the warm tears running down her face. She turned the page over and read on.

The family could not return to their Soviet-dominated land because of political and religious persecution by yet another dictator, the feared Joseph Stalin. There were stories of people returning to their homeland only to be put into prison or killed because they had the audacity to be captured.

The United Nations Refugee Relief Centre had the approval of many countries to take these displaced people. Zoya and her parents were destined for Australia.

It had taken them three days by train and truck to travel from Germany to Italy. After three weeks in Naples, they finally boarded the SS Nelly, a converted US army carrier. The men slept at the bottom of the ship and the women and children on top.

The boat sailed through the Suez Canal, stopping in Port Said in Egypt, then on to Freemantle in Western Australia before arriving in Sydney on the 24th March 1950 with sixteen hundred 'New Australians' on board.

Unclean and lice-ridden, many suffering from malnutrition, trauma and depression, they were loaded onto a bus and then a train bound for Bathurst, hardly appreciating the beauty of the Sydney Harbour.

Arriving at the camp in Bathurst, eight families were put in one room, with blankets suspended from rafters for privacy. Bread and golden syrup had been the first meal many had enjoyed in a place of safety and peace, or as close to peace as one could describe.

Zoya Veloski had grown up in many such camps in Parkes, Greta and Scheyville, near Windsor in the foothills of the Blue Mountains.

Nina looked at the photo of her mother standing proudly next to Henry Smith. Yes, her story was inspirational. This one article by Henry Smith had portrayed her family's tragic past.

Nina placed the article back in the album. She wrestled herself from the comfortable armchair and walked through the kitchen and out the back door, her feet echoing on the checkered linoleum tiles.

She looked around the yard. Memories of her father were everywhere. The vegetable patch where tomato plants, cucumbers and sweet corn lay dry and withered. The flower garden he had lovingly created for his wife, Zoya. *He was such a romantic*, thought Nina. She looked beyond the rose garden at the grevilleas and bottle brush and caught a glimpse of the Nepean River. Tears ran freely as she remembered the stories her father would tell her of his own river, the beautiful Dnieper River. A holy river flowing amidst the forests and meadows and wild fields of his beloved Ukraine.

Her father had wanted to take her back and show her the region where he grew up. Below the rapids, he would say, where old river beds and small lakes made up the beautiful green country and boundless steppes of the Ukraine.

That wish had nearly come true. They had booked their tickets. Organised their passports. Nina had even bought her pink luggage.

She was now sobbing as she realised that the dream had died with her father.

Suicide. No, it wasn't possible.

But she had found her father in a pool of blood, hadn't she?

The Coroner's report had stated that it was a 'self-inflicted gun shot wound.'

Her father didn't even own a gun.

Nina started to feel dizzy as the scent of the flowers brought back the memory of her father, so pale and cold, as he lay in the open casket in the middle of the church, surrounded by candles. She felt comforted by the priest's chanting of psalms and the swinging of the censer filling the church with the fragrance of incense. As the service progressed, the Ukrainian Orthodox church with its dome shaped roof was filled with the melodious sound of five old babushkas, the remnants of a once grand choir. The church situated in Western Sydney was once the spiritual home of a whole displaced culture but as the old immigrants died out, it stood empty.

Once the absolution prayer was read and placed in the hands of the deceased, Nina joined the procession of faceless people paying their last respects, the drops from the sprinkling of holy water joining her salty tears. Nina shivered, as she recalled kissing her father's cheek for the last time.

But the sound that would stay with her forever was the empty groan as the lid was placed on the coffin. A sound louder than thunder as she saw her father for the last time. A vice had crushed her heart as she cried through heart-wrenching sobs, "I'll always love you, Papa."

Her only saving grace was her twin brother, Alex. He wrapped his arms around her convulsing body and whispered. "Pain is the glue that binds families together forever."

The candles were extinguished and the closed coffin was carried out.

Ivan Renowicz was laid to rest at Pine Grove Cemetery next to his beloved wife, Zoya, who had died five years previously of breast cancer.

Chapter 23

"What have you got on this afternoon Jill?" asked Hudson.

"I'm delving into Jackson's shipping documents. Why?"

"This Ivan fellow keeps cropping up," said Hudson. "I'm on my way to visit the daughter."

"Do you want me to come with you?" asked Jill. "Can't trust yourself around women, can you?"

"No, to the first question. Yes, to the second," said Hudson. "And thirdly, I'd like you to arrange to see Maya. See if you can get some answers on Jackson."

"You mean woman to woman, like?" said Jill. "Sure."

"Thanks," said Hudson. "Sam's gone to the airport. We'll get together sometime tomorrow."

"Do you want me to ask Maya if she's interested in you?" asked Jill, ducking a paper cup as she exited.

* * *

Jill Morellix sat in a small café in Martin Place in the centre of the city. She had arranged to meet Maya Smith who worked close by. Jill ordered her coffee just as Maya walked in. Jill recognised her immediately from the video. Her dress style was very trendy and conspicuous, unlike Jill who wore a black knee length straight skirt teamed with a plain blue blouse.

Maya ordered a latte and walked over to where Jill was waving.

Jill stood up and introduced herself. "May I offer my condolences?" she said.

"Thank you."

"Let me explain the meeting," said Jill. "It's really just standard routine, but I need to interview family members and friends."

"No problem," said Maya as she sat down, placing a large display folder on to the vacant chair beside her. "Layout for a promotion," she said with pride.

"Can I have a look?"

"Sure."

Jill had done some homework on Maya Smith and found out that she worked in one of the leading advertising agency as their Creative Director which was a recent promotion. She was dating Colin Jackson, but had her own apartment in Surry Hills.

"That's a layout for a retail client." said Maya. "I'm taking it home to add the final details."

"Who's the client?"

"It's for a company in London."

"London?"

"We have a branch in London," said Maya.

"Impressive," said Jill.

"I was actually asked to work in our London office a few years ago," said Maya.

"Why didn't you go?"

"I fell in love."

"Great reason to give up a job."

They both laughed.

"However, no regrets," said Maya. "Now, what did you want to ask me?"

"No, do go on. I'd love to hear how someone gives up a great job opportunity for love."

"Well, it was great at the start. Dinners, romance, you know," said Maya.

"No, actually I don't," said Jill. "I'm still waiting for Mr Right."

Jill could feel that Maya wanted to talk.

"When I moved in with Colin, I saw him less and less. He was travelling a lot."

"What sort of work is he into?" asked Jill.

"He owns a nursery out at Dural, the Happi Frog," said Maya. "By a strange coincidence, I had actually designed the logo for the Happi Frog long before I met Colin. He was a client at the time. I remember it vividly. The graphic artist had prepared the artwork but no one asked for my input."

"So you put your two bobs' worth in," said Jill.

"Believe it or not. If I hadn't, there would be frogs all over his advertising material."

"And nurseries have little to do with frogs," quipped Jill.

"I changed the 'y' in *Happy* to an 'i' and made it a colourful flower," she said proudly, handing Jill one of the Happi Frog business cards.

"It's a great logo," said Jill.

"I always keep it in my purse. For luck!"

"Anyway, to cut a long story, when the Accounts Executive returned from seeing the client, she congratulated me. Colin had chosen my design."

"Colin Jackson," said Jill. "I recall that he attended your father's funeral."

"Yes. He arranged everything."

"Why don't you travel with him?" asked Jill.

"Colin dashes to a place and is back in a week. It's all business." replied Maya. "And I'm not that into shopping for garden gnomes."

Jill laughed. "He goes on buying sprees for garden gnomes?"

This sent the two girls into a fit of giggles.

"Why doesn't he shop online?" asked Jill.

"He's probably a shopoholic," said Maya.

"More like a 'shop-o-troll-ic'," said Jill.

The girls were now laughing hysterically. They had certainly clicked. Not an easy task for Jill, who lived on another planet compared to Maya.

"I'm sorry," said Jill, wiping the tears from her eyes.

"It's okay. I needed a laugh," said Maya. "But seriously, Colin visits factories overseas and has most of the garden ornaments and accessories custom-made and shipped to his nursery," she continued. "And, I can assure you, there's not too many garden gnomes."

The two women seemed to have settled down and were sipping their coffees and Jill felt it was time for official business.

"There are a couple of questions I need to ask," she said. "We don't have a motive for your father's death. Can you think of anyone who would want to harm him?"

"Apart from Dad's work? No, I can't. Dad led such a mundane life. He collected antiques, loved his gardening and played chess. My childhood was filled with good times. Family outings, a variety of holidays – from surfing to skiing and everything in between." Maya took another sip of coffee. "He was a wonderful father."

"What did you mean by 'apart from your father's work'?" asked Jill.

"My father was in the process of exposing human rights abuses in detention centres and I think he stepped on the toes of people in high places."

"Did he get threatened?"

"I don't know. My mother told me that he was receiving 'friendly' phone calls from colleagues advising him not to go public with information on refugees."

"He went ahead with it anyway," said Jill. "I read an article in the daily papers where your father was calling for a review of detention centres."

"My mother would often tell him that he was living dangerously. But he took no notice."

Jill placed her hand on Maya's and said, "I'm so sorry, Maya. I promise you that we'll get the person responsible!"

The rest of the meeting passed in a friendly discussion about less formal topics, and the matter of Henry's death was left behind.

Chapter 24

After Jill left, Maya ordered another coffee.

She looked at the business card. It had changed her life.

She took a sip. The hot, sweet taste took her mind back to the first time she had shared a cup with Colin.

She had been fossicking through a kaleidoscope of pots, ornaments and plants at the Happi Frog nursery, when she was approached by a good-looking man who cheekily grinned and asked her if she wanted to see his collection of garden gnomes.

Maya recognised him from the society pages and knew of his reputation as a playboy.

"Perhaps gnomes could come back into vogue some day," she replied. "But, no. Not today, thank you."

"By the way, my name is Colin."

"I'm Maya."

"Are you looking for anything in particular?"

"Window displays," she replied. "For a client."

"Ah! My speciality."

Maya smiled. She eventually succumbed to his persistence and opened her display folder. His mind had been a torrent of creative ideas and suggestions, built upon her original designs. Maya had been impressed.

"I think you've blown my budget completely," she said.

"I think we can come to some arrangement," he said. "Let's talk in my office."

Colin led the way to his office. As he opened the door Maya could smell the richness of the timber. The room was beautifully decorated with exquisitely handcrafted Tasmanian oak and Australian red cedar furniture. The walls were adorned with paintings of Australian wildflowers and birds.

He led her past the rich brown leather chairs to a soft velvet sofa surrounded by indoor plants.

Coffee and a small platter laden with petits fours and ratafia biscuits had miraculously appeared on the coffee table.

Maya ran her hand against the rustic timber of the coffee table, a miniature version of the huge slab atop the main desk.

"It's beautiful," she said. "Redwood?"

"You know your timbers," he said.

"One of my father's hobbies," she said. "It's rubbed off onto me."

He poured her coffee. Maya added the cream and sugar.

"Now let's get down to business," he said.

"I'll deliver the plants, set up your window displays and pick everything up at the end of the promotion."

He paused. "I'll do this free of charge in return for displaying a small sign in the window advertising that all the plants have been supplied by the Happi Frog nursery."

It was an offer Maya could not refuse.

"I'll run the possibilities past my client and get back to you," she said.

The spring fashion promotion had been a huge success.

Colin had delivered an assortment of monocotyledon plants featuring showy grasses, orchids and lilies. He had decorated the windows with a tiered water display and pond with floating lilies. Ceramic pots were filled with reeds and grasses, adorned with silver and golden dragonflies. Surrounding the pond lay a variety of leaping and climbing ceramic frogs, so realistic that shoppers were seen tapping on the shop-front windows in an attempt to make them jump. The spectrum of colour was completed by eye-catching spring blooms in topaz yellow, amethyst, cobalt blue and cherry.

After the promotion Maya had rung Colin to thank him.

"I'll believe your thanks are sincere if you accompany me and a one hundred year old friend of mine to celebrate your triumph in my favourite restaurant, which happens to be in a subterranean cavern."

"Where and when?" she responded, intrigued.

"Well, it's a full moon tonight, Maya," he teased, "and during a full moon, gnomes come to life and reveal all the secrets they have overheard in their gardens."

Maya finished her coffee and smiled to herself as she recalled their first night together. Colin had arrived with a garden gnome under one arm and a huge bunch of red roses in the other.

Sex was always freely available to Maya, but romance and imagination in her lovers were rare indeed. She was smitten with an intense desire and Colin Jackson satisfied it well.

Chapter 25

Hudson noticed the *'For Sale'* sign as soon as he pulled up at the address Jill had given him. He noted the agent's address and made his way there.

"Can I speak to the manager?" he asked the young girl sitting behind the reception counter.

A few moments later, a well dressed male with a smile that could light up a stadium introduced himself. "How can I help you?" he asked, showing Hudson into his office.

"Good morning. I'm Detective Inspector Matthew Hudson." He flashed his badge. "I'd like to see the inside of one of your houses for sale."

"Which house are you particularly interested in?" queried the agent, the radiant smile fading to bored indifference.

"This one," replied Hudson, handing over the paper with the address.

"That's a deceased estate," said the agent. "The daughter is the executor. I'll give you her name and number."

Before Hudson could thank him, he was ushered out the door with a list of phone numbers for Miss Nina Renowicz.

Speedy Gonzales couldn't have done it faster, thought Hudson. Not wanting to hang around until after office hours, he decided to ring Nina Renowicz at work.

Nina sat at her computer. The Insurance Assessor's office could get extremely busy after a flood or fire, but there had been no disasters for months. At these quieter times she would have been daydreaming or investigating travel destinations. But that pastime had faded and the joy with it.

She answered the phone after putting the nail file into the top drawer.

"Miss Renowicz?" said the man's voice.

"Yes. How can I help you?"

"I'd like to speak to you about your house for sale in Emu Plains."

"I've placed the home with a local real estate agent," she replied. "How did you get my number?"

She's on the ball! thought Hudson.

"From a mutual friend," he lied. "I'm only here for the day. Can we meet for lunch?"

Under normal circumstances, Nina would never have agreed to meet a stranger. But she was bored and desperate to sell the house quickly.

"Where will I meet you?" she asked.

"I noticed a large shopping centre when I drove in," said Hudson. "Is there a café where we could meet?"

"On the ground floor, there's a place called Oscar's. I'll meet you there in half an hour," she replied. "How will I know you?"

Hudson had also noticed a florist shop. "I'll be wearing a pink carnation in my jacket pocket," he said, suddenly feeling melodramatic.

"You'll have to buy the whole bunch," said the florist in irritation.

"But I only want *one* to put in my jacket."

Five minutes later and thirty dollars lighter, Hudson was the proud owner of a huge bunch of pink carnations, wrapped in pink cellophane and boasting the biggest and hottest pink ribbon 'Miss Florist' could find.

If I was working undercover and trying to look inconspicuous, this would definitely do the trick, he thought, as he walked through the busy shopping centre.

He found the café and chose a table in the outdoor section which appeared to be reasonably private. He ordered a black coffee and waited.

Hopefully, Miss Renowicz will let me see the inside of the house without the official paperwork. And answer a few questions at the same time.

Hudson saw the disturbance before he saw Nina Renowicz. Heads turned in the café doorway and waiters stood almost to attention. Then a vision walked in. She looked around the café and soon spotted the pink carnations. She walked towards Hudson's table.

He was momentarily stunned. There was another piece of the puzzle.

It's Ruby Red!

It took Hudson several moments to recover from the shock of finally meeting the mystery woman. She looked more mysterious and alluring than he had remembered. Her blue eyes were intensified by the deep aqua uniform, inscribed with an insurance company logo. Her blonde hair was clipped back with an ornamental clasp. The ruby red lips were gone, replaced with a soft coral.

"Nina Renowicz." She held out her hand to the stranger.

"Matthew Hudson," he finally managed to mumble. He could feel his heart racing and heat rushing to his face. *Christ, don't let me make a fool of myself,* he prayed. He handed her the bunch of flowers. "The florist wouldn't sell me one carnation."

It broke the ice and they both laughed.

"Are you on a time limit?" he asked, finally able to breathe easier.

"I've taken the afternoon off."

When a waitress approached, they ordered sandwiches and coffee.

"Who is our mutual friend?" she asked, after the waitress had left.

"I'm terribly sorry," said Hudson. "I didn't want to frighten you on the phone. It was the first thing that came to mind. I'm a detective with the NSW Police Department."

Hudson saw Nina's body language change. She leaned back in her chair. Her jaw tightened and she started to fiddle with an antique rose gold and ruby ring on her finger.

"What can I help you with?" she asked, her tone less friendly than before.

"I'm working on a murder case," said Hudson. "The victim was Henry Smith. We believe that your father, Ivan, was a friend of his."

Hudson was now the detective, the initial impact of Ruby Red under control. "May I firstly offer my deepest sympathy on the death of your father, Miss Renowicz?"

"Thank you."

The waitress brought the sandwiches and coffee. Nina placed one sugar into her cappuccino and took a sip. She didn't touch her sandwich.

"It's been almost eight weeks now," she said, looking distressed.

"I realize this is a very sensitive subject," said Hudson, "But anything you can recall will benefit this case tremendously." He was hoping Nina would feel some obligation. He could see that she had relaxed slightly and was relieved when she helped herself to a sandwich.

"When was the last time your father saw Henry?"

"He hadn't seen Henry for months. I remember him saying that he was longing for a game of chess," she replied.

"May I ask if the chessboard was a permanent fixture in the house, or only came out when a game was being played?"

"The chess set only came out when Henry was due for a visit. However, sometimes if they hadn't finished a game, Henry and my father would play over the phone and the chess set could sit on the coffee table for days."

"You were obviously very distraught when you made your statement to the police. Could you possibly clarify some points for me?"

"I thought you were investigating Henry Smith's murder?" she interrupted.

"It's come to light that your father's suicide and the murder of Henry Smith occurred on the same day and in close proximity."

"Oh, my God!" exclaimed Nina. "It hadn't occurred to me. Henry's funeral was so much later than my father's.

"They didn't find Henry Smith's body for almost two weeks. And then there was the autopsy," said Hudson.

"Now I understand," she whispered to herself.

"Understand what?" asked Hudson.

"Nothing. I was just thinking aloud."

Her slight tension didn't go unnoticed by Hudson.

"What did you want clarified?" Nina continued hurriedly.

"I know this must be difficult for you, Miss Renowicz, but we are investigating a murder, and any help you can give us will be most appreciated."

"Yes, I understand."

"When you found your father on that morning, did you touch anything?" asked Hudson. "Can you piece together what happened?"

Nina took another sip of her coffee. "Normally, I'd call on my father at least twice a week before going to work. I remember arriving and the door was unlocked. I called out to him, but there was no answer."

Hudson noticed that Nina had started to frantically twirl her ruby ring around her finger. Her eyes watered and her breathing became slightly laboured.

"I placed the casserole I'd made for him onto the kitchen counter," she said. "I then headed towards the back door to the garden. Something caught my eye in the lounge room. That's when I found my father lying on the lounge. At first I thought he was asleep. But then I saw the blood."

"Did you enter the lounge room at all?" asked Hudson, after Nina had dried her eyes.

"No, I was motionless. I managed to pick up the phone which was in the kitchen and dialled triple O. I didn't move from the spot until an ambulance officer sat me down and asked me if there was anyone he could call. I gave them my brother's telephone number."

It was obvious to Hudson that Nina didn't want to go into any more detail. He beckoned to the waitress to bring two more coffees.

"What can you tell me about your father's relationship with Henry Smith?" he asked.

"My mother, Zoya worked with Henry at the Department of Immigration and Ethnic Affairs, as it was known then. My father, Ivan came to Australia from the Ukraine to visit his brother. My parents met at a wedding and they fell in love. When my father's visa had expired, my mother turned to Henry for help. Henry was instrumental in organizing permanent residency. My father was very grateful and they became friends."

She's rattled off that story as if she had memorised it by heart, thought Hudson. "Did you know Henry personally?" he asked.

"What do you mean?"

This is definitely not the time, nor the place, to ask personal questions. "Apart from playing chess with your father," Hudson rephrased quickly, "Did your family socialise with Henry?"

"No, not really," she answered evasively. "Henry would visit at Christmas time and special events such as birthdays."

"When was the last time you saw Henry?"

"I can't recall," she said. "Probably months. Now I need to get back to work."

"Just one more thing," said Hudson, thinking he sounded like the TV detective *'Columbo.'* "I would like to have a look inside the house."

"My brother and I moved everything out last weekend. The place has been professionally cleaned and repainted since ...." Her voice trailed off.

"I realise that, but I would like to have a look around, anyway," he answered.

"Sure." She opened her handbag, extracted a bunch of keys, took a key off it and handed it to Hudson.

"I'll return it as soon as I can."

"Don't bother. I have a spare one."

Hudson took out a business card and handed it to Nina. She stood up, extended her hand politely and left.

Chapter 26

The drive to the airport was slow.

Sam Gilroy was met by the Security Liaison Officer from the Australian Protective Services, under the jurisdiction of the Australian Federal Police. After a thorough examination of his ID and appropriate paper work, Sam was asked to place his belongings into a plastic tray which had to be passed through the X-ray scanner. He took off his gun belt and placed it next to his keys and mobile phone. The officer placed all Sam's belongings into a metal storage unit before walking Sam through the electronic security screening system.

Not much of a liaison officer, thought Sam. *Didn't even introduce himself.*

Feeling quite naked without his gun, Sam followed the officer to a restricted area, where he was handed over to the Protective Services Officer, Osip Hashuwenic.

At least he has a name, even though I can't pronounce it!

Sam followed Osip through several security doors into a small office, but not before he had surveyed the huge security monitoring station. It was filled with screening equipment, computers and security officers. It resembled a spaceship. Not that Sam had ever been inside a spaceship, but he had visited NASA when he lived in the States and his favourite movies were science fiction.

"I've got the tape set up that your department requested," said Osip as they finally reached their destination.

Sam was filled with awe at the volume of people passing through the airport.

"What on earth do you look for?"

"We have trained operators with good observation skills scanning and focusing on anything out of the ordinary."

"Such as?"

"Abandoned objects. Someone acting suspiciously, like constantly looking over their shoulder, sweating, chewing their nails ..."

"I'd be arrested immediately," interrupted Sam. "Sorry, go on. This is interesting."

"Most people walk through the security line with very little emotion," continued Osip. "If the traveller deviates from this behaviour, they merit a closer look."

"Some people could just be nervous about flying."

"Our officers are well trained in behaviour analysis. There are also other indicators. For example, here we are, looking at people making their way to the Bali terminal. Most of them are wearing casual clothing, shorts and floral shirts. If they appear to be overdressed for the type of weather, we may consider that suspicious."

"What if they're going to Bali on business?"

"As a general rule, most people wear casual clothing when they travel internationally."

"There she is," said Sam suddenly, pointing to the screen.

"Is that the person you're looking for?"

"Yes. One of them."

Osip went to his computer and within seconds Susan Harvey's passport appeared on the screen.

"Can you verify that she got on the plane to Bali?" asked Sam.

"Sure can. If you hang on a minute, I'll even give you the return date."

"I need to find her male travelling companion."

"Have you spotted him yet?"

"I don't know what he looks like."

"They're bound to be seen together at some stage."

"Not necessarily," said Sam. "He's married. And not to Ms Harvey."

"Oh, like that, is it? That could make it a bit difficult. Do you have a name?" asked Osip.

"Try Mr Harvey. Apparently they registered at the Four Seasons Resort in Bali as husband and wife."

"No. There's no Mr Harvey registered as leaving for Bali on that day. I'll just check previous and post dates."

Sam waited just a minute or two as the officer scanned data on the screens.

"Negative!" said Osip.

"Does anyone look suspicious to you?" asked Sam.

"Let's have a look. They look like a very relaxed group. There's no-one wearing a disguise. There's no one hiding under a hairpiece."

Osip started to laugh and Sam realized he was having him on.

"Can we go through all the passengers?"

"There's two hundred of them. It will take a while.

"If we eliminate women, couples, children and anyone under forty," said Sam hopefully. "Although, Susan Harvey could be a *'cougar'*, and then maybe we'll have to drop the age."

"Do you want me to eliminate foreign passport holders? It will narrow the field down considerably."

"Sure."

It took Osip no time to short list fifty-two males travelling alone. As each name and face appeared on the screen, Sam shook his head.

What was he supposed to look for?

"Can you pick out a cheating husband in that lot?"

"We're not *that* good," chuckled Osip.

"Can I have a list of the names?"

"No. Not without a court order. Sorry."

"I guess it's like looking for a needle in a haystack, without a name," said Sam frustrated.

"At least I've verified Susan Harvey's alibi."

"Thanks for your help," said Sam. *Who cares if the iceberg' is having an affair?*

He left the airport with one thought on his mind. Australian cops are too soft. He could make Susan Harvey co-operate.

I've left your messages by the phone," yelled Jill as she followed Hudson into his office.

"Maya Smith and Colin Jackson are having it off," said Jill, waiting for a reaction from Hudson. She didn't get one.

Jill continued. "The serology and ballistics reports are on your desk. You have a meeting with James Kerr in fifteen minutes. And some journalist by the name of Phil Phillips rang. What a name! I'll bet he changed it by deed poll."

"Get on with it. Or get out!" yelled Hudson.

"Gee, what side of the bed did you get out of today? There's also an e-mail for you from the Four Seasons Resort in Bali. They've confirmed that the Harvey woman stayed at the resort for four nights but they won't give us the name of the bloke that stayed with her without a police order."

Hudson turned to his screen and brought up the email. "According to this," read Hudson, "the resort arranged Susan Harvey's flight back to Sydney. There is no information on her bed partner, as you said. That's being very diplomatic, but I suppose hotels have to be careful. I'd love to know who this bloke is. Okay, Jill, make the formal request to the Indonesian police for them to find out."

"Sam had no luck at the airport," said Jill. "It stands to reason. If he's married, he probably travelled on another flight. Why are you so suspicious of this woman?"

"I don't know. Probably because she looks like everyone's aunty, and she's a genius, according to work colleagues."

"What is a genius supposed to look like?"

Hudson ignored her. He reached for the report prepared by the Police Forensic Science Laboratory.

Category of bloodstain: High energy pattern. Blood stain patterns were found in the left front seat of the car. The presence of blood pooled on the back of the left front seat indicates that the victim had bled profusely.

Taking into account the variables, e.g. spot sizes, quantity, shape and location, the conclusion was that the bloodstain appeared to be of a 'high energy pattern' indicating that the source of the bloodstain would have possibly originated from a gunshot wound. The shot could possibly have been fired from the left window to the back of the neck area. The blood type is AB positive ...

"It's confirmed. Henry Smith was in the passenger seat when he was shot," said Jill.

"Who was in the driver's seat?"

"Obviously someone he knew."

"Obviously." Hudson's train of thought was interrupted.

"Just a reminder, Mr Grumpy. You have a meeting with Kerr. I'm off...."

Hudson looked up and thought. *Please don't say 'like a bucket of prawns in the hot sun.'*

"I'm off like a bucket of prawns in the hot sun," yelled Jill. "Have a good weekend."

Hudson sighed, then broke out laughing. Jill Morellix, whatever else she was and regardless of her appalling lack of respect for senior officers, was not boring.

Chapter 27

Jill was studying the shipping documents from the Customs Department of the Happi Frog imports.

Nothing unusual for a nursery, she thought. Terracotta pots, glazed pots, Anduze planters, pots and garden urns, water features and fountains, bronze, stone, cast iron and marble statues and sculptures, bird baths, a great range of ornaments, frogs, swans, mermaids and the inescapable garden gnomes.

She smiled to herself as she thought of the gnomes in her mother's garden. Hideous things. Sitting and staring from behind pot plants and shrubs.

Her mother, Raylene, felt that these gnomes brought good fortune. To top it all off, she had placed night lights along the garden path, in strategically marked spots around the front garden. It made those little creatures even less attractive and the neighbours sniggered behind her mother's back. But that did not deter her. She loved them and still collected them at garage sales and nurseries.

Jill decided to take the files home for the weekend. She could have a closer look without all the interruptions in the office.

* * *

"Hi, Mum," said Jill, throwing her jacket onto the chair.

"Hello, luv. Did you 'ave a good day?"

"Not too bad. I was talking about you today, Mum. You and your garden gnomes."

"You weren't makin' fun of my garden again?"

"No. I was just telling one of my colleagues that those pointy-hatted statues could be used as a weapon. What are those things made from anyway?"

"The antique gnomes were originally made from terracotta. Nowadays they're made from cement, ceramic clay or resin. I even 'ave one made of bronze."

"Are any of them made from plaster of Paris?" asked Jill.

"I don't think so. Plaster of Paris is a good medium for makin' moulds, but not outside ornaments. Why all the interest in gnomes? I thought you hated them."

"Oh, I do hate them," replied Jill. "Even more so since you've highlighted them with solar mushroom lights."

"The lights are there so that your father can see where he's goin'."

"He's usually too full to see where he's going," Jill retorted.

"That's not nice, Jill."

"I'm interested in the trolls, because I'm working on a drug importing case."

"And you think they're hidin' them inside the gnomes."

"Are they hollow?"

"Most of them are. Don't you remember that drug bust in Blacktown a few years ago, where snakes were concealed in garden gnomes and pottery figurines. The customs people found one of the snakes movin' in the packagin'," said Raylene with a shudder.

"Gross," said Jill.

"Your dinner's in the oven, luv. I'll just go and water the garden while I've got some time."

"Thanks, Mum. We'll have a game of scrabble later."

Garden gnomes and scrabble! I need to get a life, thought Jill. She took the paperwork out of her brief case and started sifting through it, hoping to find that one detail to tie Colin Jackson to the cocaine importation.

Early Saturday morning, Jill called out to her mother, "How would you like a trip out to the Dural nursery for morning tea? I'll even treat you to a new gnome."

"That would be lovely, dear."

"We'll leave after breakfast."

As Jill drove through the gates of the Happi Frog nursery, Raylene couldn't contain herself. "Isn't it breathtakin'?" She jumped out of the car even before Jill had put the handbrake on.

"Steady on, Mum, we've got all day. Anyone would think a hairy spider had got into the car."

"I just love springtime. Look at those blooms. What must they be feedin' 'em?"

"Probably cow manure."

"Look at the wave of colours, Jill. White camellias and azaleas, yellow daffodils, a sea of mauve lilacs and lavender and bluebells. And then a burst of colour from the Livingstone daisies and gerberas. I don't know where to start!"

Jill and Raylene walked past the flowering grevilleas and their beautiful trailing branches with bright red and yellow flowers then stopped at the roses.

Raylene fondled each rose despite the sign not to.

If she talks and smells each rose we could be here for a week, thought Jill.

"Look at this soft apricot rose, it's almost like a camellia."

After lifting each tag to find out the names of every flowering shrub and tree, Raylene finally sat down in the greenhouse to admire the orchids.

"I must say, they are captivating," said Jill. She sat down next to her mother. Two hours into their excursion and Jill was ready for coffee.

They walked past the infamous laboratory and potting shed where Constable Ryan Cooper had poured tomato sauce onto the floor near his locker.

"The café is right in the centre, Mum. You'll be able to watch the plants grow from there."

Jill smiled to herself as she thought of Hudson's face when the mystery door was opened.

"Sometimes I think you take the mickey out of me, Jill."

"Never, Mum. I was thinking of something else."

"The coffee smells good," said Raylene. "I'll have the lemon meringue pie with the coffee, thanks Jill."

They sat, enjoying the coffee and admiring the huge pot of spring flowers in the middle of the café. Raylene amused herself by identifying the individual flowers.

"Okay, Mum. Now we have to do the business side of the trip. You know what to ask the salesperson?" said Jill, walking into the covered area where frogs and trolls stared at her from their designated shelves.

"Leave it to me, Jill. I'll 'ave all the answers, before you know it."

"Can I help you?" asked the sales person, watching Raylene fondling one of the statuettes. "Do you like garden gnomes?"

Oh! No! Don't ask her that, Jill screamed to herself. *You'll be sorry.*

The salesman was doomed. Raylene told him in great detail about her collection. She even had names for some of the non-roaming trolls, which she shared with her new victim.

"You've got quite a nice collection here," she said.

"Yes. We have a good variety of garden ornaments," said the salesman, careful to avoid asking another question.

"Do you have any made from plaster of Paris?" she finally asked.

"No. They don't make garden ornaments from plaster of Paris. Even though plaster of Paris does dry hard, it will wear down if exposed to the changes of weather. So, not suitable for outdoors. The outdoor ornaments are mainly made from resin," continued the salesman, happy to get a word in. "It's a durable synthetic polymer that is weather resistant."

He looked around for an escape. "Now, if you'll excuse me, I'll attend to this gentleman," he said as he made a quick getaway.

"Thanks Mum," said Jill. "You were great. I'll let you wander around by yourself, while I grab another coffee."

Jill made her way back to the café. She could observe the operation of the nursery from this glass cage. Jill felt sure that the drug surveillance team had had numerous cups of coffee from this vantage point.

She watched as trucks, large and small, loaded up plants and garden equipment from the nursery. The distribution centre was very active as well, with forklift trucks loading boxes onto trucks. One truck caught her eye. The truck was white with a large, circular green logo on the cabin door featuring the name *'Rotating Plants.'* The name rang a bell, but she couldn't quite place it. She watched the tall, good looking driver as he loaded large pots onto a hydraulic lift at the back of his truck. The plants were lush and green. Jill actually recognized some of the palms and ficus. She smiled to herself as the mother-in-law's tongue was hurled onto the truck.

God help anyone I marry, she thought.

"I'm done," said Raylene, interrupting Jill's thoughts. "I hope you've got plenty of room in your car?"

"Why? What did you buy? Please tell me you didn't buy that giant gnome," said Jill, pointing to a statue being carried out by a salesman heading towards her car.

"It's okay Jill, I'll nurse it."

"I'm not driving through town with that troll sitting on your lap."

"It might break if we put it into the boot."

"Well, you get into the boot with it," said Jill.

Fortunately, the dozen plants and the giant gnome fitted easily into the boot, with Raylene donating her cardigan and trying desperately to grab Jill's cardigan to act as a buffer between her purchases.

It was a quiet drive home. Jill was lost in thought about what she had seen at the nursery. When they got home, Jill switched on her computer.

Raylene was upset. "I wish you'd find somethin' else to do besides work on a Saturday night," she said, pouring herself a glass of wine. "Why don't you go out with your friends?"

"I'm fine, Mum," said Jill, retrieving the paperwork from under her bed and sitting down at her computer.

Intriguing, thought Jill, as she searched through the business registry at Fair Trading. *I'll check this out in the morning.*

The next day, it was mid-morning by the time Jill got up, had breakfast and headed towards the front door.

"Where are you off to?" asked her mother.

"Just checking out another nursery," replied Jill. "I'll have lunch out, Mum. See you tonight."

Jill followed the Great Western Highway before turning off into Castlereagh Road. She soon left the homes and industrial complexes, which gave way to open fields, and followed the sparkling Nepean river. The river would eventually become the mighty Hawkesbury and then flow into the sea just north of Sydney. But here it was still and slow. She passed a number of small-acre farmlets until a large, dull looking complex came into view. Jill slowed the car and checked the map.

"Yep, this is it." The building was a large corrugated iron box of a place with an extremely high roof, set in the middle of two acres of plants and trees of every description. The building was surrounded by a heavy duty chain-link fabric fence over two metres high, with three barbed wire strands on straight posts. The gate was secured by chains and padlocks.

Strange storage shed, she thought.

Jill then detected the faded letters of the business name on the side of the building facing the road. '*Durable Stock Feeds*', she read.

Well, it probably was a stock feed mill once, she thought. *But it's obviously been converted into a storage area for plants. How can I get a closer look without arousing suspicion? There's probably a security camera in amongst those steel posts.*

Jill had travelled no more than one hundred metres when she spotted a sign on an adjoining property, '*Eggs for sale.*' She drove in without hesitation.

The farmlet had a small cottage, fronting the corrugated iron poultry shed of saw-tooth design. There were two mangy dogs tied up with chains on each side of the egg room. Jill hopped out of the car and pushed her way through the plastic streamers designed to discourage flies from entering. She was greeted by a stumpy farmer with several days of growth shadowing his face. A plump woman in a white coat was busy grading eggs. From their accents, Jill guessed they were Maltese, as were many of the poultry farmers around Sydney's west.

"What can I do for you?" asked the poultry farmer.

"I was passing through, saw your sign and thought I'd get some fresh farm eggs," said Jill in a friendly and conversational way.

"No problem," said the fellow. "What size you like?"

"The big ones, thanks. Two dozen."

"No problem. We have the biggest and the best, eh Mary?" said the farmer to his wife, who scurried away to pick up two cartons.

"How's business?" asked Jill.

"No bloody good anymore, since they deregulated the poultry industry. Politicians say, 'eggs come cheaper,' but you know what happen? One, two farmers take over all industry and now supermarkets make all the money. We barely survive. By the way, I'm Charlie."

Yep, he has an audience and he wants to talk, thought Jill, giving Charlie a look of deep concern.

"Do you get your feed from next door?" she asked.

"No, no," replied farmer Charlie, shaking his head and waving his arms around. "That not a feed mill anymore. The Council, that Penrith Council, you know, don't want any pig or poultry farms in the area. Most of the farms have gone to housing estates now, anyway."

"So who supplies you?" asked Jill.

"I mix my own. I buy a lot of the gear from the mill when it closed. A mixer, some cross augers and a couple of smaller silos. Big company take away large silos and weighbridge. Big money, weighbridge," he said, rubbing his thumb and fingers in a 'money, money' motion.

Mary had packed the eggs and taken Jill's money. Jill was making movements towards the door when she asked, "So all the equipment was sold?"

Mary joined in the conversation. "Yes, they sell and move away, but I know they kept the hammer mill and grain grister. I know they keep the thing. You can hear the thing banging away sometimes. Don't know what they do in a nursery, maybe crushing fertilizer. Stinking smell sometimes."

"Fertilizer does stink," said Jill with a smile. "Blood and bone and all that."

"Yeah," said Charlie.

Mary piped up and added, "My daughter says it smells like her nail polish stuff."

Acetone, thought Jill. "It must be big business. I noticed they have a big cyclone fence around the property."

"Locked up every night," said Charlie. "Caretaker sometimes stays all night. But you know what, anyone can get in. From behind. No back fence, only river. They have fence, but flood washed it away," Charlie remarked with a big belly laugh. "Anyway, long way from road, so no problem."

Jill thanked them and headed off past the two sleepy dogs that lazily wagged their tails, into the refuge of her car. She was trying to figure out a way to get into the mill for a sneaky look. She spotted a lane heading towards the river. An old car was parked at the dead end. She saw a fisherman staring intensively at the water in the hope that something would attach itself to the three rods he had set up. She got out of the car and made her way down the path, ignoring the mud and stones that would do nothing good for her shoes.

Jill made her way along the bank, which was surprisingly clear of vegetation until she came to the rear of the mill. The cyclone fence had not been washed away but had been mangled and the vegetation had grown around it, securing it in its crushed state. She manoeuvred herself around a lowered area in the fence and made her way toward the mill.

She was thinking of a dozen-and-one excuses should anyone catch her snooping, one of which would be 'the bored wife of the fisherman, stretching her legs.' Her eyes suddenly focused on a small grey object a couple of metres to her left. She jumped involuntarily as a lizard blew out its frilly neck and showed her some fine teeth protruding from its large yellow mouth.

"Shit!" she cried out loud, as the bearded dragon scurried off. "I hope there's no bloody snakes around as well!"

The building had one window, which would have previously belonged to the office. Jill peered through and saw large storage boxes marked '*Export*'. The whole area was filled with enormous flower pots, fountains and marble statues. She could also see a forklift truck. As she walked around the side of the building she realized what an enormous storage area it was, possibly fifty metres on each side of the square shape.

And it was all owned by the Happi Frog nursery.

Jill had her mobile phone at the ready for photos if needed. But she had to get in. She walked around the other side of the building and noticed that one of the metal panels was loose. She could try and squeeze in through there.

She glanced around apprehensively and let out a deep breath, not knowing what she would find inside.

She didn't see the motion-sensing security camera that was tracking her every move.

Chapter 28

Forty kilometres away, Colin Jackson was momentarily startled as the mobile phone he had connected to the Castlereagh storage complex buzzed. He was frightened by that because it signalled possible intruders to the property. It was linked to the security devices around the facility and could show him the images from the cameras directly to his mobile phone. He steeled himself, knowing that he had to take a look at the phone. There was too much at stake.

With an effort he raised himself on his right elbow, and with a sweaty left arm made a sweeping gesture in a furtive attempt to locate the mobile on the bedside table.

Maya stopped moving, opened her eyes and glared furiously down at him.

"Don't you *dare!*" she hissed.

The last time he had interrupted Maya *in flagrante delicto,* she had slapped his face so hard that the red glow of her handprint was still there two hours later. A man remembers a thing like that. Sex wasn't just fun for Maya, it was life and death. Jackson knew from experience that this particular game would be played for an hour before she reached her climax, and he dare not take time away from her obsession. After she came he might entice her down from her heightened state with a cold glass of Dom Perignon and lobster tail, but even then she wouldn't allow him out of her sight. To Maya, power was sex and sex was power over men.

Every Sunday, Jackson's apartment became a pleasure dome, a fantasy venue. All this sexual energy worked well for Jackson, as he used Maya's willing body and her imagination to feed his own lust. Once he had entered Maya's lair he knew there would be no escape until he had satisfied her completely, if only temporarily. But Jackson was a very willing prisoner and playmate with her array of adult toys and forbidden games.

Jackson had set up security cameras, including some triggered by motion, to guard his property and other assets, including Maya. He had video cameras set up at his unit, his office, the distribution centre and storage facility. He could access it anywhere, anytime on his mobile. The camera feed was recorded automatically onto the hard drive of his computer. He also had video cameras in Maya's apartment. At first he had been angry that she entertained other men, but after a while he enjoyed watching her.

Maya was addicted to sex, to the opiate-like endorphins it released in her brain, but like most chemical addictions, a progressively higher quantity was needed to achieve her euphoric high.

If Maya devoted her life to Venus the goddess of love, Jackson worshipped at the temple of Juno Moneta, the Roman goddess of money.

You are quite a woman, Maya, but only a woman and that warehouse is the source of all the cash that pays for these playthings.

But he was smart enough not to say it aloud and ruin his chance for a happy ending in Maya's game.

It was only a stray cat last time, Jackson thought to himself. *I'm better off concentrating on the wild cat I've got right here. Shit! There goes that damn alarm again!*

Chapter 29

Jill's hand was bleeding from the cut she received from the sharp edge of the corrugated sheet when she lifted it to crawl into the disused mill. It was all worth it. She had found the clandestine laboratory. She had found the stash.

She was totally absorbed in collecting as much evidence as she could when she heard a car pulling up outside the complex. She switched off her mobile and crouched behind one of the large wooden crates.

Someone had entered the storage shed.

Jill shielded her face with her t-shirt. She was fearful that the white chalky powder residue that hung in the air might make her sneeze.

She heard running water. A jug switching itself off. The smell of coffee. The scent of cigarette smoke.

All she could do now was sit and wait.

Jill reflected on the last twenty-four hours, as she sat hidden from the man who had disrupted her plans. She had stayed up all night at home, cross-referencing piles of shipping documentation until she stumbled on one item which kept cropping up in each shipment.

Those wretched garden gnomes made in the plaster of Paris compound, she thought.

The huge quantities of these trolls were disproportionate to the orders of other garden ornaments placed by the Happi Frog nursery. Jill had also recalled Maya's comment previously that the nursery did not import too many garden gnomes. Jill afforded herself a smile as she thought of her mother, who was probably the only person who kept the troll business going.

Jill had Googled 'plaster of Paris' on the computer, and stumbled on an interesting case in South America where cocaine powder was mixed with the plaster of Paris mixture and sculpted into ornaments then transported into the United States of America.

She desperately wanted to send the photos to Hudson's mobile but didn't dare switch the mobile phone back on. Before she could reset the phone to silent, it would most certainly 'beep' to let her know there were messages. She knew there would be messages, especially from her mother asking when she'd be home for dinner. Jill would have to wait.

The stranger sat in the office part of the old mill, between her and the escape route. The only sound in the stillness of the mill was her heart pounding.

The sun had set and the place was in total darkness, apart from the light in his office. She peeked out from behind her box and saw that he was a heavy-set man with shoulder length dark hair.

Damn, I'm frozen. Thank heavens I had that huge hamburger for lunch. Jill stretched her cramped legs and rubbed her cold backside. She had been squatting behind the crate for almost three hours.

Chapter 30

It was almost 6:00 pm before Maya showed any signs of slowing down. Jackson had refilled her glass on several occasions. The second bottle of champagne was nearly empty.

"We haven't played on the patio, yet," she murmured at Jackson, as she slid the glass doors open. She turned all the lights on and called out to Jackson. "Bring the glasses out here, Colin."

"It's quite cool out there, darling."

"No way. Sunsets are for lovers. Where's your romantic spirit?"

Jackson remembered the first time Maya had requested love-making on the patio in broad daylight, claiming that the railing height was conducive to a climax. Jackson had refused.

Maya had packed her bags and left. Jackson had let her go. There had been no contact for over a week.

The following Saturday night Jackson had gone to the International Tank Nightclub after a race meeting with a group of friends. Maya had walked in with a male companion.

She didn't waste any time, thought Jackson as he watched Maya escort her date to the secluded piano bar with its velvet-lined cubicles.

Jackson ordered a double scotch to take his mind off Maya. But ten minutes later, eleven at the most, Jackson was making his way to the dimly lit piano lounge. He arrived at the alcove where Maya and the date were almost on level two. Maya very rarely wore underwear, and level one was discovering that phenomenon. One look from Jackson and the date decided to go to the bar at the other end of the club.

"I was just trying to make you jealous," said Maya.

Jackson had caved in to Maya yet again. Now neighbours at his unit in North Sydney were treated to an erotic sideshow whenever it took her fancy. She was such an exhibitionist.

"I'll just get another bottle, petal," he called out, grabbing his mobile and dashing to the bathroom.

"Don't be too long."

He switched the mobile on. The camera was sending through the inside of the old mill. Nothing appeared abnormal. Kevin, the caretaker, was in the office area, packing the snow. He pressed a button and Kevin answered.

"Hi, boss," said Kevin, "What's up?"

"What the f... is going on? The alarm went off twice today."

"I switched it off," claimed Kevin.

"What time was that?"

"Early afternoon, I think it could have been....." Kevin droned.

"I don't f.... pay you to think. Check the place! Make sure it's secure or you're a dead man. You hear me?" Jackson spat into the phone.

"Sure, boss."

Jackson reached for the stash taped under the sink. He was desperate. Viagra and cocaine would keep him going. He had to distract Maya.

"Maya, darling. If you close your eyes, I'll bring you a present," he teased. Jackson kept a myriad of toys stashed in case of an emergency.

She loved all her toys. Her favourite was the hands-free wireless 'butterfly.'

"You work it out," he said, handing the package over to Maya. "I'll go and organize dinner." He prayed that this would work and buy him some desperately needed time out.

Jackson disappeared to his stash. He lay down on the bed and thought of the toy he had just given Maya and smiled.

The young woman in Bangkok who sold him the toy had insisted on giving Jackson a demonstration.

"This toy is different to all the other vibrators," she said as she inserted the eight inch shaft. "This toy rotates and thrusts. See for yourself," she said, grabbing Jackson's hand. "There is a variety of speeds, all by remote control. And they come in small, medium, large or extra large like the one I am using."

Jackson had glanced around the showroom, feeling extremely embarrassed. There were several live demonstrations happening simultaneously and onlookers participated as if it were a kitchen appliance, or some new power tool being demonstrated.

"And I'm saving the best to last," she said, like a true salesperson. "Come closer so that you can feel it." Jackson moved closer as Miss Bangkok removed the wireless shaft and demonstrated its chilling and heating abilities.

By this stage Jackson was treating the demonstration in the same way as the people around him. Asking questions and feeling the appliance. The shaft was made of a clear pliable material. *Probably silicone*, he thought at the time.

Jackson ordered the small and extra large.

* * *

The nose candy had finally kicked in. He didn't need sex, this was so much better. He was all ready when Maya walked into the room with her new toy.

Chapter 31

Without any warning all the lights went on in the storage shed.

Jill could hear the man walking around. His shoes crunching on loose debris. She froze. This time with fear as beads of cold sweat formed under her eyes and around her temple. She forced herself to remain motionless, but her heart was pounding. She hurt all over, but her mind was sharp. *Take him on or make a dash for the opening.*

A few more steps and he would certainly see her.

A loud noise startled her. It took micro-seconds to realize that it was heavy rain pounding on the tin roof. She could now afford to shuffle around to the back of the crate.

He was still there. She could smell the smoke from his cigarette. She waited for the confrontation and held her breath.

Suddenly the lights went out. He had returned to the office.

It was almost nine o'clock before Jill saw the office lights go off and the movement of a torch. He was finally leaving. Jill heard the door being bolted, the car starting up and driving off.

She felt emotionally and physically drained as she slowly stood up and stretched. The place was now pitch-dark. She turned the mobile on and sent the cell phone photos to Hudson's mobile.

As she adjusted her eyes to the darkness, Jill tried to visualize the route she would take. With hands stretched out in front of her and a little light from the mobile phone, she made her way along the wall, towards the office, towards the loose corrugated sheet.

Please let me find it.

She ended up crawling around on the ground feeling each panel for the one that was loose, touching dust and cobwebs as she made her way towards freedom. Something touched her hand.

Jill screamed momentarily, followed by a shudder, as her mind painted pictures of large hairy spiders waiting to snare a moth. This one felt big enough to snare a mouse. Or was it a mouse? She didn't want to find out.

Jill thought of something funny her father used to say whenever she retreated in terror from a hairy spider.

"Jill, how can you pour hot wax on your legs, wait for the wax to dry, then rip it off and now tell me you're scared of spiders?"

Jill finally felt the sharp edge of the loose sheet. She pushed her head out, gasping for the fresh night air as she squeezed her shoulders through the corrugated sheet, along the wet grass to freedom.

The night was starless. She couldn't see a metre in front of her.

She was being guided by memory. As Jill gingerly shuffled for approximately twenty metres, the ground vanished. She hit bottom with a crash, hitting something hard and waves of excruciating agony swept through her. She let out a loud scream before darkness mercifully descended upon her.

Chapter 32

"Did you have a good one?" said Hudson, looking up from the mountain of paperwork covering his desk.

"Not long enough," said Sam

"We've been told to lay off Colin Jackson and the Happi Frog nursery and find some real criminals to chase," said Hudson, handing Sam a copy of a memo sent to Kerr from his Superintendent. "I spoke to Nina Renowicz ....."

"Ah! Yes, the mystery woman. I read your report." Sam smirked. "What a doll!"

"We finally have an ID on this Ruby Red," said Hudson. "It's Nina Renowicz, the daughter of Ivan."

"Good grief! The suicide! She was the one who found him, wasn't she? Did you interview her?"

"I did. Miss Renowicz stated that she did not enter the room, nor did she touch anything. She also stated that the chess set would only come out if Henry Smith was visiting. Interesting, isn't it?"

"We could possibly rule out suicide," said Sam.

"Possibly," agreed Hudson. "There are more dead ends in this investigation than a '*Cold Case*' episode on television."

"Never watched it."

Hudson grinned. "Let's consider a hypothetical situation," he said. "First, *if* Henry Smith killed Ivan

Renowicz then someone could have killed Henry out of revenge. Or second, *if* Henry Smith was a witness to the killing then someone had to silence him. Either way there has to be a third party involved in this fiasco."

Their conversation was interrupted by the phone. Hudson picked it up. It was Raylene Morellix.

"Is Jill there?" she asked abruptly.

"No, not yet. It's a bit early, Mrs Morellix. What time did she leave home?" asked Hudson. "The trains could be ..."

"No!" interrupted the distraught mother. "Jill didn't come home last night."

"She's a big girl. Have you tried her mobile?"

"I rang her mobile until late last night, but there was no answer."

"Have you tried her friends?" asked Hudson, sensing that Mrs Morellix could not be consoled.

"I'll wait half an hour until everyone arrives, and then I'll ring you back."

"Thank you."

Hudson replaced the phone and turned to Sam. "That was Jill's mother. Jill didn't come home last night."

"Let's see if she comes in with the gang," Sam replied. "But as you said, she's a big girl, maybe she was just having a wild night with some lucky bastard in the western suburbs."

Hudson nodded.

The troops were starting to stagger in, one by one. But Jill was not among them.

Hudson walked into the main office where everyone congregated with their first cup of coffee, comparing weekend activities. "Has anyone heard from Jill?"

"Not yet," came several replies.

"Her mother rang, claims she didn't come home last night."

"There are plenty of doughnuts, Boss! You don't have to pull another disappearing act on us again."

Hudson shook his head at their lack of concern and walked back to his office. He rang Raylene Morellix back. "Give me the details of what she did over the weekend."

Raylene told Hudson about their outing to the Dural nursery on Saturday and that Jill went off to another nursery on Sunday.

"Did she say which nursery?"

"No, only that she wouldn't be home for lunch."

"Was there anything unusual that happened on the weekend. Any phone calls?"

"No. She worked on her computer most of Saturday night."

"Why did you and Jill go to the Dural nursery?"

"It was supposed to be a day out. But Jill wanted me to ask some questions about garden gnomes," said Mrs Morellix.

"What kind of questions?"

"She wanted to know if the gnomes were made from plaster of Paris."

That girl is nuttier than a Christmas cake, thought Hudson. "Why on earth did she want to know that?" he asked, trying to keep the irritation out of his voice.

"I don't know. She never tells me nothin'."

"Were the garden gnomes made from plaster of Paris?" Hudson couldn't believe he was having a conversation about gnomes. *Hopefully, those goblins have carried Jill off to a place of no return.*

"No, they weren't. The salesman told us that plaster of Paris wasn't suitable for outdoors. You don't think anythin's happened to our Jill, Mr Hudson?"

"No, I'm sure she'll come bouncing in any minute. I'll keep in touch, Mrs Morellix. Please don't worry."

"Sam, can you keep trying Jill's mobile?" Hudson yelled across the room as he hung up the phone.

There was a lot more he could do; Put out an all points bulletin on her car, get the computer technician to check her computer, but Hudson waited. He had a reputation as a habitual bungler to live down. Didn't he? He settled at his desk and tried to make an inroad into the endless paperwork.

It was now mid morning. Still no sign of Jill.

Sam started to pace.

"We would have heard from her by now," he said to Hudson. "There's nothing on my mobile, and I've checked with reception. Is there anything on your mobile?"

"Jill's never rung me on my mobile before." Hudson looked around his desk. "Where did I leave that contraption? It's in the bloody car, Sam."

He threw Sam the keys.

Sam was back from the underground car park in what seemed like seconds.

"Are you training for the marathon?" said Hudson.

"I'm worried about her," said Sam seriously. "South Sydney were playing Penrith Panthers on Sunday, and she never misses a Rabbitohs game. We usually go together, but I haven't heard from her at all."

Hudson switched his mobile on.

Within seconds, he yelled out to Sam. "Call Kerr, pronto. I'll meet you both in the interview room. Hurry, Sam."

Hudson plugged his mobile into the computer, just as Kerr and Sam walked in. He downloaded the images and brought them up on the monitor.

Kerr studied the screen.

"It's a classic clandestine laboratory, all right," he said. "And a bloody complete one at that. Who sent these images?"

"They're from Jill," replied Sam.

"That's a centrifuge machine there on the counter, which is used to separate particles from a suspension by means of high speed rotation. On the other side of the room is a diffusion pump. Those large steel vessels against the wall with condensers attached are used for..." Kerr hadn't finished his sentence as he exclaimed. "Where on earth is she?"

"Jill told her mother that she was going to visit a nursery," said Hudson. "The equipment definitely looks over the top for a nursery."

"By a satellite orbit or two," replied Kerr. "One of the machines looks like a dessicator which is a drying chamber," he continued. "There's also a commercial heating mantle and several reaction vessels. The diffusion pump could be a vacuum. I also recognize that large machine on the counter. It looks like the one Ryan Cooper photographed at the Happi Frog nursery."

"We haven't heard from Jill since Friday night," said Hudson.

"She could be in trouble, Matt," said Kerr. "Especially if she's stumbled on something as elaborate as we're seeing here."

"Put out a general alert on her car, Sam." said Hudson, picking up the phone and dialling an internal number.

"Find him!" Kerr heard Hudson yell to whoever was on the other end.

"Jill's mother said she'd been working on the computer all night Saturday," said Hudson, replacing the phone. "She took off on Sunday morning and hasn't been seen since. I've just rung for Bailey Brisco. I'll go out with him and have a look at her home computer."

"Is he that new fellow in forensics computers?" asked Kerr.

"Yes, one of those nerdy technocrats."

The phone interrupted him. "Bailey, this is an emergency," said Hudson. "Meet me in my office."

He pressed the disconnect and dialled Raylene Morellix.

"Jill, is that you?" she cried into the phone before Hudson answered.

"No, it's Matthew Hudson. Can we come over and have a look at Jill's computer?"

"Oh please! You have to find her."

"We're on our way," said Hudson and slammed the phone down.

"Put the siren on, Bailey."

Chapter 33

"Who the hell is that?" said Jackson.

The images from the motion sensor camera materialized onto his screen. "She's snooping with a friggin' camera. She's got to be a cop."

Jackson picked up one of his mobiles.

"I'm sending you an e-mail," he said to the recipient of the call. "See if you can identify the woman and e-mail me back."

The phone rang back almost immediately.

"It's Jill Morellix. She's a detective with the Crime Command. What's this about?" asked the caller.

"Never mind that for the moment. Has there been any police activity?" asked Jackson.

"I haven't heard anything," said the caller.

Jackson hung up without any goodbye formality and dialled the next number.

"Kevin, get your arse over to the mill and torch the place."

"What? You want me to torch the lab?" queried Kevin. "What about all the ...?"

"Torch it! There's enough acetone in there to blow the whole place up. Make it look like an accident."

Jackson dialled the next number.

"Hello, Diane. Colin Jackson. Can you get me two first class tickets to Buenos Aires, today?"

"Let me check. Er... yes! There's a flight tonight at 8.00 pm. Do you want me to book that?"

"Yes, thanks, Diane.   Just charge it to my account."

"I'll e-mail your booking confirmation."

"Thanks. I'll give you the second name later."

His last call was to the ZenKazZoo Agency.

"Hello, babe."

"Hi, sweetheart."

"Can you come home, Maya?"

"Normally, sweetheart, you know I would, but I'm to my neck in work," she said softly.

"Maya, it's real important. You know I wouldn't ask if it wasn't."

"Colin ...."

"Just do it Maya. Now!"

"Okay! I'm on my way. I hope it's worth it!" she said.

"It is," he snapped and switched off the phone.

Chapter 34

"It may take me a little while, Hudson," said Bailey. "Why don't you go and have a coffee with the Jill's mum?"

"We don't have a little while," said Hudson anxiously.

"I'll have all the information shortly. The computer is not password-protected. I just need to retrieve the most recent files that Jill has been looking at."

Mrs Morellix brought in a tray of coffee and freshly baked scones with butter and strawberry jam on two small dishes. Bailey was grateful that the coffee and scones had stopped Hudson from breathing down his neck.

"I'll print everything out as I'm going along. You sift through it to find what you're looking for," said Bailey.

"Okay," said Hudson, his voice harsh with tension. He sat down and tried to concentrate on the scones without success. Ten minutes later, he looked up as Bailey set the printer going.

"Got something?" he asked.

"Have a look," said Bailey and handed over two printed sheets.

Hudson didn't have to look far. "Eureka! That's got to be it," he exclaimed. "She's found a storage shed belonging to the Happi Frog nursery at Castlereagh, near Penrith. Let's go. Let's move it!"

They both grabbed another scone as they dashed for the door.

"Thanks, Mrs Morellix. We'll be in touch."

Their siren soon blended in with other sirens heading in the same direction. It was unclear who was overtaking whom, but the race was threatening the safety along the highway.

Hudson took the radio microphone. "What the hell is going on?" he asked the emergency services controller.

"Major fire at a nursery, Sir," replied the calm voice of the despatcher.

"Holy shit!" said Bailey.

"Step on it," commanded Hudson.

The State Emergency Services had placed barricades to stop any traffic along Castlereagh Road. Two ambulances were on standby, and several police cars were on the scene. Two fire trucks were at the scene, with fire crew flooding the burning building with water.

Hudson and Bailey got out of the car to encounter a symphony of chaos.

Billowing smoke hung like a giant blanket, blocking the sun from view and spewing chemical vapours into the atmosphere. A large crowd stood behind the barricade, paying little attention to the policeman with the megaphone who was continually asking people to leave the area.

Hudson could hear the many comments from the spectators.

"It sounded like a bomb going off!"

And another. "The flames were over a hundred feet high!"

The stories kept growing with each account.

"I thought it was an earthquake!"

Hudson quickly walked over to one of the patrol cars and introduced himself. "Was anyone in the building at the time?" he asked.

"No-one's come out of the building, Sir," replied the Constable. "The fire crew's got the fire pretty well under control. There's not much to burn in an iron shed."

Hudson approached the Chief Fire Officer.

"How long before I can have a look around?"

"If it's vital for you to come in," the Fire Chief said. "Then probably another thirty minutes."

Hudson looked at his watch. "It's possible I have an officer in there," he said.

"It's going to take us at least until tomorrow to do a full search and report," said the fire officer. "But I can tell you, there's nobody alive in there."

Hudson felt his blood run cold.

Kerr arrived with his team and joined him. The fire had started to subside and the team moved in closer. White dust filled the air, choking the detectives. Shattered glass lay around like bits of confetti.

Hudson's phone rang. It was Sam. "Where are you?" asked the young American

"I'm in Castlereagh, near Penrith."

"That's a coincidence," said Sam. "That's where a patrol car has just reported sighting Jill's car."

"You're kidding?" said Hudson. "Give me a direct reading."

"I'll give you the patrol car's number. You talk to him. I'm on my way."

It took Hudson a couple of minutes to realize that Jill's car was about five hundred metres from where he stood.

He raced over to the fire officer. "Can I get to the barricade on the other side? It's urgent."

The officer signalled to one of his men who escorted Hudson to the location of Jill's car.

Once on the other side, Hudson ran over to Jill's car. It was unlocked. There was nothing inside except for two dozen eggs. Another fire crew member arrived and handed Hudson a multi-coloured mobile phone.

"We found this near the burnt out shed. The chief asked me to bring it over."

"That's Jill's phone!"

Please, God. Don't let Jill have been in there!

Chapter 35

Charlie and Mary were standing at the back of their property. They had a good view of the current happenings. The fire had subsided, but the smoke was billowing in their direction, distressing the chickens and the dogs.

They watched as Hudson took out a carton of eggs from the back of the abandoned car, which they presumed must have belonged to the lady.

"That must be her car," said Mary. "Look, our eggs."

"Please stay behind the barrier, sir," said the SES man to Charlie.

"That car," said Charlie. "We knows what happen to the girl."

Hudson was frantic as he raced towards the burnt out shed. "Jill Morellix. She could be inside. We need to have a look."

"The medical team is being escorted in now," said the chief. "We should get some more information shortly. We have no way of knowing how stable those metal beams are."

It was now almost 2:00 pm. As Hudson lit the last cigarette in his packet, he noticed what looked like a poultry farm in the distance. At the same time, sirens blazing, Sam screeched to a halt beside him.

Hudson grabbed Sam's arm and headed in the direction of the poultry farm.

"Hello, hello," yelled Charlie to the two plain clothes men coming towards him. "Are you the police?"

"Yes, I'm Detective Inspector Hudson and this is Detective Sergeant Gilroy."

Before Hudson could ask about the eggs, Charlie and Mary spoke in unison.

"She buys eggs. She break her leg. We call ambulance. She go to hospital."

Hudson spontaneously kissed Mary, who blushed and stepped behind her husband. Hudson and Sam shook Charlie's hand before rushing off to their car.

"Bailey, you drive towards Penrith hospital. Sam, you ring ahead and see if she's there. I'll ring Kerr and let him know where we're going."

With sirens blazing, they arrived at the Nepean hospital in Penrith.

Sam walked in first and practically leapt on to Jill in an embrace that resembled the reunion of lost lovers. Jill started to cry. Sam sat down on the chair beside her and held her hand. Her head was bandaged and her leg was up in plaster.

"So, you found the plaster," said Hudson. "Your mother told us you were on a mission to find the plaster of Paris." said Hudson. He bent over and kissed Jill. "We didn't have time to buy flowers," he said. "We were too busy putting out fires. Have you rung your mother?"

"I've just got off the phone to a very relieved mother. I've asked her and Dad to bring me some clothing. Oh! I forgot!" Jill reached for her bedside phone and made a call. "Thank heavens you haven't left yet, Mum. Make sure you bring me a skirt. Yes, Mum, I do have one somewhere. Yes, I do wear skirts, Mum. A long skirt, please. Thanks. See you soon."

She replaced the phone and grinned at Hudson. "I suppose you want a report, sir?"

Hudson suppressed a snort. *The Westie girl has guts.*

Jill related her experience of the previous day. How she fell over in the dark and broke her leg, climbing out of the trench when she regained consciousness with the first streaks of dawn and crawling all the way to Charlie and Mary's home.

Mid-stream through her story, Jill asked, "What were you saying about a fire?"

"The old mill went up in flames just before midday. We were hoping to collect your ashes," said Hudson, laughing more with relief than the joke. "They're treating the fire as very suspicious. One neighbour reported seeing a truck leaving the premises shortly before the first big bang."

"Jackson seems to be always one step in front of us. There's got to be a leak in the department," said Jill.

"Don't go paranoid on us, Jill," said Sam. "Anyway, what on earth did you stumble on to lead you there?"

"When I looked through the shipping documents, I noticed that there were large quantities of plaster of

Paris gnomes with every shipment. Don't laugh when I tell you that my mother has those trolls all over our garden and they are not made with plaster of Paris."

"I think we'll recommend your mother for the commendation," said Sam.

"She deserves it. So does that poor salesman she cornered at the Happi Frog. The mill was full of them. It was obvious that the statues were being crushed. There was white powder all over the place. Plus there were boxes and boxes of vacuum-sealed bags containing white powder. I've got a sample bag in my jeans pocket. The nurses had to cut my jeans off. Lucky no one searched the pockets. They would have called the police."

"We could still arrest you for possession," said Hudson.

"If that wasn't bad enough," said Jill. "They also cut up my Rabbitohs jersey."

"There's an omen," said Sam.

Hudson's mobile rang. It was Kerr.

"I think 'Operation Snail Trail' is coming to a close. We have enough incriminating evidence to put him away for a long time."

"What did you get?" asked Hudson.

"He was importing the cocaine in plaster of Paris ornaments which he crushed using a hammer mill and then grinding it into a fine dust with the grain grister. He then extracted the cocaine by placing the powder in an alkaline solution and mixing it with a solvent; in this case it was acetone."

"That must have been what caused the explosions," said Hudson.

"Yes, it was. There were remnants of drums scattered all over the place, including paperwork with his company's name and logo, which survived the fire."

"What did they use the acetone for?" asked Hudson.

"It makes the mixture separate into two layers. The upper layer containing the dissolved cocaine," said Kerr with authority. "He's been importing cocaine for quite a while. And always one step ahead of us."

"We've just been talking about that," said Hudson.

"When he knew we were on to him, he started double-glazing the ornaments with lead glaze so that sniffer dogs couldn't detect the cocaine," continued Kerr. "Although I don't think the dogs could have picked it up anyway. I'll keep you posted. My boys are trying to locate Jackson now. How's Jill?"

"The patient is immobile, but doing fine," said Hudson.

"Give her my regards."

"Inspector Kerr sends his regards," said Hudson, putting the phone away. "And I've got to go. You be careful, young lady."

Jill waved lightly, starting to look half asleep.

Hudson left. Sam stayed behind.

Chapter 36

Maya arrived at Jackson's unit only to be greeted by a packed suitcase at the door.

"Where are you off to now?" There was venom in her voice. "You son-of-a-bitch. You rushed me home so you can have a shag before you run off again. Well, I won't be here when you get back!"

The eternal manipulator, thought Jackson.

"Calm down, babe. You're coming with me this time. You know that trip I've always promised you. We leave tonight."

"Tell me you're joking." She studied his face. "You're not joking. Where are we going?"

"It's a surprise."

How long are we going for?"

"As long as you want. You know how you love surprises. Just pack. I've organized a cab for 5:00 pm."

"What will I pack?"

"Just take your passport and some clothing. We can buy whatever you need when we get there."

He handed Maya a glass of Moet and downed another scotch, his third for the day. "Don't ring anyone. Let's hang on to the surprise for a little while," he said.

"You *are* serious," murmured Maya, pouring another glass of champagne.

"Happy anniversary!"

"Darling. You didn't forget."

Jackson had looked at the calendar and by chance he noticed that their third anniversary was coming up.

What a stroke of luck that was!

"It's quite a coincidence," said Maya, putting her arms around him. "I actually put in for a month's holiday, hoping we could spend some time together. I love you, Colin."

They exchanged a long lingering kiss.

"I love you too, babe."

"It won't take me three hours to pack, Colin," she purred as she unbuttoned her blouse.

I'm definitely not in the mood, thought Jackson. "I've got lots to organise, babe, before we go. We'll have plenty of time on this trip for whatever you want," said Jackson, walking away into his office. He knew full well that Maya would be right behind him. She was insatiable and as always, she got her way. He could no more resist that beautiful body than he could abandon his bank accounts.

An hour later, as he lay on the lush soft sheepskin rug with Maya resting on his shoulder, he thought of Argentina, energetic and seductive. His villa in Buenos Aires, the wealthiest and richest city in South America. He would be royalty in Argentina. All the snow and stardust a man could ever want. A tsunami of toys, including his plane and yacht. His millions stashed away.

All thanks to Henry Smith.

Chapter 37

Jackson was starting to feel relaxed now that he and Maya had made it to the international airport at Mascot. In fact he was feeling rather smug, confident that he would be enjoying the sophisticated night life in some club at La Boca long before the cops could piece together all the clues that explained his cocaine importing scheme.

The airport was not busy at this time of the evening as they walked towards the First Class check-in desk.

"You've trekked Nepal and now you'll get the best," said Jackson, putting his arm round Maya's slender waist.

"You mean..... Machu Picchu," squealed Maya. "Are we going there first?"

"No. We'll do that later. Firstly, we'll visit those mysterious statues staring out to sea on Easter Island?" he whispered into Maya's elegant and fragrant neck.

"LAN Chile airlines will stop there and at Santiago. It might be fun to make love on the beach there. I'm sure your naked body would turn the heads of even those moai."

"Colin, you are so romantic. We should have done this together a long time ago," purred Maya. "I'm getting quite excited."

"Sign this Immigration card. I've filled it out for you. Then all we have to do is show our passports and boarding cards and we can take it easy in the departure lounge. It will be a while before they announce that our flight is boarding. So, we can occupy ourselves by planning how we can join the mile high club when we cross the South Pacific."

"I hope we can do more than planning in the departure lounge."

The spell broke as two men blocked their way to the check-in desk. One of the men displayed an official badge. "Are you Colin Jackson?" he asked.

"Who are you?" asked Jackson.

"I'm Detective Inspector James Kerr. And this is Detective Senior Constable John Crosby. Are you Colin Jackson?"

"Yes, I am. What's this all about?"

"I am placing you under arrest for the importation and dealing of a prohibited substance. You are not obliged to say anything, but if you do, it may be taken down in writing and used in evidence against you," intoned Kerr.

Jackson could feel his world starting to crumble around him. His dreams of a life in Argentina had evaporated. A waterfall of white sound seemed to fill his ears.

"Put your hands out in front of you," continued Kerr. He handcuffed one of Jackson's wrists then turned him to secure the cuffs behind his back.

Jackson didn't resist. He stared ahead, lost in a whirlwind of thought.

Maya stood by pale with fright and close to tears.

"Don't say a word to them, Maya," commanded Jackson. "Just take the bags and go home. I'll ring you later. It's all a mistake."

"Not so fast. I'll take those," said Detective Crosby, pouncing on the bags like some giant bird swooping on a mouse.

Jackson kept protesting that the bags belonged to Maya, but that did not deter the detective from confiscating both the backpack and the pink cabin luggage.

As the drama unfolded at the airport, other police officers were executing warrants to search Jackson's home, as well as the Happi Frog nursery.

Bewildered staff offered no resistance.

At the police station, Jackson asked to make a phone call. "I'm not giving you anything but my name and address until I do."

"Your father has trained you well," said Detective Inspector Kerr. "Yes. You can make one call."

"Dad, it's Colin. I've been arrested at the airport."

"Where, exactly, at the airport?" asked the barrister.

"Just before we checked in."

"You idiot. There goes any chance of bail."

The barrister hung up. He was seething with anger as he realized that his supply of cocaine, his river of gold, had abruptly dried up.

Hudson took a sip of his coffee as he read the headlines:

SENIOR COUNSEL'S SON HELD ON MASSIVE
DRUG CHARGES

Federal and State police have claimed to have dismantled a very sophisticated drug importation syndicate worth millions of dollars.

The arrest of Mr Big followed a three year investigation.

"Why are they referring to him as Mr Big? Why not 'the snail'?" muttered Hudson and read on.

Colin Jackson, the 32 year old son of a leading and prominent barrister was intercepted at the airport where he was boarding a plane for Argentina. Bail has been refused as Jackson is considered a flight risk. The maximum penalty for this offence is 25 years imprisonment and/or a $550,000 fine.

This clever operation had police and customs officers baffled for over three years. In that time, it is estimated that over fifty million dollars worth of cocaine had been imported into Sydney, the cocaine capital.

The cocaine was mainly destined for the high earning professionals and socialite set.

"Why do these journalists portray drug trafficking as clever and then glamorise it?" Hudson was intensely irritated, despite the success of the arrest.

```
Firearms  have  been  confiscated  from
his unit in North Sydney.  More arrests
are pending.
```

Hudson reached for his cigarettes and headed out the door.

Chapter 38

Alex Renowicz read the Sydney Morning Herald article in mounting horror.

'Senior Counsel's son held on massive drug charges,' blared the headlines. The Australian had the same headline, but the item was relegated to below the fold on page two.

The words swam before his eyes like wind over a pond's surface. "What the hell am I going to do now?" he asked the unresponsive walls of his kitchen. He was terribly afraid.

Alex dropped the paper on his kitchen table. In a dreamlike state he gripped the handle of his half drunk cup of coffee. He had no inclination to finish it. His mind was totally locked on what could happen to him. He spotted the bottle. His throat was dry and he poured himself a large glass of vodka.

For a bizarre moment Alex felt a wave of hatred for Colin Jackson as he replayed the events of the last two years in his mind. Events that would lead to his own demise.

* * *

It was the start of the autumn racing carnival at Randwick Racecourse near Sydney. A beautiful sunny day, clear skies, with a hint of autumn in the crisp air.

Alex had arrived early for the Doncaster Handicap, one of the richest races to be held at Randwick. He wanted to soak up the atmosphere, the colours, the sounds and the smells before the crowd of punters arrived.

Today he would pick a winner.

His favourite spot was the parade ring where he could watch the horses parade and check out their form. Alex would look at the alertness of the horse, the shine of its coat and the muscle tone in the legs, belly and rump. Of course, he would also consult the form guide, and the tips from various celebrities and race callers.

Before the first race, Alex was standing in a prime position at the front of the parade ring breathing in the satisfying smells of freshly mowed grass, leather and manure when he heard his name being called.

"Alex! Alex!"

He turned to the sound. It was Henry Smith. Alex strolled over, to be greeted effusively by Henry, who was with another, younger man.

"Colin, I'd like you to meet the son of an old friend of mine. This is Alex Renowicz," said Henry Smith. "Alex, this is Colin Jackson."

"Hello Alex. You don't look like you're dressed for a big day out at Royal Randwick," said Jackson, himself a picture of sartorial elegance in a tailored suit and Italian tie, snappy hat, and a leather binocular case hanging from a strap around his neck.

"Oh, no!" stammered Alex. "I'm not a member. I just come along to have a few bets with the rest of the plebs."

The sudden embarrassment Alex felt was quickly banished when Jackson said, "Why don't you join us in our private box anyway? The club always has ties and a range of coats of various sizes stashed away for little emergencies like this."

It seemed to Alex as if he had been blessed by the angels that day. He was exhilarated by the chance to live a day as a member of the upper class, watching the races from on high and rubbing shoulders with famous sports people and glamorous socialites.

"What kind of work do you do, Alex?" Jackson asked him during the course of the afternoon.

"I'm a Nurseryman," he replied, expecting a put-down.

"That's fantastic! It could be that our meeting today was preordained. I'm involved in the nursery business as well. I own the Happi Frog nursery at Dural."

"That *is* a co-incidence," said Alex. "I buy a lot of my stock from your nursery."

"I'm actually mixing business with pleasure today," said Jackson. "I'm involved in various businesses, one of which is the indoor plant hire trade and I've just acquired this club's business."

"Ah! Yes! The rotating plant business. I've heard it's booming," said Alex with interest.

"Henry tells me you need a little help with your business. How would you like some of the action? It pays well."

"Yes, of course, but..."

"We can work out the details later. The main thing is that you've come recommended by Henry as being trustworthy, so it's a done deal. How have those nags been treating you?"

"Not so good. I've kind of run out of cash," Alex replied.

"No problem," said Jackson. "Here's two grand. Consider it an advance on your salary. Enjoy yourself. I'm sure your luck is about to change."

And that's how Alex's Pots & Plants nursery became the Rotating Plants business.

Jackson had supplied Alex with a brand new Isuzu pantech truck, the initial plants and a huge variety of fancy pots.

Everything was going well. Alex picked up one set of plants from various venues and replaced them with fresh ones each week. He would bring the old plants back to his nursery to rejuvenate them for the next rotation. It was easy work. Easy money. Until one day Jackson mentioned Alex's gambling debt.

"How much do you owe me now, Alex? I need to call it in, mate," said Jackson.

"About twenty-five grand. I've been on a rotten losing streak. It's sure to change, but I can't pay you back right now."

"I need it right now, Alex."

Alex recalled the ripples of shock that ran through his body, leaving sweat in his thighs and armpits. For a few seconds, he experienced simple panic at the thought of losing Jackson's business, but that was soon overwhelmed by a hideous fear that he could lose everything.

Jackson broke the silence. "There is a way out, Alex. I'll give you a pay rise so you can pay me back faster."

And that was how Alex became a cocaine courier.

"There are a lot of wealthy people that go to the races, Alex, and win big time. They like to celebrate their good fortune with their friends, there and then. Once it would have been with expensive French champagne. Now it's with 'Florida snowflakes.' But the problem is how to get it into the venue, and I've got the perfect plan. Hide it in plain sight. One minute it's under their noses, next minute it's up their noses."

"How do I fit into this plan?" asked Alex.

"We lay the cocaine on top of the soil in the pot plant and cover it with pine bark mulch. You pick up the plants at our Castlereagh storage facility then you deliver them to the specified venues."

"Which specific venues?" interrupted Alex.

"My private box at Randwick, a few private residences, small law firms, a few exclusive clubs and some top restaurants."

"When you collect the plants, there will be money hidden where the cocaine was, and you deliver the plants back to the Happi Frog nursery. Archie moves the plants to the back of the office block where I harvest the money and you get a little share. If you get greedy and develop sticky fingers, I'll feed your arm into the mulching machine."

Alex had no choice. And the scheme had worked well, so far. Alex had allowed himself the delusion that he was doing nothing wrong and that he was only the delivery man. A businessman.

It was only after he had met 'Big Kev' at the Castlereagh storage facility that Alex felt he was in too deep. Kev had given him the gun. "As a security measure. To discourage the two-legged rats," he told Alex.

It was the start of the ruin of his life.

* * *

Alex was brought back to the present when the knuckle of his right index finger suddenly developed a sharp pain. He realized his finger had gone white from gripping the coffee cup so tightly. He saw the vodka glass at his side. He put down the cup and gulped down the vodka, feeling almost nauseated as the liquor ran through him.

He picked up the newspaper again, the newsprint leaving black marks on his sweaty fingers.

This headline meant that his income had been slashed by ninety per cent, but his gambling debts had not gone away.

He thought of all the misery, the torment and destruction he would now cause his family.

His stomach knotted, Alex cupped his head in his hands, leaned forward on the kitchen table, and for the first time since his father's tragic death sobbed with an uncontrolled helplessness.

Chapter 39

Silverwater.   Named for the magical silver reflections of the morning light on the waters of the nearby Parramatta River.   But there was nothing magical about the small one-bed cell where Colin Jackson sat. On remand.

The Metropolitan Remand and Reception Centre is housed in the Silverwater Correctional Complex about twenty kilometres west of Sydney.

Richard Jackson, Senior Council wanted nothing to do with his son. So Colin Jackson hired the best law firm money could buy, Justin, Stark and Taylor, led by the distinguished barrister, James Justin-Stark, SC.

Simon Taylor, the senior lawyer, had just arrived at the Remand Centre with the news that bail had been refused.

"We're organizing an appeal to the Supreme Court," said Taylor, opening his briefcase.

"How long will that take?"

"Five weeks."

"I've spent a week in this cesspool.   I'm not spending another five weeks in here watching weevils dance the Zumba in the stuff they call porridge."

"We're doing everything possible for your release on bail," continued Taylor, ignoring Jackson's temper tantrum. He handed Jackson the first of a series of forms, together with a pen. "You realize Colin that conditions will apply. First, you will have to agree to surrender your passport. Second, you will have to live within an allocated area, with a curfew and report daily to the local police station. And, third, you will need to enter a drug rehabilitation program."

"I'll sell my grandmother to get out of here."

"We're lining up some prominent business leaders to lodge funds as security for your bail. We should have no problems."

"But there's no guarantee, is there?" asked Jackson.

"No. There are no guarantees. Amendments to bail laws have made it more difficult for people accused of drug trafficking or other serious crimes to await trial on the outside."

"What if I cut a deal with the police," said Jackson.

"What do you mean? Plead guilty? No way," said Taylor.

"No, no! I mean give them information."

"You mean plea-bargain?" said the lawyer. "Why? What have you got to bargain with?"

"Information on a murder," replied Jackson, warily.

"They'll probably charge you with obstruction of justice. There is no need to complicate things, Colin," continued Taylor. "We're working on a suspended sentence anyway. With a fine. A very hefty fine, I might add."

"I can't stay in here until the trial. I'll go bats playing table tennis and draughts."

"I could definitely guarantee release on bail if the police don't offer any objections," said Taylor.

"I can't see them doing that," said Jackson. "They've been trying to nail me for years. Talk to Detective Inspector Matthew Hudson."

Jackson began signing each form placed in front of him. "Let him know that I've got some information for him. He can come and see me anytime. I'm not going anywhere."

"I must advise you against this, Colin."

"I insist."

"Okay, then. I'll ask him to contact you. That's the best I can do."

"That's fine. I'll talk to him alone."

"Be careful, Colin. Don't make it sound like a bribe."

"Sure, sure," said a cocky Jackson. "Everyone has a price."

Still on crutches, her leg in plaster, Jill arrived in the office amidst cheers and accolades.

"If you had broken your leg earlier, you could have got onto the plaster of Paris drug bust sooner," said Sam, with humour. "Instead of chasing gnomes around the countryside."

Everyone laughed. The team took turns in signing her plastered leg with messages that couldn't be read out in public.

"If you come back to work, it's a desk job," said Kerr. "I'll make Matt chain you to the desk if I have to."

Jill pulled a face. "Oh, I love it when you talk dirty."

"She's recovered," said Sam.

They had a huge morning tea for Jill, with the Police Commissioner commending her for bravery and good work.

"Come on, Hoppy," said Sam. "I'll fill you in with the latest developments."

"Any more on the affair between Zoya and Henry? That would have thrown a spanner into the works," said Jill. "I'll bet that's why Henry gave Ivan permanent residency, so that Ivan could marry Zoya and get him off the hook."

"That's what Hudson thought."

"This is developing into quite a circus," said Jill. "Talking of circuses, where's Hudson?"

"He's gone to Silverwater, at the request of Jackson's lawyer," replied Sam. "Hudson told the lawyer that James Kerr was in charge of this case, but the lawyer said Jackson wanted to see him, alone."

"I wonder what that's all about?"

"I don't know. All I know is that James Kerr has been working his butt off to make sure that Jackson stays behind bars. It's so frustrating when these rich bastards get off with a couple of years, and then serve even less."

"Especially when the maximum is twenty five years," said Jill.

"Kerr is making sure that it doesn't happen. But the prosecution is up against a very powerful team of defence lawyers," said Sam.

"Who is Jackson using? His father, I presume?"

"No, he's not. Don't ask me why."

"Who's he got?"

"He's using James Justin-Stark, SC. Nothing but the best."

"And the most expensive."

Hudson met Simon Taylor in the reception area of the Silverwater Correctional Complex. As they made their way to the Remand Centre, Hudson asked, "What's this about?"

"Jackson wants to cut a deal," replied Taylor.

"You've got to be kidding."

"This is all off the record, Inspector," said Taylor. "Client privilege and all that."

This guy's been watching too many re-runs of Law and Order, thought Hudson. "Shouldn't you be talking to the prosecutor?" he asked.

They entered the office and waited for Colin Jackson to emerge.

I'm here now, so I might as well witness Jackson's grovelling, thought Hudson.

They only had a few minutes to wait before Jackson was brought to the interview room by two large warders. They sat their prisoner at the desk opposite Hudson and Taylor and moved to the back of the room.

"I'm not saying anything if those two are here," said Jackson.

Taylor nodded at the two warders. "It's okay," he said. "I think the Inspector and I can handle him."

"Detective Inspector Hudson," said Colin Jackson, holding out his hand as the door closed behind the warders. "Thank you for coming."

Hudson shook his hand briefly. He sat down again.

Taylor started the conversation. "As you are aware, Detective Inspector Hudson, we are taking the request for bail to the Supreme Court."

"We'll oppose it," said Hudson firmly. "On the grounds that he would be a flight risk. And we'll cement it with the fact that he could interfere with witnesses if released on bail."

Hudson didn't take his eyes of Jackson, who sat there with a smirk on his face. Hudson wished he could push that face into a pile of something disgusting and smelly and he immediately thought of the piles of manure at Charlie and Mary's chicken shed. It was Hudson's turn to smile to himself as he pictured the scene.

Jackson leaned over the table and faced Hudson. Simon Taylor left the room, saying he was going to the canteen for a coffee.

Surely he's not going to offer me a bribe, thought Hudson, wishing he was wired.

"Have you solved your murders, yet?" asked Jackson.

"Which murders are you referring to?"

"Your current ones."

"I didn't come down here to discuss my cases with you, Jackson."

"I may be able to help you."

"If you have any information on a crime, you can't withhold it."

"I'm only offering to help."

"In return for what?" asked Hudson sarcastically. "A letter of recommendation?"

"No, you don't have to go that far. Just don't oppose my bail request. Mind you, I'm sure I'll get bail with or without your help. I just thought I'd be a good citizen and help out."

Good citizen. That's a joke, thought Hudson. He knew that Jackson's lawyers would go all-out to have him released on bail. *He's probably conned a priest or two to give him a reference and his dad's influence can work wonders. Any information this creep may have on the murders could save millions and bring justice and peace to so many people.*

"Okay, agreed, providing my colleagues also agree. What have you got?"

"We'll keep everything above board," said Jackson. He beckoned to his lawyer who had just returned to the room.

"I've agreed to help Detective Inspector Hudson with information," said Jackson. "As soon as I'm released on bail."

Hudson was just about to protest, but realized once again that 'the snail' was one step ahead of him. He knew he'd have to wait about five weeks for his information and there was no guarantee it would be of any use.

He walked out without shaking hands.

Chapter 40

"We've got enough evidence here to put Jackson away for a very long time." Hudson heard James Kerr tell his team as he walked into the conference room.

Kerr had set up photos of the Castlereagh storage complex and the aftermath of the fire. There was a great deal of interest in the display as detectives gathered around the photographs of incriminating evidence. Bags of cocaine were strewn all over the back of the storage complex. There were remnants of drums that had contained acetone. And last but not least, the paperwork that had escaped the fire, paperwork that would finally seal the fate of Colin Jackson.

"Come on in, Matt, you're just in time," said an exhilarated James Kerr. "We've got all the evidence we need, right here." Kerr pointed to the display. "The Arson Squad detectives were very thorough in their investigations and confirmed that the fire was deliberately lit."

"This is excellent," said Hudson.

"How was that bastard, Jackson?" asked Kerr.

Hudson could not reveal his agreement with Jackson to anyone, especially not Kerr who was on an absolute high.

"Jackson wanted to know if we were going to object to his release on bail," said Hudson.

"Object!" said Jill. "We'll be putting in a recommendation that he never be released!"

"We've just finished interviewing neighbours around the site," said Kerr. "And they gave us a full description of two trucks and a car seen in the area. We investigated the car. The driver is now a person of interest in this investigation."

"Have you spoken to this person?" asked Hudson.

"Not yet, but they are in *big* trouble," said Kerr, trying hard not to laugh.

"What's so funny?" asked Jill as the team roared with laughter.

"Sorry Jill. It was your car they were describing."

Kerr continued, after the laughter died down. "The two Isuzu pantech trucks have been seen in the area, picking up plants, and dropping off plants on a regular basis. Both trucks are white, but only one truck has a green logo displaying *'Rotating Plants'* on the doors.

"That truck," said Jill. "I've seen the logo. Where's Sam? Saaam!" she screeched in a voice that could be heard two blocks away.

Now that she has hero status, she's taken over the place, thought Hudson.

Sam entered with two coffees. "You shrieked. I mean *called?*" he said, handing a mug of coffee to Jill.

"Sam, you mentioned someone running a rotating plant business some time ago. Who was it?" she asked.

"That was Alex Renowicz, Ivan's son. Why?"

You could hear a pin drop as the room fell silent.

"I saw that truck at the Happi Frog nursery, when I was there with Mum," said Jill, breaking the silence.

"Where's this leading?" asked Sam.

"Okay, let's think about this," said Hudson. "Alex has a small nursery. He is probably buying his plants from the Happi Frog, and using the old mill as a storage area. He could have had a legitimate reason to visit the mill at Castlereagh."

"It was a legitimate nursery storage area, all right," said Kerr. "They had an automatic sprinkler system for the plants and a large storage area for the pots. However, it's now obvious that they smuggled the cocaine in contained in the plaster of Paris gnomes, and out to clients in the pot plants." Kerr pointed to the photographs on the wall again. "We found small sealed bags of cocaine, hidden inside the pot plants and covered with pine bark mulch."

"Did the eye witness see both trucks on the day of the fire, or only one?" asked Hudson.

"Only one, but the woman couldn't remember if it had a logo," replied Kerr. "I'd better interview this Alex Renowicz as a matter of urgency."

"I'll come with you, James," said Hudson. "I need to talk to the detectives in Penrith, regarding the Ivan Renowicz case, anyway. Sam, can you organize a warrant for Alex Renowicz's files?"

Hudson turned to Jill. "Jill, you've got nothing to do. Can you check the paperwork from the Happi Frog and see if Alex or his business comes up? Just don't go traipsing off again."

"What else have we got?" said Kerr.

"Sam and I visited Susan Harvey. She went to Bali the day after Henry Smith disappeared," said Hudson.

"That's pretty suspicious," said Kerr.

"We're keeping a watchful eye on Ms Harvey," said Hudson. "We also found out that Henry had an affair with Ivan's wife, Zoya, prior to *their* marriage. They're both deceased now, so I don't know if that tidbit will have any bearing on the case."

He added the information to the rest on the chart on the wall and then prepared to leave.

Hudson had organized the meeting with Alex at 9:00 am. Kerr lived in Parramatta, so they decided to drive separately, and meet at the nursery.

Kerr arrived first and made himself known. He then introduced Alex to Hudson when he arrived.

What an uncanny resemblance to Henry Smith, thought Hudson. *Totally different in looks to his twin sister, Nina.*

They sat down with the coffee Alex had organized.

"Did you know about the recent fire at Castlereagh?" asked Kerr.

"Yes. That was horrible," replied Alex. "I couldn't believe it."

"Were you involved with the storage plant, at all?"

"I stored the pot plants that needed rejuvenation, at the complex," answered Alex. "My place is too small for the large pots."

"So you knew Colin Jackson?"

"Yes, I did. I can't believe he's been arrested. I don't know what will happen to my business now."

"How did you meet Jackson?" asked Hudson.

"At the Randwick races," replied Alex. "Colin Jackson was there with Henry Smith one day, and Henry introduced us. They invited me to the private box area. Wow! That was something else," exclaimed Alex, obviously remembering something that was a turning point for him. "I feel Henry was instrumental in helping me out, because of his friendship with my father."

"Do you think you'll keep the rotating plant business going, Alex?" asked Hudson.

"I don't think so. Jackson had all the contacts. I just delivered and picked up the plants. He paid me for the work. If I lose that I'll be back to my small nursery, which isn't all that profitable."

"Who was the caretaker at the storage complex?" asked Kerr.

"That was Kevin. I don't know his last name."

"Did you have your own key to get into the place?"

"Only the outside area and the small shed. The old mill was a storage area for the garden ornaments, which belonged to the Happi Frog."

"Did you know anything about the drugs on the premises?" asked Hudson.

"No, nothing at all. I read about it in the newspapers. As I said, I just picked up the fresh plants at the Happi Frog and delivered them to various businesses. I then brought the old plants back to the storage complex at Castlereagh for rejuvenation."

There was a break in the conversation, as Kerr and Hudson made notes.

"Were you in the area at the time of the fire?" asked Kerr.

"No. I was delivering on the North Shore. I heard it on the news."

"Do you know where Kevin lives?" asked Hudson.

"No, sorry, I don't."

"Can I get a list of the clients that used the rotating plants business?" asked Hudson.

There was a slight hesitation before Alex went to a small filing cabinet and retrieved a list of names and addresses.

"Thanks, Alex."

"Do you keep a diary, Alex?" asked Kerr.

"Yes. I do."

"Alex, I have a warrant here to confiscate your filing cabinet, your diary and your computer," said Kerr. He handed the document to Alex who looked shattered.

"But... *why?*" asked Alex.

"Matters about another case," replied Hudson without expression.

Alex could only stand watching as Hudson and Kerr carried out the small filing cabinet and computer into Kerr's station wagon.

"We'll be in touch," said Hudson to a bewildered Alex and walked away.

"What do you think?" asked Kerr as they stood by his car.

"I don't know. And I don't trust my gut feelings anymore," said Hudson. "I'll meet you back at the station, James. In the morning."

Hudson had organized to visit Nina Renowicz whilst in the area.

Nina greeted him at the door.

"It's nice to see you again, Miss Renowicz," said Hudson. He had decided to meet her at the unit. *It would be more conducive to questioning in privacy*, he thought. His heart was beating a little faster at her appearance and by the warmth with which she had greeted him. "I'm sorry it's under such unfortunate circumstances."

"Can I get you some coffee?" Nina asked as she escorted Hudson to the balcony of her unit which overlooked the majestic Nepean River.

"That would be nice," he replied and waited, admiring the view and trying to still the reaction she caused in him.

"As I mentioned on the phone," said Hudson, after Nina joined him and placed a tray on the small table. "New evidence has come to hand which we are now pursuing. May I also mention that this visit is just a general enquiry. My team is gathering information from many other sources."

"I'll help in any way I can," replied Nina.

"Thank you."

Hudson took out his note pad. "We suspect that your father could have been murdered."

Hudson noted that she didn't look surprised. He continued. "There is evidence that there were two people in the house at the time of your father's death."

She took a sip of her coffee but said nothing.

"I'm sorry to break the news to you in this way. It's vital that you level with me, Miss Renowicz."

She appeared to be deep in thought before she spoke.

"I know Henry was in the house on or before the day my father died."

"How do you know that?"

"I found a large brown envelope on the kitchen table. It had my name on it. I automatically picked it up and put it into my handbag when I arrived."

"What was in the envelope?"

"Henry had organized our passports, visas and letters of invitation for our trip to the Ukraine." She started to cry. "Papa was so looking forward to it."

Hudson took a deep breath. The sight of this woman crying was intensely disturbing.

"I have to ask you this, Miss Renowicz. Do you think Henry Smith was capable of murdering your father?"

"No! Never!" she said indignantly. "How could you even suggest such a thing?"

Hudson watched as Nina closed her eyes and placed her hands on either side of her face, rubbing her temples in a pained, circular motion.

"Please excuse me," she whispered and left the room.

Hudson looked out at the tranquil river set against the blue wall of the mountain range. The river shimmered in the sunlight. It was a peaceful scene with the weeping willows swaying in the breeze, and the only sound breaking the silence was the call of the bellbirds. He was mesmerized by the beauty and serenity of the landscape. It was a sharp contrast to his own reality which was filled with violence and twisted plots.

"It's beautiful, isn't it?" she said behind him.

It was obvious to Hudson that Nina had splashed her face with water. Her hair was wet and pulled back with an ornamental clip.

"Yes. It's a great part of the world," replied Hudson. *God, but she's beautiful!*

"I'm sorry. I never believed my father committed suicide. But I can't accept the alternative. Henry was a good person, very empathetic and compassionate. However, my father did comment that Henry had secrets."

"What did your father mean by that?"

"About twelve months ago, Henry came to visit. He brought a small leather case with a medal in it. He asked my father to keep it. My father, who was a historian was intrigued by this medal and asked Henry how he came by it. Henry told him that as a child in Argentina, he found the medal amongst the rubbish his parents threw out prior to their migration to Australia. Henry had retrieved the medal and hidden it in his suitcase. He said his wife, Ruth, had found the medal and would not permit it to stay in the house."

"Do you know the significance of the medal?" asked Hudson.

"No. Only that it belonged to Henry's father. I'm not that interested in medals or trophies," she added with a smile. "What I meant to say is that I don't believe in competition."

"What? Competition is healthy. It gives you self-confidence and encouragement," said Hudson, shifting in the chair.

"I don't believe that. Competition simply means that one person succeeds if another fails."

"Not at all! It's a contest in skills and knowledge."

"Yes. They use their skills and knowledge to triumph over others."

"So," said Hudson. "You don't believe competition promotes motivation and gives people self-esteem?"

"At the expense of losers feeling inferior," replied Nina.

"And you don't believe that it promotes teamwork and positive participation?"

"It promotes rivalry. Competition brings out the worst in people."

"You have just killed my cycling career."

They both laughed.

"We've gone right off the track," said Hudson. "How on earth did we end up debating whether competition was health or unhealthy?"

"You asked me the significance of Henry's medal."

"Why? Was it a sports medal?" asked Hudson.

"Definitely not! It was a World War II decoration, German. When I found out that Henry died." She crossed herself. "I felt the only place for the medal was to be buried with him."

"You weren't curious at all?"

"Not at the time. My father collected all sorts of historical souvenirs, especially war memorabilia. I wasn't interested in that either. I hope we don't get into a debate about war now?"

"No. I have a feeling you would win," said Hudson.

"There are no winners, only victims," replied Nina.

"I agree. Not that I've experienced it personally."

"I think you do experience human tragedy in your police work. It must affect you, even though you're not aware of it."

"Quite the philosopher, aren't you?" said Hudson.

"Philosophy. That's what I loved about Henry's visits." She stood up and walked into the lounge room, returning with a leather-bound book. "We would all sit around the coffee table with a bottle of vodka and coffee and debate philosophy. Mainly the Russian philosophers, Gurdjieff and Ouspensky." She turned away. Tears were rolling down her face. "How I miss them all." She hugged the book close to her chest.

Hudson sat silently. He felt an impulsive urge to put his arms round her. She looked so vulnerable.

He reached for his folder and made a few notes. *She has certainly cleared up a few mysteries. But opened up a Pandora's box as well,* he thought.

"How did Henry die?" she asked suddenly, wiping away her tears.

"I can't discuss that at this stage, Miss Renowicz." There was so much he couldn't discuss. He couldn't tell her that he had just raided her brother's nursery. Nor could he mention the revelation that Henry Smith had an affair with her mother.

Instead he stood up. "Thank you for the information." He held out his hand. "I am so sorry for your loss, Miss Renowicz."

"Thank you."

"If you think of anything else, please do not hesitate to call me."

"I will."

"I hope we meet again, under more favourable circumstances," he said. "Goodbye, Miss Renowicz."

"Nina," she whispered.

As Hudson drove off, he could see her in the rear vision mirror. She was standing in the doorway watching him.

Chapter 41

James Kerr walked into Hudson's office with two Chelsea buns and two coffees.

"Where did you steal those from?" asked Hudson, helping himself to the bun and coffee.

"I hijacked the bakery van."

"Very funny. What's the occasion?"

Hudson took a bite of the bun which was still warm and dripping with butter. The sweet taste of glazing, fruit and cinnamon melted in his mouth as he washed it down with coffee. "This is a bribe, isn't it?"

"Not at all! I'm just celebrating a win. The case is finally falling into place."

"That's good. You can help me with my murder investigation now."

"The frog did it," said Kerr, roaring with laughter at his own joke.

"You're full of it, today!"

"Listen," said Kerr. "You'll love this. We picked up Kevin Zaylen, the caretaker of the storage complex."

"The gnome crusher?"

"Yup. Would you believe, he's married to Helen, the over-qualified horticulturalist who worked in the potting shed. And, wait there's more. Archie, the old gardener, is Helen's father. They were all involved."

"It's quite a family affair," said Hudson.

"Anyway, Jill spent the weekend going through Alex Renowicz's files," continued Kerr.

That girl is a workaholic, thought Hudson.

"Alex is definitely involved," said Kerr. He placed a printout of the rotating plant clients onto Hudson's desk and pointed out the legitimate recipients of plants. "These clients have their full business name, address and contact numbers listed. All are supported with invoices and appropriate documentation. These clients," he said, pointing to a list of generic names, "have no documentation."

Hudson studied the list which consisted of a variety of establishments such as yacht clubs, sports clubs, racecourses and restaurants.

Jill had also highlighted a number of private homes, penthouses and mansions around the exclusive Eastern Suburbs and the North Shore of Sydney. No names, only addresses and dates. It was now obvious that the cocaine was being smuggled into these venues in the pot plants.

Gathering evidence by door-to-door knocking would prove futile. The contraband would be long gone.

"That was an incredible way of distributing the cocaine," said Hudson.

"And collecting the money," said Kerr.

"Jill has done a great job."

"Speak of the devil, here she comes." Kerr beckoned to Jill out in the corridor.

"Don't give him any information," said Jill as she walked in. "Unless he promises to take me sailing on that yacht."

"What yacht?" said Hudson.

"When we confiscated Jackson's assets...."

"Already?" interrupted Hudson.

"Yes. Under the civil recovery of the Proceeds of Crime Act 2002, we can remove the access to assets generated from Jackson's criminal activities, without the necessity of securing a criminal conviction. Amongst the assets suspected of criminal origins was a yacht, named the '*Nymph*'."

Hudson was listening intently. "And you want me to check it out?"

"Yes, if you would," said Kerr. "We're up to our necks with searching Jackson's home and the nursery. Not to mention extracting data from his laptop."

"Did the technocrats break into his computer, yet?" asked Hudson.

"No, not yet. It will take a while to break the passwords before we get to his files," said Kerr.

"Jackson's files will probably be coded, also," said Jill.

"Let me know as soon as you have any information," said Hudson. "I'm damned sure there's a connection between Jackson and Henry Smith's murder."

"Coming back to the task at hand, Matt," said Kerr. "You will have a look at Jackson's yacht?"

"Only if he takes me with him," exclaimed Jill.

"Yes, she deserves it," said Kerr. "She rang all the Marine and Yacht Clubs and found out where it was moored. You might find something interesting."

"Okay, let's go now, before I get bogged down with more paperwork."

"I've got the car out front," said Jill.

"How did you know I'd agree to go and take you?"

"Because you love a challenge!"

Hudson shook his head and muttered something unintelligible.

* * *

Giant eucalyptus trees and towering Sydney red gums lined the steep descent into Apple Tree Bay. The morning light flickered through the branches as they swayed in the updraft of the coastal sea breeze, giving the impression that the road surface was somehow mysteriously moving, as Hudson and Jill made their way down the winding road to the Delacruise Yacht Club. The road clung precariously to the sandstone escarpment which dropped thousands of feet into the valley below.

All of a sudden the greenery gave way to a blaze of aqua, as the idyllic blue waters of Apple Tree Bay hit their eyes.

"This is absolutely breathtaking," observed Jill as she wound down the window.

They rounded the next corner and the marina came into view dotted with a plethora of luxury cruisers, yachts, catamarans and sailing boats.

"How the other half lives," whistled Jill.

Hudson parked the car and they made their way towards the Yacht Club which boasted a fully licensed restaurant, an outdoor function area and a café.

Everything was still closed, except for the café. The aroma of the coffee wafted onto their senses and they succumbed to the temptation. They ordered two coffees with freshly baked scones, jam and cream.

There goes the diet, thought Hudson, remembering that he'd already devoured a large Chelsea bun that morning.

After the coffee, Hudson and Jill made their way towards the moorings, past the yachts and cruisers until they reached Berth 18. The '*Nymph'* was moored in a secluded spot at the end of the mooring.

"Wow!" Jill exclaimed. "We've got a tinny at home that would look like a toothpick moored next to that. You've got the keys, Sir. Let's take her out."

"Settle down, Jill. We're here to do a job."

Hudson helped Jill manoeuvre her crutches across the removable ramp as they boarded the 17-metre yacht. It was like stepping into an alien environment filled with foreign objects.

"Don't trip over all those ropes and gadgets," cautioned Hudson. "I'll check the top deck. You make your way below deck, and yell out if you need a hand."

After a thorough search of the top deck, Hudson made his way down into the galley. He entered the single large saloon finished in wood oak panelling, a fully equipped seating area richly upholstered in royal blue velvet.

"Nothing out of the ordinary up on deck. Apart from the life jackets, the usual things you would expect to find on a boat, like diving gear or fishing rods, are nowhere to be seen," he said to Jill, who had stretched out on one of the luxurious seats. "I see you've made yourself comfortable."

"I don't think Jackson fits the mould of an angler."

Hudson went through the storage cupboards. Nothing but kitchen appliances, some crockery and wine glasses.

"I've checked out the fridge. Half a dozen bottles of wine. No food. Let's hit the bedroom."

"Sounds good!"

"Give it up, Jill."

The very clever use of ergonomics gave the cruiser a very large master bedroom with a queen size bed, a toilet/shower and plenty of storage space.

"I guess we tackle the storage areas," said Hudson.

"A bit more action in here," said Jill. "Wardrobe with clothing, both male and female. Swimwear. Towels. Linen. Toiletries."

"Can you see any drawers under the bed, Jill."

"No. That's a huge bed, though. Maybe the mattress lifts up."

"Don't you go lifting anything. I can manage the mattress."

Hudson lifted the mattress and slid it to one side. The mattress was resting on a solid marine board. Hudson lifted the mattress off completely and stood it up against the wall. He lifted the board and let out a loud whistle.

"Get on the phone to Kerr. Get him to bring the boys in."

Chapter 42

Jackson lay on his bunk staring at the barred window and his lack of freedom. He hated the prison food, the routine and the violence that engulfed the place. As he watched the sun filter through the leaves of the tree branches above him, he thought of Maya.

She was still refusing to visit him.

A face appeared at the grille. "Visitor for you, Jackson."

Jackson jumped off his bunk and followed the warder to the visitors' room.

He was shattered to find it was only Hudson. He held out his hand in a mock greeting that was totally ignored by Hudson.

"I've got some good news for you," said Hudson.

Jackson's face lit up. He immediately thought of his impending bail.

"Tell me. I'm all ears," he said with a grin.

"The good news for us is that we've now solved the double murder. The bad news is that you don't have any cards left to play," said Hudson.

Jackson's arrogant grin faded.

"We found the Luger on your boat," said Hudson. "Your fingerprints were on it." He paused. "Ballistics have matched your gun to the bullet recovered from the small time drug dealer you wasted."

Jackson sat motionless, staring at the table.

"And," continued Hudson, "your gun is identical to the one we found in the home of Ivan Renowicz. Both guns have been traced back to you, Jackson."

Hudson knew he was stretching the truth regarding the ballistic fingerprinting of the bullet. But he needed to outfox Jackson. Just this once.

The colour had drained from Jackson's face and panic replaced the smugness.

Hudson continued. "We've arrested Kevin Zaylen. Right now, he's singing like a canary."

More deadly silence.

"It's going to be a long time before you go sailing on the *'Nymph'* again, Jackson. Or spend a day at the races dressed in fine clothes. Or spend a night with Maya....."

Hudson hadn't finished the sentence when the silence was shattered as Jackson shouted.

"It was Kevin who wasted the dealer! It was Kevin who gave the gun to Alex! It was Alex who shot his father! I'm not taking the rap for anyone!"

Hudson desperately tried to keep his composure. But the cold numbness engulfed him.

"We'll see what the trial brings out," he said.

As Hudson walked out, he heard Jackson screaming, "What about the deal, Hudson? We had a deal."

Two burly prison officers appeared from nowhere and headed towards the visitors' room.

Hudson got into the car and hammered the dashboard with his fist. He looked out at the sports oval adjacent to the Remand Centre.

I should have been a professional footballer, chasing balls, he thought. *Not chasing felons.*

He didn't want to believe what he had just heard. *Why should I take the word of a criminal?* But he could not dismiss what Jackson had shouted to him.

Chapter 43

Jill hobbled into Hudson's office minus the crutches.

"You look like the Hunchback of Notre Dame," Hudson said with a welcoming smile.

"Thanks, you don't look so hot either. Something happen at the jail?"

"Let's just say Jackson is not a happy camper. When's the plaster coming off?"

"Next week. I see you've moved the board around."

"I've just been given a red herring and I'm trying to....."

"We seem to have lots of fishy stories in this case," interrupted Jill. "Let me throw another red herring your way."

Hudson gave her a steely glare.

"I'm serious," she added quickly.

"Jill, I'm up to my neck trying to make sense of this evidence. I've got no time for your comedy routines."

Jill placed the report on Hudson's desk. "I've dissected Henry Smith's file....."

"I wish someone would dissect you! Jill, we don't have the time for this."

"There's something not quite adding up," she said, ignoring his words.

"What did you dissect? A garden gnome or a stick insect?"

"There's a discrepancy."

"What sort of discrepancy?"

"It's the blood. Remember that last report from forensics about bloodstains in the car found to be AB positive? There is also a heap of jargon on DNA stuff from Doctor Ting. Sir, I don't know how you can say that Doctor Ting's reports are simple. I don't understand a word of it."

"Will you stay on track! Please."

"I also went through Doctor Roberts' report."

"Who the hell is Doctor Roberts?"

"Doctor Roberts removed Henry Smith's gall bladder last year."

"So what?"

"There's no mention in the autopsy report that Henry Smith had a gall bladder scar."

"Will you get to the point!"

"My mother has an enormous scar on the right side of her body, just above the hipbone and below the rib cage," said Jill as she pointed the position of the scar on her own body.

"Why are we having a conversation about your mother's gall bladder operation?"

"Because Henry Smith didn't have a scar."

"He probably had laparoscopic gallbladder surgery," said Hudson, tapping his pen impatiently. "Doctors can do the operation with a lighted scope attached to a video camera. I think they make a small incision near the belly button."

"That would explain it, then," said Jill, rather disappointed. "As well as the lapa...whatever, I found that Doctor Roberts' file was quite comprehensive, and the blood type in his report stated that Henry Smith was O positive."

"And?" said Hudson.

"Work with me, please Sir. You're not listening! What did I just say about the blood found in the car?"

"I don't know. Tell me."

"The blood stains found in Henry Smith's car were AB positive," said Jill finally.

"Probably just a typing error."

"I don't think professional people make kindergarten mistakes like that," said Jill.

"I'll check it out. Now can I get some peace?"

Chapter 44

Mike Adams watched carefully as his boss placed his coffee mug precisely midway between the inbox and the pen rack on Mike's desk, eased himself into the seat across from him, carefully arranged his blue tie down the middle of a rather prominent waistline and finally looked at him. The next fifteen minutes could be torrid, Mike knew. His boss was a meticulous man and disturbances to standard operating procedures were not easily tolerated.

"Okay, Mike," the boss began. "A case investigator's job description is to investigate and collate all the reports and then submit them for my approval. Tell me why you have summoned me from my much bigger and suitably appointed luxury office to this junior's hovel to talk to you."

Mike stifled a grin. He and Gareth Jones were not close, but he liked his superior's sardonic humour. "Something about this case smells," said Mike.

"So does your medical degree from a chickenshit university like Sydney," replied Jones. "Unlike my degree from the infinitely superior school at Melbourne. What exactly is it that has offended your olfactory senses?"

"The case is Henry Smith."

"The saga of Henry Smith. I know of it. Okay, run the details." Jones was all business now. There was a great deal of mutual professional respect here and he knew Mike would not have called for his review unless it was serious.

"Crime scene officers got the identification fast," began Mike. "The wallet containing personal identification, a driver's licence and credit cards were found on the victim. Henry Smith's wife later identified his body.

"Yes. Yes, I read the reports," said Jones. "Carry on."

"His fingerprints were also confirmed from an electronic passport, which was found in the glovebox of the car."

"So?" asked Jones. "I'm convinced you positively identified Henry Smith."

"The post-mortem examination was performed by Doctor Ting and the autopsy report revealed a gunshot wound to the suboccipial region."

"Yes, I read all that in the reports. There is nothing new in that," interjected Jones.

"I'll come to that in a moment. Hear me out."

Jones nodded, took his coffee mug and sipped at it, his eyes fixed firmly on Mike. Outside the honks and traffic noise along the road past the Glebe Coroner's Office provided a subdued backdrop to the growing tension in the room.

Jones put down his coffee mug exactly where it had been before and sat back, rearranging his tie again.

"The blood in the car was examined by forensics and the results of the blood spatter found in the car came back as AB positive, which matched the pathology findings. The blood type also matched the type recorded in the biometric information contained in the electronic passport.

"And so we get to it," said Mike. "It has been brought to my attention by Detective Inspector Hudson from homicide, that there's a discrepancy in Henry Smith's blood samples."

"What kind of discrepancy?"

"It has come to light that Henry Smith's blood type was O positive. This information was apparently in the file of Henry Smith's GP."

Mike paused. He knew that he had recommended fast-tracking the release of Henry Smith's body for Maya's sake. He would now have to pay the price.

"Could it be just a laboratory error?"

Mike shrugged. "It could, but unlikely. I'll check it out immediately."

Jones picked up his coffee mug and rose to his feet. "Do that, Mike. It smells even worse than a medical degree from Sydney."

Chapter 45

Mike Adams answered the knock on the door the following morning to a very dishevelled looking Neville Ting. His ashen face and sunken eyes blended into his white laboratory coat, giving him a ghost-like appearance.

"I thought it better if we discuss the results here," said Ting.

"Understandable," replied Mike. "A positive result, I hope?"

"Unfortunately, no!"

Mike poured two coffees and handed a mug to Neville.

"I just left histology and the victim's blood samples are definitely AB positive. I spent hours with the Chief at the Forensic Science Lab last night, testing and re-examining the blood stains found in the car and comparing them to the victim's blood type. All the blood samples have been confirmed as AB positive.

"I also spoke to Doctor Roberts and he confirmed that Henry Smith's blood group was O positive. Henry Smith donated blood to the Red Cross and they also confirmed that his blood type was O positive."

Mike placed his large hands over his face hoping this fiasco would disappear. *Why had no one picked up the discrepancy?*

As if reading his thoughts, Doctor Ting added. "I'd like to mention here that Doctor Roberts' report came directly to your office. I hadn't seen it at all, until yesterday."

"I should have picked it up, Neville."

Neville Ting was quiet for a few minutes. Choosing his words carefully, he said. "The fingerprints, Mike. They belonged to Henry Smith. I matched the victim's fingerprints against the ones in Henry Smith's passport."

Mike lifted his hands off his face, ran his fingers through his hair, and walked around to his desk. Shuffling through his drawers with no idea what he was looking for he turned to Neville. "It's like the domino effect. One missed clue and it all tumbles down. We have no alternative but to exhume Henry Smith's body."

An eerie silence had engulfed the room. Time stood still for Mike Adams and Neville Ting as they both contemplated the consequences.

Mike Adams was first to break the silence. "There's enough cause for the Coroner to grant an exhumation. I'll let him know that the cause of death is questionable, that the identity of the victim is questionable, and that the second post-mortem could possibly bring new facts to light."

Chapter 46

"Bloody horrible start to the week," Mike Adams muttered into the rim of his travel mug. The hot, aromatic coffee tasted exquisite on his tongue and he replaced the mug in the cupholder on the dashboard. The clock above the windscreen said 4:00 am, and he was very warm where he was.

But as he looked out into the night, the doors to the garage opened in the distance, the internal lights revealing the backhoe and a team of workers filing out into the chilly pre-dawn.

Reluctantly, Adams turned off the car engine and got out. The sharp cold hit him immediately and he zipped up his heavy ski-jacket to his neck and pushed down the trilby hat more firmly. His hands in the jacket pocket, he crunched over the frosty lawn of the cemetery to where the screens around the grave of Henry Smith had been erected the previous evening. In the distance, the muffled clatter of the backhoe's diesel engine broke the night's stillness as the machine drove out of the garage and along the path towards him. As it neared, the acrid smell of exhaust fumes wafted past his face and he coughed.

Another small truck appeared; its headlights shone through the nebulous mist that seemed to cling to the gravestones, and every so often frost sparkled like diamonds scattered over the neatly kept lawns. The truck stopped close to the site.

Before him rose a scene from *Close Encounters of the Third Kind* as bright halogen lights, powered by a portable generator illuminated the screens that had been placed around the grave site. The three cemetery workers added to the feeling of an alien landing, dressed as they were in impervious protective bib-and-brace outer garments and white gum boots. Their upper bodies were clad in disposable garments fastened at the neck and wrist, and white PVC industrial gauntlets covered their hands. A disposable mask and protective eyewear covered their faces.

As Mike Adams accustomed his eyes to the powerful lights, another figure emerged from the shadows and then another, all dressed in black, gliding towards the light like phantoms emerging from the door of a haunted house.

One of the men came nearer and held out his hand. "Doctor Adams, I'm Clive Baxter, the cemetery Curator." Adams took his out of the pocket and shook the proffered hand. "I'll need to have that Exhumation Order," Baxter continued. Adams nodded, zipped down his jacket and reached into his suit breast pocket, the cold cutting a sharp edge into his chest as he did so. He pulled out the envelope and handed it over, quickly zipping up the jacket again.

Baxter turned to the other shadow. "This is Dan Grieves from the Department of Health. Mike Adams, Case Investigator from the Coroners Office." Both men shook hands. Clive Baxter opened the envelope, examining the contents by the floodlights.

Another set of car headlights flickered over the scene as a vehicle entered through the gates. As it approached along the winding path, the beams lit up a series of gravestones and some statues, a few still with bunches of flowers by them. The hearse, Adams realized, as he moved towards the three men who alighted.

"Morning all," said Adams. "Quite a crowd for this time of the morning." As he spoke, he wondered what it was that caused people to create forced cheerfulness in such grim circumstances. Nonetheless he greeted them all with a smile and a few nods.

"Not one more than absolutely necessary to meet legal, religious and safety requirements, Doctor Adams," responded Clive Baxter. "Cemetery workers, an Environmental Health Officer, a Clergyman, and two Funeral Directors to receive the coffin. And, of course, the Smith family solicitor. Have you met Charles Dawkins? No? Mike Adams, this is Charles Dawkins."

The pair shook hands. Adams was starting to shiver as the cold seeped into his bones and he wished he had worn a thicker jacket. The priest was deep in conversation with the health officer, their breaths condensing in the air each time they spoke, reminding Adams of the exhalation of the humpback whales he had seen migrating up the coast a few days ago.

"This gives me the creeps," Dawkins confided. "But the family wanted some representation. I suppose you're used to this sort of thing."

"I'll never get used to it, but it has to be done. I just wish they'd get on with it. I'll see what's holding them up," said Adams and he moved towards the digging crew.

"I don't know about you, Jonesy," he heard one man say to the other as they leaned on their shovels. "I don't mind the early start. Double time and ya get to finish early. Plenty of time to go fishin' after lunch."

"Speakin' of food, I could do a nice plate of bacon and eggs about now. I only had a cup of coffee this morning," said Jonesy.

"Excuse me fellas," said Mike Adams, interrupting their conversation. "When are we starting the exhumation?"

"Soon as the health officer gives the word. He's in charge. We just do what we're told, mate."

As if on cue the health officer, having settled his problem with the priest, approached the workmen and said, "Okay. Let's do it."

One of the workers hauled himself up to the controls, turned the key, then pressed the preheat button. Ten seconds later he pressed the starter button and the engine sprang into life with a raucous shattering of the stillness. The thumping of the diesel combined with the rattling of a loose fitting coverplate seemed out of place in these surroundings.

Clanking forward on its caterpillar tracks, the back hoe moved to a position just short of the foot of the grave; the bucket and arm were extended over the grave site, then scooped backwards. The roar of the backhoe fluctuated as the bucket dug into the cold earth and hauled out large clumps of dark soil, swinging a few degrees to one side and dumping the soil on the other side. The backhoe operator quickly and skillfully removed the soft soil as the priest mumbled inaudible incantations from his prayer book. The smell of fresh earth mingled with the smell of exhaust fumes as the machine swung sideways to spew out its load.

Two of the men standing by the side lit up cigarettes whilst they waited their turn and the aromatic smell across his face made Adams long for the habit he'd abandoned years before. In the freezing night, those cigarettes and the backhoe's engine were the only source of warmth, but making no inroads into the cold of the operation. Adams hated exhumations. They made him feel chilled and depressed, even in the summer.

The oily smell of diesel fumes mixed with odour of the industrial deodorant and the images of bacon and eggs produced a feeling of nausea in Adam's stomach. It was obviously too much for Dawkins too, who retreated behind the nearest tree, probably to throw up.

For a further twenty minutes, the scene continued, the machine digging out soil, everybody else motionless. It wasn't long before the soft clunk of steel on wood was heard. Then Grieves held up his hand and the engine died to an idle. Grieves waved it away and the machine reversed from the graveside and began moving back to the garage. Two of the silent men picked up shovels and carefully eased themselves down the side of the deep grave. They began shoveling gently, throwing out the soil to the ground level until one of them made a sound. Under their feet, stems of flowers appeared, still whole after being buried with the coffin, sad relics of the funeral a few weeks before. Even more carefully, the two men simply pushed the remaining soil off the coffin lid to the side but then one of them let out a shout. He bent down and picked up an object. It appeared to be a small cloth packet. He held it up to Grieves who shook his head and pointed to Adams.

The man turned to Adams, who advanced to the edge of the grave and took it. Despite the curious stares of the others, Adams pushed the package into his jacket pocket. It was probably evidence and needed examining in private, away from the public gaze. But a core of excitement ran through him as he recalled Matthew Hudson telling him about the object that a beautiful woman had tossed into the grave after the funeral ceremony. His hidden hand explored the object through the cloth cover. It was metallic, that was certain, with raised patterns along one side.

I can't wait to get back to Glebe and find out what's in here, he thought. *I can always hand it back to the family after I've examined it.*

Below him, the coffin was now clearly exposed. The men with spades and shovels dropped into the void and cleared further, until ropes could be attached to the coffin which was then lifted out of the gravesite, rising like a phoenix into the light of the living world.

A few moments later it lay on the grass. The wood still looked fresh, a few stains from the earth down one side, but no further evidence of deterioration, such as Adams had seen when exhumations occurred years after the funeral.

It was now the turn of the two undertakers, also in protective clothing, to approach the grave with their trolley, on top of which was an outsized coffin, which they placed on the ground. Henry's original coffin was cleared of soil by the workers, then they and the undertakers put the original coffin with Henry's remains into the outsize one, closed the lid and lifted it onto the undertaker's trolley.

Mike Adams noticed that he had been holding his breath for most of the time during these final manoeuvres, and when he did at last inhale, he had a whiff of putrefaction that all the man-made chemical smells could not disguise.

A queasy-looking Dawkins had returned from behind his tree. "What happens now?" he asked Mike Adams.

"Now the workers secure the grave site for safety, then return to their clubhouse in the workshop area and cook up their greasy breakfast. The undertakers drive Henry Smith's remains to our office in Glebe and the rest of the world gets out of bed and goes about its business oblivious to the goings on here," Adams replied. "You had better treat yourself to a strong cup of coffee, Mr Dawkins. You look like shit."

Adams turned to the curator. "Thanks for the co-operation, Clive," he said, and shook hands once more. "Somebody will call you when the autopsy's done."

Baxter nodded. "Bloody awful business, these things," he replied. "I'll be glad when it's done and we can tidy the place up again."

A kookaburra laughed in the distance, apparently amused by these human follies, as the rosy fingers of dawn appeared in the sky over Chatswood. Mike Adams left Dawkins to thank the other officials and take his leave.

The lights were turned out, the truck's headlights resumed their service as the only lights around. Mike Adams walked back to his car, eager to start the engine and get the heater going while he poured another coffee from his vacuum flask. The entire episode had chilled his soul with more than just the cold of the frozen pre-dawn morning.

He drove his car into Entrance Drive and left the chill of the Macquarie Park Cemetery and Crematorium.

His day was only beginning.

Once back at the Coroner's offices, Mike braced himself for the autopsy, which Neville Ting would conduct.

Chapter 47

The medal has finally been retrieved, thought Hudson as he helped himself to a coffee.

"Where is everyone?" he asked.

"They're in the conference room, Detective Inspector Hudson," replied the receptionist. "Mike Adams and Doctor Ting are in there as well."

Hudson nodded and carried his coffee into the conference room. The meeting had already begun, to Hudson's slight irritation, but he said nothing.

Adams addressed the group. "Because of some questions raised after the first autopsy, we found it necessary to exhume Henry Smith's body. We did so yesterday."

"What was the reason for the exhumation?" asked Jill.

"There was an oddity in the blood type."

"And you didn't see all this at the first autopsy?"

Mike Adams looked embarrassed. "No! We didn't."

"Pretty ratshit job, wasn't it?"

Not frightened of authority, our rough diamond. Hudson smiled to himself.

Adams looked furious, but Ting broke in.

"We were very busy that week. We were short staffed, and we had just assigned a new pathologist," he said calmly. "Yes, we missed key signs, and I take full responsibility. I will be supplying a full report to the Minister of Health, the Public Prosecutor and the Police Commander. There's not much more I can tell you, until the second autopsy is completed. We should have the results within a few days."

Shoddy evidence management, thought Hudson. Aloud he said. "Thank you, Doctor."

He turned to Mike Adams. "Mike, you have something for us?"

"As Doctor Ting said we will have the results by next week."

What is Adams not telling us? thought Hudson. "When you exhumed the coffin, was anything else found in the grave?"

Adams was taken aback, but reacted instantly. "Oh, you mean, the pouch? Yes. It was a small family memento, nothing of consequence."

"What precisely was the memento?" asked Hudson, sensing that Adams was being evasive.

"It was just a non-descript medallion, probably meant something to the mourner. I am sure it is of no interest to us or to your investigation."

"All the same, Mike. I'd like to have a look at it."

"I'll look for it, but we may have disposed of it already. I've given a description of the medallion in my report to the Coroner. As I've said before, it was nothing of consequence."

Like hell you'll look for it, thought Hudson. But out loud he said. "Yes, if you would look for it, Mike."

Adams gathered up his paperwork. Without another word he strode out of the room, followed by

Ting, apparently oblivious to the mounting anger in the detective.

Before Adams had reached the door, Hudson cut him off.

"Cuff him," he said to Jill.

"What are you doing?" hissed Jill.

"Watch me," replied Hudson and placed himself in Adam's path, making him stop, an astonished expression on his face. "Mike Adams, I'm placing you under arrest for obstructing the course of justice."

Adams had allowed himself to be led away with a look of amused bewilderment. However, when his wallet and mobile had been removed and the cell door closed behind him, bewilderment soon turned to anger. Adams demanded that he be allowed to make a phone call. He rang the Coroner, Gareth Jones.

The Assistant Commissioner of Police had enjoyed a quiet morning. He was feeling quite mellow and looking forward to a quiet lunch at the City Tattersall's with a local member of parliament and a colourful racing identity, when his phone rang.

"Gareth Jones here. What the hell is going on in your part of the woods?" bellowed the Coroner.

Totally perplexed, Andrew Pelt replied, "Steady on Gareth. What's the problem?"

"You're aware of the Henry Smith case and the subsequent exhumation? Well, that Inspector of yours, Matthew-bloody-Hudson just slapped a pair of handcuffs on my offsider, Mike Adams. Locked him up for some trivial finding at the exhumation. This is totally unacceptable, Andrew!"

"Fill me in Gareth. What trivial finding? What did he charge him with? He must have given him a reason."

"Obstructing the course of justice, or some such meaningless, paltry reason. To answer your first question, the trivial finding was a St Christopher medal tossed into an open grave by a mourner."

"Go on."

"Hudson, for some unknown reason, thought something surreptitious was going on and demanded to see the medal. Adams assured him it was nothing of consequence, and that lunatic, Hudson, decided that Adams must be part of some devious plot and had him arrested."

"Do you have the medal with you?"

"Yes. It's on my desk," replied the Coroner.

"Look, Gareth. I can only apologise. Our guys are under a lot of pressure to solve the murder of this government official and they're probably clutching at straws."

"The press would have a field day if this got out," interrupted Gareth.

"Leave it with me. I'll have Adams released immediately. Can you send the medal to Detective Hudson, ASAP! And again, please accept our apologies."

"Okay," said the Coroner, his voice resembling a deflating tyre. "I hope this kind of thing won't happen again."

"I can assure you it won't go any further."

"Thanks, Andrew."

The Assistant Commissioner's quiet morning had suddenly steered a different course, high blood pressure replacing the mellow mood and an appetite for good food and good company replaced by a flaring ulcer.

He dialled Superintendent Wilson, swearing under his breath at Hudson's egotistical stupidity.

Mike Adams walked through the door of his unit. His anger had not died down since being released from his cell. His mobile rang. It was Maya Smith.

"Is it true?" she asked.

"Unfortunately, yes," said Mike, unable to mask the anger in his voice. "I was arrested by that arrogant bastard, Hudson.

"Are you okay?

"I'm fine. Thank you, Maya."

"Could we meet for coffee?" asked Maya.

"I'm not coming into the city today, Maya. I've decided to have a quiet day at home." He poured himself a scotch.

"Do you want some company, Mike? I could bring some lunch."

"Yes, I'd like that."

The next morning Adams came to work whistling and greeting staff.

"Obviously we all need to spend a night in the cells," said Gareth Jones.

Chapter 48

Like hell, I'll apologise.

If days could get more dismal for Hudson, today was one.

Maya Smith had rung him with abuse that could only be described as lava flowing out of a volcano.

He had been trying to organize an interview with Alex Renowicz who appeared to have performed a *Houdini* act and vanished from the face of the earth.

And he was about to have a conversation with Mike Adams. He picked up the phone.

"Mike Adams here."

"It's Hudson, Michael."

Adams was silent for a moment. "Yes, Inspector," he said.

Some tension and no forgiveness, thought Hudson, hearing the slight grate in Adam's voice.

"Ringing to apologise?" said Adams, the anger still evident.

"No, I'm not. I need to talk to you."

"Go on."

"In person."

"Make an appointment."

"Don't be a fool, Michael. You need to hear this," said Hudson, his voice displaying a threatening tone. It worked.

"I'll see you when you get here," said Adams, the chill very obvious.

"Give me half an hour," said Hudson and hung up without another word.

When Hudson arrived at the Coroner's office, Hudson was shown to Adam's office. The two men didn't shake hands.

"What can I do for you?" asked Adams, sitting formally behind his desk.

"We are currently investigating the death of Ivan Renowicz," said Hudson. He placed the Police and Medical reports on Adams' table. "I believe the Coroner dispensed with an Inquest into Ivan Renowicz's death on your recommendation."

Adams shifted uncomfortably in his chair.

"We also have Jackson in custody, as you know. He seems to be well informed of our investigations." Hudson placed the phone records from the Silverwater Remand Centre on Adams' desk. "Mike, you lied about the medal. I have a signed document from Nina Renowicz about the contents of the pouch," said Hudson, stretching the truth somewhat.

"What do you want, Inspector?" said Adams. He wiped his forehead with a handkerchief.

"The truth, Mike. All of it."

Mike Adams stood up. He walked over to a small cupboard, took out a key and opened a small safe hidden under the counter. He took out a small pouch and handed it to Hudson.

Hudson opened the pouch and retrieved a large medal. He recognized it immediately as an Iron Cross.

"It's a 1939 Third Reich Knight's Cross of the Iron Cross," said Adams. "These medals were awarded to senior German officers during the duration of WW11. Henry Smith's father was a recipient of one of these medals. His name is inscribed on the back."

Hudson turned the medal over. "Frederick Schmidtz," he read out loud.

"I did some research," said Adams, "and traced the name of Schmidtz to Henry Smith. My only crime is that I wanted to protect Maya and her mother," said Adams.

"Mike, I know you're essentially an honourable man. However, I know I'm not out of line in suggesting that information of a sensitive nature has been passed onto Jackson. And, before you deny it, I have confidential evidence that puts you right in with the Jackson operation. Whether you realize it or not, I might be able to help you keep a lid on it." Hudson knew he was playing a bluff. But Adams didn't know that.

"Tell me, before it goes any further," Hudson continued. "What is it that Jackson has on you?"

Adams seemed to shrivel. The pressure-cooker tension permeated the atmosphere, hanging between them, waiting to erupt. Adams took some deep breaths and appeared to regain his composure.

"You probably already know that Jackson and I were at Uni together," he said in a calm voice.

Hudson didn't reply.

Adams continued. "I came from the country and I guess the distractions of the city got to me. We were pretty wild young blokes. Jackson didn't help. He was a real party animal."

Hudson could hear the tone of defeat in Adams' voice.

"One night, after a heavy session of drinking and partying, we drove off with two campus chicks in a Mini Moke. For some crazy reason, we decided to drive up to the headland at Narrabeen. I was driving and doing a pretty wacked out job of it, but we made it to the headland. Jackson took his girl for a walk. I jumped out of the car and asked Margaret O'Malley ..."

Adams paused and turned towards the window. "I've never forgotten her name," he murmured. "I didn't have the handbrake on. The Moke rolled over the cliff with Margaret in it. Jackson took the rap. He hadn't had that much to drink. His father cleaned up the mess. Tragic accident. I've always been in his debt. And yes, I did call him when I thought he was in trouble. But, as God is my witness, I didn't know he was involved in drugs and murder."

Hudson was enjoying watching Adams squirm.

"You know what, Mike," he said finally. "You let yourself get involved with a bunch of real stinkers. We've got our man, and I don't see any benefit to anyone, including the general public, in tearing down the office of the Coroner."

Hudson saw Adams relax for a moment. "I think we'll let it die. Let's just say, you owe me one. Let's hope I never have to collect." Hudson emphasized the 'I.'

The relief in Adams face was conspicuous as he held out his hand to Hudson. Hudson shook it and left the office, taking all the files with him.

And he wins the girl! The emphasis on *'he'* was whispered with venom.

Chapter 49

Gloomy secrets come out at the darkest moments.

Hudson dozed off in the early hours of the morning, only to be woken up by a lick to the ear. That was Tyson's morning ritual. If that didn't get Hudson up, it was a full body launch of thirty-five kilos and a full face lick. Hudson covered his head with the blanket, yawned, stretched and felt the stubble on his chin.

"Yeah, yeah, I know you want a walk."

Tyson bounced off the bed, pleased he had his human so well trained.

Raisin toast and coffee was all Hudson could stomach this Sunday morning, the first day off in ages. His phone rang. To his surprise, it was Nina Renowicz. She sounded worse than he felt.

"I'm sorry to ring you on a Sunday, Matthew. But I need to talk to you."

"What's the matter, Nina?"

He couldn't remember addressing her by her first name before. Nor had she ever called him Matthew. He shook his head. *What had brought on this familiarity?* he thought. He didn't know but he felt okay about it.

"I'd like to talk to you about Alex."

Yes. I need to talk to you about Alex too, thought Hudson.

"What is it?" he asked, bracing himself for an onslaught, given the developments of the last few weeks.

"Could you come over?" she asked.

Hudson, a little bewildered, replied. "Sure. Could we meet in the park below your unit? I'd like to bring my dog. He's desperate for an outing."

"Yes, that would be great. It's a beautiful day here."

"I'll see you in a couple of hours. Say around 11:30."

A little later, Hudson joined the Sunday drivers. Tyson settled into the back of the car, pleased to be included in the outing.

Hudson thought of Nina. Her beautiful, gentle blue eyes. Everything about Nina was gentle. The touch of her hand, when she had handed him a cup of coffee. Her voice, gentle and soft. He had to admit she was very attractive and he felt comfortable with her, despite the circumstances. But this was official business.

He arrived at the park adjacent to the Nepean River at the foot of the lower Blue Mountains. Tyson headed straight to the water and ploughed right in. Hudson picked up a stick. As he threw it into the water for Tyson to fetch, he heard Nina's voice behind him.

It had only been a week since he had last seen her. He was shocked by her transformation. Gone was the gentle person and the harmonious sparkle in her eyes.

In its place was a woman in obvious pain, pale and drawn.

She hesitated then raced into his arms, and in the next moment her entire body convulsed with sobs. He held her tightly until her body went limp, seeming almost lifeless.

Strangers. Thrown together by the most unfortunate circumstances. Their only bond was a hideous crime.

Hudson didn't know what to feel. This wasn't in the police manual. He held her close and gently patted her back.

Suddenly, Tyson was between them, shaking vigorously and showering them both with river water.

"I'm sorry," said Hudson, calling Tyson to heel.

But Tyson would have none of that. He placed both his paws on Nina's white slacks.

"It's okay." She bent down and hugged Tyson. "You are gorgeous."

She picked up a stick and threw it for Tyson. Tyson retrieved it and sat at her feet. She threw it again.

She was covered in mud, but Hudson noticed that the colour had come back to her face and she was giggling.

"My fault," she said. "I could have picked a better outfit than white."

"Tyson loves the water," said Hudson.

He sat down on the grass next to Tyson, who had finished playing and was happy to lie down and guard the stick. Nina sat down on the grass next to Hudson.

Tyson immediately left his stick and laid his paws on her lap.

"I'm so sorry to impose on your day off."

"It's fine. This beats playing ball with Tyson in the park."

Nina had composed herself now. "Matthew, I really need your help. Could we have lunch? I can make us something," she said, her voice soft and shy.

"What about your new best friend?"

"He can come too." She looked down at Tyson. "I'll make you a hamburger."

Hudson brought out a towel from the car and wiped Tyson down. Tyson followed Nina.

Turncoat! thought Hudson, trying not to laugh.

While Nina went into the bedroom to change, Hudson took Tyson out onto the balcony and settled him down in a sunny spot.

A few moments later, Nina emerged. She had changed into a pair of blue jeans and a red singlet top. She had applied fresh makeup, and her blonde hair hung loose around her shoulders. Hudson felt slightly guilty for staring.

"I hope you like foreign food," she called as she walked through to the kitchen.

Hudson watched her defrost some mince meat.

"That's for Tyson," she said. "I'll make him that hamburger."

"He'll be happy with it raw."

"Are you sure?"

Tyson was definitely sure and devoured the meat in three giant gulps.

Nina poured two glasses of Chardonnay. "That's all I have, I'm afraid," she said apologetically before disappearing back into the kitchen.

She brought out two large steaming bowls. "They're called '*vareniki*.' There's potato, cabbage and bacon inside the pastry."

Hudson dipped the *vareniki* into the sour cream.

"They're delicious," he said. The only way he could describe them was a cross between gnocchi and ravioli, but that wasn't even close.

Nina took the dishes inside when they had finished. Hudson followed. Tyson was curled up, asleep.

Nina came out with two coffees and they both settled on the lounge. He felt relaxed in this homely atmosphere.

It wasn't long before the magic spell was shattered.

"It's Alex," she said. "My twin brother. I've lost him."

"Nina. What is it? What's happened?" asked Hudson, stirring to attention.

"It was an accident."

"What was?"

"It shouldn't have happened. It was an accident."

Nina's body shook ever so slightly as if a chill had passed down her spine. Hudson put his hand over hers and said, "Take your time, Nina."

Tears glistened in her eyes. She took a deep breath and slowly gave Hudson an account of the last few days.

"Alex said it was an accident," she repeated. "He had called in to see Papa to fix the back door which had unhinged. While my father got up to make the coffee, he found a gun in Alex's toolbox. When Alex finished fixing the door, he came back inside only to be confronted by my father waving the gun. Alex told me that my father called him a 'no-good gangster.'

"Alex said he tried to tell Papa that he was only looking after the gun for someone. But my father called him a gambler and a good-for-nothing liar. Alex said he pleaded for the gun and my father told him to 'get out'. He called him *'chort, chort,'* which means 'devil.'"

"Alex then told me that Papa said the strangest thing. It just doesn't make sense. My father told Alex that he wasn't his father, and that Alex was evil, just like his grandfather."

"It was probably the reaction of a father disowning a rebellious son," said Hudson reassuringly. "Then what happened, Nina?"

"Alex said my father started to push him and that Alex had tried to take the gun off him. They struggled and the gun went off." She started to cry.

"What did Alex do then?" asked Hudson with deep concern in his voice.

"He panicked and fled. Oh, my God! Matthew, my father could have been saved. Why didn't Alex ring for an ambulance? Papa died alone."

Hudson reached for her hand. "Nina, the wound was fatal."

Hudson held her hand for what seemed an eternity. She finally pulled her hand away.

"Did Alex tell you about the illegal drug dealings?"

"Yes, he did. What will happen to him, Matthew?" she asked as a sheet of panic washed over her face.

"I don't know. I need to talk to Alex. Where is he now?"

"He's taken his wife and children to the Abercrombie River, to a place we used to go as children."

"Can you reach him by phone?" asked Hudson.

"No. There's no reception there. It's very remote."

"Did he say how long he would be gone?"

"About a week. He said he needed to think. My father's house has been sold, Matthew. We'll have money to fight this." She was talking rapidly.

It's not that easy, thought Hudson. With this new revelation he knew he would have to contact the local police in Taralga in an attempt to find Alex Renowicz.

Hudson sat down next to Nina. "We'll have to bring Alex in." His mind was in turmoil. *Did Henry Smith walk in on that?*

He didn't know at what stage he had stood up. But she was in his arms and he held her close. "I'll have to go. I'll call you tomorrow."

The kiss was gentle and spontaneous.

Chapter 50

Jill stared at Hudson's face. "There's something different about you, Sir."

"Like what?"

"You're being nice. It's weird."

"What's so weird about being nice? I'm always nice."

"Yeah! Right! When you're not yelling or throwing things."

"Before I forget," said Hudson, glad to change the subject. "Can you look after Tyson next weekend?"

"Sure, no problem."

Hudson gathered his files, opened the door for Jill then headed for the conference room.

"That's what I mean," said Jill as they walked along the corridor. "You have never held the door open for me before. You usually slam it in my face."

"That's because you're an invalid."

"I don't believe that for a moment. You've become over-protective all of a sudden. Did you ever find out what was in the pouch?" she asked.

"Yup! It was a St Christopher's medal, after all. I'll be apologizing to Mike Adams in the not too distant future."

"There you go again. I would have taken bets last week that you would never admit that you were wrong in arresting Adams."

"I said distant future. *'Distant'* being the operative word."

As he entered the conference room, Hudson looked around. It was unusually quiet. Coroner Gareth Jones, Mike Adams and Doctor Neville Ting sat at one table.

The three musketeers.

Superintendent Wilson, Kerr and Sam occupied various seats around the conference room. The rest of the team stood against the back wall.

What's going on? thought Hudson. *It's like a morgue in here.*

"Is everyone here?" asked the superintendent, as he slowly got up and moved to the front of the room. Superintendent Wilson or 'Koala' as he was known behind his back, not due to his nature but to his bald head and frizzy grey hair that stuck out just above his ears.

Koala finally addressed the group. "Have I got everyone's attention? This morning I had a meeting with Coroner Jones and there have been some startling revelations in the Henry Smith case."

He scrubbed a hand down his face and let out a long, jagged breath. "We need to brace ourselves for a media onslaught, if it comes to that," he said slowly.

Media onslaught? thought Hudson.

"I'll come straight to the point." The superintendent took a sip of water.

I wish you would!

"As you are all aware," continued the superintendent. "We exhumed Henry Smith's body last week. The forensic scientists are still working on the cadaver. However, I can tell you that the information I am about to divulge has been confirmed beyond reasonable doubt."

He walked to the desk where the three musketeers sat and picked up a folder. He slowly opened the folder and flicked through a few sheets of paper.

The suspense is killing me. If he draws it out any longer, we'll have to read it for ourselves in the late edition.

The Koala finally lifted his head, looked around the room, and in a loud clear voice said, "The body in the coffin was not that of Henry Smith."

Chapter 51

This case is like a marathon of vanishing bodies, thought Hudson.

He smashed his fist against the evidence board and swiped the photos and bulletins to the floor. He slammed the door of the conference room and roared at the staff as he headed towards his office.

"All leave is cancelled as from today," he shouted to his bewildered staff.

Jill and Sam followed him into his office. This was not a day to challenge Hudson.

"What a mood swing," Jill whispered to Sam.

"Back to his old self," said Sam with a smile as they entered the office.

"Jill, could you make sure that the family is properly informed?" snapped Hudson. "Get Senior Constable Bloomfield to do the deed. Make sure she takes a social worker with her. Sam, we need to know who that John Doe in the coffin is. Keep in touch with Adams and Ting. Also, get me the list of personal items found in Henry Smith's car. His wife said he never went anywhere without his laptop or mobile."

"There was no laptop or mobile found," said Sam.

"How the hell did they get it so wrong?" asked Jill.

"His wife positively identified his body," said Sam.

"She also identified his clothing and the engraved wedding ring," Jill stated.

"That's right, Jill," said Hudson. "She identified his clothing and the wedding ring. There is no way she could have identified his body. I remember seeing the photos taken at the crime scene and Henry Smith's face was distorted beyond recognition. Facial bones and teeth had been shattered by the exit gunshot wound and his whole body was bloated."

"But the fingerprints belonged to Henry Smith," said Sam. "The accuracy of fingerprinting is over ninety percent."

The detectives looked from one to the other.

"Susan Harvey. Susan-bloody-Harvey," repeated Hudson. "Who else could manipulate something as elaborate as a John Doe's fingerprints into Henry Smith's passport? How the hell would she get access to the machines?"

"Don't forget. She was the queen of hackers and security," said Jill.

"Well. Leave Ms-bloody-Harvey to me," said Hudson, grabbing his coat and heading for the door. "Get the car, Jill. I'll meet you out front. We've got to have answers before the story gets out."

Some time later, Jill pulled into the loading zone at the Department of Immigration.

"I'll bring her out in cuffs if I have to," said Hudson, getting out of the car and striding into the building.

Before Jill had time to gloat about watching the iceberg melt, Hudson was back. "Warm up the siren and head out to Berowra," he ordered.

"What's going on?" asked Jill, as she crunched the car into gear. She steered her way out to the road accelerated hard as Hudson switched on the siren.

"She's gone," said Hudson.

"What do you mean *gone*?"

"Susan Harvey resigned the day after Sam and I questioned her, and...." warned Hudson. "Don't say '*I told you so!*'"

"I wouldn't dare," said Jill. "But you are so losing it with women."

"What do you mean?" snapped Hudson.

"Well, where do I start? You didn't question Maya about why Jackson was at her father's funeral."

"It wasn't appropriate at the time," said Hudson.

"Of course. You were on a date!"

"It wasn't a date!"

"You didn't ask Ruth Smith about the marital bed!"

"How could I? The Rabbi had arrived."

"You always have an excuse, Sir. What about you letting the iceberg escape without getting the name of her Bali companion." Jill was on a roll. "And ..... you failed to interrogate Helen Zaylen after the raid on the potting shed. Do you want me to go on?"

She doesn't let go of anything, thought Hudson.

"You have a fear of rejection, Sir," continued Jill. "You handle women like porcelain. Except me, of course."

"You're one of the boys, Jill."

A gloomy silence ensued.

Hudson lit a cigarette. "I've just given this case a new code name," he said, happy to change the subject.

"What?" asked Jill.

"Evanescence."

"What does *that* mean?" asked Jill.

"To vanish gradually from sight," said Hudson. "Like vapour."

"Gradually? These people are disappearing like a deck of cards in a hurricane," said Jill.

"Why didn't anyone from the Immigration Department ring us when she resigned?" asked Hudson slapping his hand against the dashboard. "Didn't anyone think it was odd?"

Hudson and Jill arrived at Susan Harvey's address in record time, despite the city running at its peak with shoppers.

As they walked down the long driveway towards three single-storey units, a man suddenly appeared from behind the bush, startling Jill.

"Jacob Burns," he said, as he approached them. "And this is Milo. I'm the caretaker." Jill noticed the white ball of fluff under his arm.

"Detective Inspector Hudson and Detective Senior Constable Morellix," said Jill. Hudson was still in a mood.

"I heard the sirens," said Burns. "Figured it would be the law."

"Which unit is Ms Harvey's?" asked Jill.

"She's left. Gone. Almost three weeks ago."

"We'd like to have a look at her unit," said Hudson impatiently.

"I've got an extra key," Burns said. He pulled a large parcel of keys from his pocket, examined them carefully and eventually pulled one off and handed it to Hudson. It had a tag with "Number 3" plainly marked.

"I thought you would have," muttered Hudson. "Jill, you stay and get some info from Burns. I'll check out the unit."

"You won't need the security code," yelled Burns as Hudson walked away.

Jill took out her notebook. "Do you know where she went?"

"Nope. Not a word to anyone," replied Burns. "Kept pretty much to herself."

"Did you see her leave?"

"I was looking out the window when a cab pulled up. A minute later, she came down with a large suitcase which the driver put into the boot. She then raced back into her unit and came out with a pet travel capsule. It was empty. Mind you, I hadn't seen her tiger for almost a week. My Milo has been most relieved."

"Can you remember the date?"

"It was definitely a Wednesday. I had my lawn bowls gear on. Playing in the Pennants that day, I was. Last month on the 9th. We got up. Terrific game and not only ..."

"Congratulations, Mr Burns," said Jill, cutting the trivial chatter short. "Do you remember the time?"

"About 8:00 am. I left shortly after that."

"Can you remember the company name of the taxi?" asked Jill, her fingers crossed hoping that Jacob Burns was sharp enough to remember.

"It was a white sedan. The writing was on the door." Burns was trying hard to remember.

Please try, you old goat. It would save so much work, thought Jill.

He rubbed his chin with his free hand. "No," he said slowly. "The memory is not as good as it used to be."

Damn! "Thank you, Mr Burns," said Jill as she slowly headed for Unit Three.

"It was a Premier Cab," he shouted after her.

"Thank you very much, Mr Burns." She went back and handed him her card, before ringing her office. She entered the building and joined Hudson at Apartment Three.

"How did you go with Mr Burns?" he asked.

"Great! He remembered the name of the taxi company. I've asked Admin to chase up the passenger's destination details. How's it going in here?" asked Jill.

"She was certainly meticulous," replied Hudson. "There's a place for everything, and everything in its place."

"More like obsessive compulsive," observed Jill.

"You could take a page out of her book," said Hudson with a smile in his voice.

"I'm tidy. I know where everything is."

"You might, but no-one else can ever find anything on your desk."

"They don't know where to look."

"I've finished in the bedroom," said Hudson. "Found nothing of interest. She's certainly travelling light. Left most of her clothes. There's also some men's clothing in her wardrobe. See if Burns knows anything about any male visitors. I'll continue here."

Jill walked out and located Jacob Burns' unit. She knocked on the door and heard a dog's bark from inside. But there was no answer. She gave up and returned to see Hudson.

Back in Susan Harvey's apartment, Hudson was rummaging through a large bookshelf as Jill entered.

"Have a scout around the kitchen," said Hudson. "Don't look for the obvious. Look for something unusual or out of place."

Jill was looking through the kitchen cupboards when her mobile beeped and a text message appeared from headquarters with the details from the cab company: Date, name of passenger, phone number, pickup address, time, number of passengers and destination.

"Guess what," she announced, coming back to the room where Hudson was. "The destination for Susan Harvey was Berowra railway station."

"Damn!" said Hudson.

Jill returned to her search. As she replaced the cutlery drawer something caught her eye. It was a small white card protruding from the minute space between the electric stove and the Formica bench top. Jill eased it out with a knife. She walked back to where Hudson had emptied the bookshelf.

Hudson stood up and took the business card from Jill. It had the Australian Government insignia at the top and the name Chad Tohlafitti as the Manager of the Villawood Immigration Detention Centre.

"That was the last place anyone had heard from Henry Smith," said Hudson. "Lock up. We're off."

Chapter 52

"I'll stay in the office and do the usual checks on Susan Harvey's phone accounts," said Jill, handing Hudson the car keys.

"I'm off to Villawood. Tell Sam to keep me posted with any updates."

Hudson drove past the towering walls of barbed wire and entered the Visitors Reception area of the Villawood Immigration Detention Centre. To the left of the reception area stood a large building surrounded by a number of cyclone fences. From a previous visit he knew that this was the high security section and housed single males. To the right were several two-storey, brick residential buildings grouped around a grassed courtyard.

In the centre, at the back of the buildings stood the remains of a burnt out building, its roof and walls collapsed in a heap. Next to it a shell of a building, the interior burnt out. Temporary buildings had been set up in a large grassed area behind the compound.

As he entered the reception area he noticed the large sign stating that no cameras, no video recorders and no mobile phones were allowed into the compound.

Hudson produced his identification, filled in a form and was escorted to an office where he was met by Chad Tohlafitti, the same name on the business card he had found in Susan Harvey's unit.

"Just call me Tofti, everyone else does." The man was huge, nearly two metres tall and built on a wide scale. He would have been intimidating but for the brilliant smile that seemed a fixture on his dark face.

Tofti was quite happy to talk about the compound. He explained that approximately four hundred refugees and asylum seekers were housed at Villawood, most of whom had to flee their countries because of human rights violations.

"As you are aware, we are going through a transition process due to the recent protests," said Tofti. "What can I help you with today?"

"I'd like some information on one of your volunteers, Henry Smith."

"Yes," said Tofti. "The detainees had been asking about him. They were missing his program. And I only found out the other day that he was deceased. Tragic."

"Yes, it was tragic," replied Hudson. "I believe Henry Smith was here during the protests."

"Yes, he was. Henry arrived at the usual time on the Saturday morning. He set up his woodwork just outside the multi-purpose recreation building. About 3:00 pm the alarms went off and it wasn't long before we realized that we had a riot on our hands.

"There were several visitors on site and we hurriedly evacuated them, before securing the compound. Henry Smith signed out at around 4:00

pm. By then the fire fighters and the riot squad had arrived and the place was absolute bedlam. Miraculously there were no injuries," he added. "However, we lost several buildings."

"Do you have security footage of the visitors arriving and leaving?" asked Hudson.

"We do have footage of the arrivals. Unfortunately, the security cameras were damaged by protesters hurling roof tiles around that time. Why do you ask?"

"Was everyone accounted for on that day?"

"There were over a hundred fire and rescue workers and police attending the riots. We had to evacuate staff and visitors. It was bedlam. But to answer your question. One detainee has not been accounted for."

"Who is the detainee that is missing?" asked Hudson. *Please tell me his name is Houdini.*

"It's in the hands of the Federal Police," replied Tofti.

"Can you give me a name?"

"Franco Alavarez," said Tofti with hesitation. "We have not made this public as yet."

"Surely he would be regarded as an escapee?"

"Alavarez was not a high priority case."

"Why not?"

"He wasn't a refugee, as such. Alavarez had overstayed his visa and had applied for permanent residency. All he needed was the application to be approved by Immigration, which Henry Smith was handling."

"Do you have any paperwork or photographs of Alavarez?" asked Hudson.

"It's all been handed over to the Feds."

"Did Alavarez have any visitors during his stay?"

"Apart from Henry Smith? No," said Tofti.

"Do you know how Alavarez left the compound?"

"We believe he left during the kerfuffle somehow." Chad Tohlafitti looked embarrassed. "There was pandemonium and chaos. You understand."

Yes I do, thought Hudson. *I'm up to my ears in people disappearing.*

He thanked Tohlafitti and left.

Chapter 53

Hudson stormed into headquarters. "Round up the mob," he barked at Jill. "Conference room, now."

For a few moments the office looked chaotic as the investigators made their way to the conference room.

"Nothing concrete yet on John Doe," said Sam before Hudson had a chance to ask.

"Jill. Anything?" asked Hudson.

Jill pulled out her notebook. "Susan Harvey made phone calls daily to the Australian Quarantine Inspection Services. I rang them. They're out at Eastern Creek, west of Sydney. Just behind my place at Doonside," she added. "On the Wednesday in question, Ms Harvey's cat, Jaspa, was picked up by an International Pet Transport Service and taken to Pet Carriers International in Mascot.

"After three solid hours on the phone," said Jill in frustration, "there was no Susan Harvey leaving the country and there was no cat on any flight."

This left an opening for Sam to jump in and say. "How the hell did you lose your pussy?"

Everyone cracked up laughing. The tension had finally been lifted.

Tears were still rolling down Jill's face as she added. "I was still chasing the cat around Mascot International Airport, when Sherlock Holmes over here," Jill pointed to Detective Senior Constable Lockey, who took a bow, "suggested I try domestic flights."

"Bingo! The cat and the bat flew to Darwin. Then I lost her somewhere between Darwin and Melbourne."

"She's either paranoid or trying to cover her tracks," said Sam.

After the frivolity died down, Hudson picked up a file. "I think I may have a make on John Doe."

This got the attention of every detective and a flood of questions followed.

"I'm not a hundred percent sure at this stage," said Hudson, "But I should have some more information soon. It's getting onto the Federal Police that's holding me up."

Hudson addressed Sam. "Could you go back to the airport? Get the court order first and this time, check the international male passports to Bali as well."

"Do you think Henry Smith was the mystery man?" asked Jill.

"If not, where the bloody hell is he?" retorted Hudson. "And while you're there Sam, can you follow up if Susan Harvey left the country? She wouldn't have gone to all the trouble with Australian Quarantine if she wasn't serious about leaving the country. She may also be using a false passport."

"I'm sure she could organise a stack of passports," said Jill.

"But," said Sam. "There's not too many pussies leaving the country."

"Get young Cooper on to it. He's good at chasing pussies," yelled one of the officers.

The team roared laughing again.

"That's it, forget Susan Harvey. Follow the cat."

Chapter 54

Richard Jackson SC was sitting in his commodious office studying a brief when the intercom buzzed.

"Yes?"

"There's a Detective Inspector James Kerr wishes to see you," came the reply from his personal secretary.

"Tell him to make an appointment. I'm busy," snapped Jackson.

The large timber panelled door to his office burst open and there stood Inspector Kerr, together with a uniformed constable and a rather large German shepherd.

"Richard Jackson," said Kerr. "I have a warrant for your arrest. Conspiring to import a prohibited substance. You do not need to say anything, but if you do it may be used in evidence. I also have a search warrant for these premises."

"This is outrageous!" bellowed Jackson. "I'll sue you for harassment."

"You can try," said Kerr. "You should have been nicer to your son."

At the same time, the German shepherd started sniffing and sat next to a large drawer situated at the right hand side of Jackson's mahogany desk.

"Open that bottom drawer, Sir."

"And what if I don't?"

"Then I will have to handcuff you as being uncooperative. Open the drawer and avoid the indignity of being cuffed."

Jackson removed a small key from his waistcoat pocket, held it out as if to give the key to Kerr, then ceremoniously dropped it to the floor. Kerr bent down to pick it up and as he did so Jackson flicked out his left foot in a short, but well timed blow that caught Kerr on the eyebrow.

The dog growled and made a lunge at Jackson, but was restrained by the constable.

Kerr stood up and touched the area. No blood.

"Oh, I beg your pardon," hissed Jackson. "An accident."

Kerr's right hand shot out like lightning, grasping Jackson's left hand in a vice-like grip. He swung the barrister around and rammed his arm into a hammer lock. With his free hand he grabbed Jackson's head and slammed his face down into the middle of his work desk.

"Yes, accidents do happen, Sir."

"I'll have your badge for this, you bastard," Jackson stuttered.

A crimson pool of blood had spread across the blotter on his desk pad.

"Why is that, Sir?" asked Kerr. "I'm sure my colleague here will verify that the accident was your own fault."

"Absolutely," said the dog handler. "I saw the whole thing."

Kerr slapped the cuffs on the now shaking Senior Counsel, and frog-marched him out the door. Before kicking the door shut, he turned to the smiling dog handler and said, "Secure and search the area please. I'll escort Mr Jackson myself, just to make sure he doesn't have any more accidents."

Some days are diamonds, and some days are pearls. This one is a five carat diamond.

Chapter 55

"I hear you're filling up the jails fast, James," said Hudson.

"Yup. I'm netting some very prominent fish," said Kerr. "They're all out on bail, and squirming like worms at the end of the hook. My hook."

"You're into the marine biology this morning, James. Jill's right about you. She thinks you've missed your vocation in life as a writer."

"I wish."

"I believe Jackson's lawyers have applied to the Supreme Court for his release on bail," said Hudson.

"I'm still going to oppose it," said Kerr.

"I don't like your chances. Money talks. Is Colin Jackson at the top of your chain?" asked Hudson.

"No, not at all. Mind you, he is a major distributor," said Kerr. "But there is definitely a Drug Czar out there. Someone behind the scenes responsible for the production, transportation, money exchanging and banking."

"I believe it's much harder to nail these guys."

"It sure is. The trend now is to run a smaller operation, involve fewer people and keep out of the spotlight. These smaller operations are mobile and more elusive."

"What's the story on Jackson Senior?" asked Hudson. "Is he behind the operation?"

"I thought the same thing," said Kerr. "But after giving him the third degree, I'm convinced he's only a user and distributor to the rich and famous."

Hudson was quiet for a few moments.

"I'm thinking of paying Jackson another visit," he finally said.

"What for? He'll give you nothing."

"I'm desperate, James. I need a break. The analysts haven't got into Jackson's computer, yet."

"They have managed to break into a few files only to find that everything in Jackson's files is coded," said Kerr.

"It's frustrating," said Hudson.

"It is. We've called for reinforcements from the Australian Federal Police to try and decode these files. They have massively-powerful computers and if anyone can decode the files, they can. Nobody can design a perfectly safe code, not even the military and the spooks. Just wait a few more days."

"I haven't got a few more days," said Hudson. "I've got to find out where Henry Smith is and who was his replacement in the coffin. And I need to decipher the circumstances in order to determine the motive. And everything keeps coming back to Jackson. If you recall, Henry Smith assisted Jackson with his business dealings in Argentina."

"Yes, I remember. Helped with translations, I believe," said Kerr. "Surely Henry would have had to know what was going on."

"I'd say so. That's why I want to go and see Jackson. Bluff him into helping me."

"How?"

"By offering not to object to his bail request."

"What?" Kerr exploded. "You've got to be kidding, Hudson?"

"Look, James," said Hudson. "You can bet your life his lawyers will have references from very prominent people. Jackson will surrender his passport. He will agree to visit the local police station every day. He'll agree to join a rehabilitation programme. I've seen it all before. Jackson will get bail."

"I can't give in to that bastard," said Kerr, shaking his head.

Hudson stood looking out the window and lit a cigarette. *So arrest me. Suspend me. Fire me. I don't give a damn.*

After a long bout of silence, Kerr finally said. "Go for it, Matt."

"Thanks, James. I owe you one."

"I've done my job. The rest will have to be dealt with by the courts."

Chapter 56

Hudson heard whistles and shouting as he emerged from his car and headed towards the reception centre.

"He's out there," said the officer, pointing to the open field behind the complex.

Hudson could see that a game of football was in progress.

"Thanks," he said. "I'll go out and watch the game."

The game was a raucous affair, as players tried to dribble and kick the ball while being tripped up or pushed. It was a soccer game of sorts, but there were no rules.

Hudson was a little bemused as he recognised that the whistle-blowing referee was none other than Colin Jackson.

A makeshift scoreboard stood on a chair behind the goal posts and read: 'Silverwater vs Villawood' in large white chalk letters.

It was obvious to Hudson that the prisoners were playing the recently arrived detainees from the Villawood Detention Centre.

With the game over, the inmates headed towards their living areas. Hudson walked over to Jackson.

"Didn't know you played soccer," he said

"I don't." Jackson didn't seem inclined to converse.

"I need your help, Jackson."

"Screw you, Hudson. Why should I help you?"

"Then do it for Maya." *I hope the rumour that Maya is having it off with Mike Adams hasn't reached Jackson.*

Jackson was silent.

"You probably heard by now that the person we buried was not Henry Smith," said Hudson.

"Shoddy work if you ask me."

"Do you know anything about Henry's disappearance?" asked Hudson.

"No. It was a bombshell to me."

Hudson and Jackson had reached the visiting area and sat opposite each other at one of the outdoor settings.

"You have a court hearing next week," said Hudson. "If you help me, I guarantee we won't oppose your bail application."

"Why should I believe you? You double-crossed me before."

Hudson extended his hand towards Jackson. "You have my word," he said, looking Jackson straight in the eye.

Jackson reluctantly shook hands.

"You still have the Magistrate to contend with, Jackson."

Jackson didn't reply but seemed to have relaxed a little.

"I believe that Henry Smith helped you with language translations for your nursery business?"

"Yes."

"He would have had to know what was going on?"

"He did."

"How did this partnership evolve?"

"I don't want to incriminate myself."

"This conversation is off the record," said Hudson. "However, if you feel threatened by any of the questions, you can refuse to answer."

Jackson looked away.

"Your father would have warned you about coercive questioning. It can't be used against you in a court of law."

Jackson smiled. "My father has been a great help," he said sarcastically. "I've had no contact with him since I was picked up."

"Getting back to the partnership," said Hudson.

Jackson leaned forward. "After Maya and I became an item, I would often go to the races with Henry. That's when I found out that he was a user. Henry couldn't live a day without candy cane."

Hudson was stunned.

"Especially given his age," said Jackson.

"There are no traditional stereotypes when it comes to users," said Hudson. *I don't remember anything about drugs in the toxicology report,* he thought.

Jackson continued. "Because Henry was such a habitual user, I thought it was strange that his tox report was negative."

Took the words right out of my mouth, thought Hudson. He looked at Jackson.

"Maya had a copy of the autopsy report," said Jackson.

Mike Adams again, thought Hudson.

"I know for a fact that the body produces benzoylecgonine as a result of cocaine intake and this can stay in the body for weeks," continued Jackson. "And the dead guy came up negative."

Jackson was on a roll.

"How do you know so much about drugs?" asked Hudson sarcastically.

"I studied medicine before changing to agricultural science. Preferred plants to people."

"After you found out that Henry was a user, what did you do?" said Hudson, trying to keep Jackson on track.

"I ignored it. For Maya's sake."

"Okay. So when did the Spanish translations begin?" asked Hudson.

Jackson paused. "This better be off the record."

"Guaranteed."

"Henry approached me a few months later. He told me that his family in Argentina owned a garden décor factory and would I like to import my garden accessories at a much cheaper rate. Business was slow and I took the punt. Henry made several trips to Argentina to set up the operation."

"You're not trying to pass the buck, are you Jackson?"

"As God is my witness," said Jackson, striking his chest as if making a pledge.

"How did it become..." Hudson was choosing his words carefully, "more than a nursery business?"

"When my shipments arrived there were several boxes marked for Henry's attention which he picked up from the nursery. The business evolved from there."

"Are you telling me that Henry Smith was behind?..."

"You figure it out," said Jackson. "I've said enough." Jackson stood up.

"We've hacked into your laptop and decoded the files," said Hudson, stretching the truth severely. "I'm just trying to fill in the gaps."

Jackson sat down again.

"So much for passwords and encrypted files," said Jackson.

"We have some hi-tech hackers," said Hudson, hoping Jackson wouldn't ask any unanswerable questions.

"Henry was responsible for the financial side of things," continued Jackson. "His family in Argentina were responsible for production and transportation."

"And you handled the distribution," said Hudson.

"I'm giving you more than the bail application is worth," said Jackson with anger.

"Just think, Jackson. You can leave this hell hole next week. The alternative is another six to twelve months until your case comes up."

Jackson stayed silent.

"Where do you think Henry Smith is now?" asked Hudson

"Off somewhere with his floozie."

"Name?"

"She worked with him."

"Did you know her?" asked Hudson.

"Met her a couple of times. She was the one that set up the digital currency and encrypted chat rooms. Cunning as a fox."

Jackson didn't expand any further.

"Do you know anything about Henry's replacement in the sarcophagus?" asked Hudson.

"Not a clue. I started distancing myself from Henry when I figured out that his family of drug cartels were moving here to expand their business. I didn't want to be associated with that criminal element."

Hudson felt like laughing.

"I swear I'll be a model citizen when this is over."

Sure! thought Hudson.

"Settle down and run a legitimate business."

Right!

"Why would Smith abandon his family and disappear?" asked Hudson.

"His marriage was a sham," said Jackson.

"Faking his death was an extreme way out," said Hudson.

"Henry was also under a lot of stress at work," said Jackson. "He was fearful of being exposed and humiliated."

"He seemed to share some of his innermost secrets with you," said Hudson.

"Look. The way I see it," said Jackson. "Henry had a very expensive habit. He was up to his neck in debt, saw an opportunity for wealth and power and took it."

Hudson's mobile phone rang. "Hold that thought, Jackson," he said.

It was Jill.

"The techies have hacked into Jackson's laptop." She was yelling so loud, Hudson had to move away from Jackson. "We have records of all shipment and payments. Names, e-mail addresses and phone numbers. It's all here!"

"Thanks Jill. I'm on my way back."

Hudson turned to Jackson.

"I have to go. Emergency. Good luck next week."

Chapter 57

Hudson arrived at Headquarters and headed for the Technology wing. Kerr greeted him at the door.

"How did you get on with Jackson?" said Kerr.

"You won't believe what he revealed. It was so worth the bail application," said Hudson. "I'll fill you in later. How's the hacking going?"

"We still have a fair way to go according to Brisco," said Kerr.

"I've memorized something Jackson said after I told him we had already hacked into his computer."

"What was it?" asked Kerr.

"He told me Susan Harvey set up the digital currency and encrypted chat rooms. Too hi-tech for me!" said Hudson.

"Excellent!" yelled Bailey Brisco from behind a plethora of screens and wires.

"What does it mean?" asked Hudson.

"Firstly, the digital currency system allows international remittances via the Internet. It's an ideal money laundering instrument because payment is instant. Secondly," continued Brisco. "Users of digital currency may also use encrypted chat rooms to conceal communications between individuals, making law enforcement scrutiny more difficult."

"I can see why *you're* excited," said Hudson sarcastically.

"Can't you see, Sir?" said Brisco. "We now know what to look for. It will make decoding that much easier."

"Good work, Matt," said Kerr.

"I'm glad I've done something right for a change."

"You've been bloody brilliant," said Kerr. "What we've got so far is that Jackson had a legitimate business which Henry Smith saw as a front for smuggling in drugs. Jackson used false invoicing, greatly overpricing goods being imported which would justify large amounts of money being transferred overseas. Now we know that they used digital currency which is a global, borderless world currency system. It allows instant transfers between accounts and payments are instantaneous.

"Anyway, I've got to leave. I've got a meeting shortly with the Australian Federal Police," said Kerr collecting his jacket from behind the chair.

"I've been trying to contact someone at the AFP," said Hudson. Have you got a contact, James?"

"Yes. Federal Agent Coombes."

"Any chance of having a word with your contact?" asked Hudson.

"It's your lucky day, Hudson, old boy," said Kerr. "Lesley Coombes is coming in this afternoon for a meet."

"What time? I'll be there."

Hudson was taken aback as Kerr and Federal Agent Lesley Coombes walked into his office.

It's a 'she', thought Hudson. *And she looks as if she's stepped right out of a James Bond movie.*

Not only was Lesley Coombes the most glamorous person he had ever set eyes on, she had the most amazing presence about her.

Graceful and full of energy. Hudson was sure that every male had followed her into his office, if only with their eyes.

He stood up.

"Lesley," she said, holding out her hand as she greeted him.

"Matthew," said Hudson. He felt instantly at ease with her.

"Tea or coffee?" he asked.

"Coffee please. If it's no bother, Matthew."

Jill knocked, stuck her head in the door and asked if anyone wanted tea or coffee. Hudson smiled to himself. *She's either a mind reader or the biggest stickybeak.*

"Two white coffees, no sugar. Thanks Jill," said Hudson.

"James said you needed some information, Matthew."

"I do. I'm trying to get onto someone who is handling a missing person from the Villawood Immigration Detention Centre."

"You've come to the right person, Matthew. I'm the coordinator for the Federal Police."

"Thank heavens for that. All I kept getting was a royal run-around from your head office in Canberra."

"I'm so sorry, Matthew. Now that you've met me, you can ring me anytime."

She's wearing a Celtic wedding ring. But who cares? Just say 'Matthew' again in that Irish accent.

The door opened and Jill walked in with the coffee.

"Thank you very much," said Lesley, standing up and introducing herself.

"Nice to meet you," said Jill. She walked out and gently closed the door.

This woman has the same effect on everyone.

"What a great team you have, Matthew."

That wasn't the real Jill, thought Hudson, but aloud he said. "Yes, they're certainly co-operative." *All of a sudden.*

"You must be an inspirational leader, Matthew. Now, what can I help you with?" she asked, her voice taking on a warm Gaelic lilt.

Move into this office, please.

"You mentioned a missing person from the detention centre, Matthew."

"Yes," said Hudson.

"I'll try and bring you up to date, Matthew. As you are aware, the Federal police and Customs have been working closely with South American law enforcement agencies concerning the importation of drugs into Australia," she said as she opened the screen on her Tablet PC Notebook.

"The shipments of cocaine have been thorny to follow, as they arrived from different destinations in South America. However, we eventually traced the Happi Frog shipments to a small organization in Argentina run by the Alavarez family and headed by the infamous and ageing Dona Laticia.

Where have I heard that name before? thought Hudson.

Lesley Coombes continued. "Detective Inspector Kerr has just confirmed dealings and contacts with that crime family from the data extracted in Colin Jackson's laptop. Your analyst has done an excellent job."

She stopped and opened another file. "Our agency has also been investigating an Argentine national who went missing during the riots."

She turned to Hudson and said. "I'm sorry this is taking so long."

"That's fine," said Hudson. *Take all the time you want.*

"Here it is," she finally announced. "Franco Alavarez."

"Yes. That's the man I'm interested in," said Hudson. "Have you found him?"

"No! We keep hitting dead ends."

"Join the club," said Hudson. "Dead ends and disappearances have been the major theme of this whole investigation."

"I'm so sorry, Matthew."

Please, let that Celtic wedding ring be a family heirloom.

"Do you have any photos of Franco Alavarez?" asked Hudson.

Before she could answer him, Sam barged in. He stopped in his tracks. "Sorry."

"Come in," said Hudson. "This is Federal Agent Lesley Coombes. Detective Sergeant Sam Gilroy."

Lesley and Sam shook hands. Sam appeared to be fighting internally to let go of Lesley's hand before mumbling. "Nice to meet you."

"Grab a seat, Sam," said Hudson. "What have you got?"

Sam looked at Lesley, then back at Hudson.

"It's okay, Sam. We're discussing the same case. What's got you so excited?"

Sam laid out a photocopy of an Argentine passport next to a photo of Henry Smith. The passport was in the name of Franco Alavarez. The two pictures were of the same man.

"It was Henry Smith, alias Franco Alavarez who went to Bali with Susan Harvey. And it's been confirmed by the Bali cops that he checked into the hotel with Susan."

Hudson hadn't noticed that Jill was hot on the heels of Sam when he barged into the office.

"Henry Smith is still alive!" shrieked Jill. "Holy Mother of ......"

"Are you Irish as well, Jill?" interjected Lesley Coombes.

"Nah! I'm a fair dinkum Aussie."

Hudson and Sam tried to keep a straight face.

Lesley went back to the Notebook. She turned the screen towards the three detectives.

The three detectives gazed intently at the photograph.

The face on the screen was of a younger, leaner man but there was a remarkable resemblance to Henry Smith.

"There's your John Doe," said Hudson.

"Faith and Begorrah!" exclaimed Jill.

"Are you sure you're not Irish, Jill," said Lesley.

"If you give me Franco Alavarez's file and his fingerprints," Jill said to Lesley Coombes, "I'll take it straight down to the Coroner's office and see if we get a match with the dead guy."

"You have such an efficient team," said the Federal agent. "Jill would make a great operative."

Jill beamed.

I'll swap Jill for you, thought Hudson, but instead said, "Thanks Jill. Thanks Sam. Great work."

"I'll leave a copy of the whole file for you," said Lesley. "Including statements from the twenty-two detainees being questioned in Silverwater. Most of the asylum seekers were terrified of Franco Alavarez. Some of them insinuated that Franco's main purpose in coming to Australia was to expand the drug and money laundering operations."

She stood up. "I need to go," she said.

Hudson held out his hand to her. "Thank you so much for the information."

"Anytime, Matthew." She turned and shook hands with Sam and Jill. "If I can get access to a printer," she said. "I'll leave this information with you."

Sam was quick to respond. However, Jill shoved past him and led the agent out.

Chapter 58

Nina had her arm around his shoulder.

Alex had made his statement and was asked to read it before signing. Detectives Inspector James Kerr and Senior Constable John Crosby sat silently across from the Renowicz twins.

"Where does Renowicz go now?" asked Sam, watching the interview on the closed circuit televesion. "His sister wants to post bail."

"He'll be in custody until the hearing on Monday," said Hudson.

"I don't think Kerr will be objecting to his release on bail. Renowicz has no priors," said Sam.

"That could change," said Hudson. "I'm in the process of investigating the accidental shooting of his old man. He could also be charged with manslaughter."

"I hope they don't have to dig up another stiff," said Jill.

"You have such a way with words, Jill," said Sam.

"I hope not. The Coroner's office in enough strife as it is," said Hudson.

"Especially Mike Adams," said Sam.

"I think Alex's biggest problem was that he met Jackson. Sharks like him can smell the weakness in others and use it to entrap and then blackmail and manipulate them," said Hudson.

"Don't forget that Henry Smith introduced them," said Jill.

"What about our Henry Smith?" said Sam. "Kills Franco and swaps identities."

"Looks like it," said Hudson.

"Nearly gets away with murder," said Sam.

"If it wasn't for the keen eye and investigative work of our Senior Constable Morellix," said Hudson. "You might be the rudest cop in the place but I'm proud of you, Jill."

"We're all proud of you," said Sam.

"Gee, thanks guys."

"You're intuitive *and* a lateral thinker," continued Hudson.

"That means you think outside the box," said Sam.

"Don't interrupt, Sam," said Jill. "Keep going, Sir."

Hudson laughed. "You're courageous, straightforward and honest." He held out his hand. But Jill leapt at him with a hug.

"You deserve all the accolades," he said as he hugged back.

"That means..."

"I know what that means, Sam," said Jill, wiping away tears.

Sam hugged her as well. "You're a real asset to the Police Force, Jill."

The phone buzzed and Jill answered, listening intently.

She hung up. "It's confirmed, Franco Alavarez's fingerprints taken from the Villawood Detention Centre's file match the ones initially taken from the body and the e-passport."

"Franco Alavarez is our John Doe," said Sam. "Henry Smith is now a fugitive."

"My theory is that Henry's gone to Argentina and Susan Harvey has joined him," said Jill.

"I believe," said Hudson, "that Franco Alavarez was here to expand the drug business. He was similar in height and colouring to Henry and he seized the opportunity for power and a new life."

"Given the distortion to Franco Alavarez's face from the gunshot wound and the bloating of the body, the big ID mistake was made," said Sam.

"Smith, alias Schmidtz now known as Franco Alavarez, is in the capable hands of the Federal Police and Interpol," said Hudson.

"Henry must have planned his exit for a while," said Jill.

"With the iceberg's help," said Sam.

"I think the drug importation was going on long before Susan Harvey and Colin Jackson were on the scene," said Hudson.

"What do you mean?" asked Sam.

"I think Henry Smith was involved with drugs long before he started to use Jackson's legitimate business as a front," said Hudson.

"It's obvious from the information on Jackson's laptop that the Happi Frog nursery was dealing with the Alavarez family in Argentina," said Sam. "In particular Laticia Alavarez."

"That's it," yelled Hudson.

"That's what?" said Jill.

"The name. I knew I heard that name before."

"Well. Dah." said Jill. "You are so behind the eight ball, Sir."

"An American saying at last," said Sam with a laugh.

"You didn't hear one word that Irish chick said," added Jill. "You were too busy drooling, Sir."

"I was not!" he retorted.

"It's obvious that the Laticia Alavarez in this case was Henry Smith's mother. She went back to Argentina and became the 'Dona.'"

"When did you figure that one out Jill?" asked Hudson.

"From that newspaper article," said Jill. "And the photograph."

"I'll add another thing to your attributes. You've got the memory of an elephant," said Hudson.

"And," continued Jill. "I'll bet Franco Alavarez was a close relative of Henry Smith. Maybe a half brother."

James Kerr interrupted them. "I'm taking Renowicz down to Long Bay. Could you look after his sister, she's quite distraught."

"Where is she?" asked Hudson.

"I've left her in the interview room."

Nina looked up at him. Her troubled and sad blue eyes searching his face for answers.

This would be so much easier if there wasn't a conflict of interest, thought Hudson.

Chapter 59

Dressed in casual dark blue slacks and an open necked, white cotton shirt with sleeves rolled up to the elbows, Matthew Hudson arrived at Circular Quay, the hub of Sydney Harbour. A vibrant and bustling place where people scurried towards the ferry terminals or made their way to the Opera House, the Museum of Contemporary Art, or the many sights that this beautiful harbour had to offer. The buskers and street performers added to the colour and activity. The hustle and bustle contrasted sharply with the quiet beauty of the ocean as it lapped against the wharf.

The harbour was shimmering on this warm summer day. The sun's reflection adding to the magic of the water's iridescence and beauty.

Hudson leaned against the railing. The Sydney Harbour Bridge, affectionately known as the 'coathanger' loomed before him, all fifty-two thousand tonnes of it.

He thought of the many migrants that used the bridge as their focus point on their arrival in Sydney.

When they had the bridge in their sight, they knew that they had made it! he had heard many a traveller declare. Now this mighty landmark had been enhanced by the bold architecture of the Sydney Opera House.

"What a great day for a bridge climb," he heard a female passer-by say to her companion. "I'll bet you could see the Blue Mountains on a day like this."

It *was* a picture perfect day.

His eyes wandered absently, observing the tsunami of colour dashing past. Women in brightly coloured summer wear and tourists in flamboyant clothing, reflecting the mood of the place.

Hudson watched her approach from a distance. She entered the sea of colour standing out in white linen slacks and a white strapless top.

"You look great," he said.

"Thanks."

"Are you looking forward to the cruise?"

"Yes, I am. It's been years since I sailed the harbour, or should I say ferried across the harbour."

Hudson felt a warm inner glow to be alone with her, but he also had the hollow, empty feeling that often accompanied the ending of a major case that had been the focus of his life and thoughts for months. And this case would remain in limbo.

They boarded the *Magistic*. Hudson affectionately put his arm around her waist and ushered her aboard. They moved to the back of the boat to watch the embarkation of guests, mainly couples.

As the cruiser left the wharf, the boat swayed slightly and their bodies touched. She smiled and he noticed her beautiful eyes and her flawless skin, touched lightly with blush. He placed his hand over hers and a shot of electricity ran through his body.

Hudson knew he was recklessly stepping into forbidden territory.

"Complimentary champagne," said the waiter.

Hudson picked up two glasses and handed one to his companion.

"Here's to a wonderful day together," he said.

"You look so much more relaxed away from work," she said with a cheeky grin.

"That's a dirty word, today," he answered, pressing his finger to her lips.

She turned her back to him and watched the Sydney skyline fading into the distance. He put his arms around her waist and kissed her shoulder. Hudson knew that the afternoon, and perhaps the evening, were heading in the right direction.

They ate from the seafood buffet and watched the famous landmarks set against a magical city skyline backdrop.

"Shall we watch the last of the views from the top deck?" she said.

They were alone.

"Do you have to go home tonight?"

She lowered her eyes and the words fell from her ruby-red lips as she whispered. "I'll stay."

Chapter 60

Susan Harvey's heart was beating faster now. The plane was due to land in less than an hour. Her life would be complete. She would finally be with her lover.

She knew he would be angry. At first.

Susan took out her precious cedar box from the holdall under her seat and shuffled through the contents. Her passport. A copy of her lover's last Will and Testament. Photographs of their time together in Bali. She closed her eyes.

A giant clap of thunder shook the plane. The pilot came on the intercom and said something in Spanish. There was a collective groan from the passengers. Susan looked at the flight attendant for reassurance. The female attendant just smiled and indicated that Susan should stay seated, pointing to the 'fasten seat belt' sign which had lit up.

The plane's engines gunned up. At first it levelled and then began to climb.

Susan's heart began to thump against her chest. She could hear it drumming in her ear as she sat motionless, clinging to the armrest. Unable to get her head around what was happening, time ceased to exist.

Then an accented English voice came on the intercom.

"Ladies and Gentlemen. This is your Captain speaking. We are flying a holding pattern around the thunderstorm until it is safe to land."

Susan breathed a sigh of relief and released the grip on the armrests. She looked down and saw that her knuckles had turned white.

The Captain's voice again. "We do apologise for the delay. We have struck exceptionally strong winds and heavy rain and we will experience some turbulence."

For thirty minutes the plane circled. To Susan it felt like an eternity.

Eventually the pilot announced the descent.

Some turbulence! thought Susan as the plane rocked from side to side in the gusting winds.

She tried to distract herself, flicking aimlessly through a magazine.

Suddenly it was still.

She needed to freshen up after the long flight.

Susan unzipped the makeup bag and at that very moment the wheels of the plane hit the tarmac with a bang causing her makeup to spill on the floor.

Susan was embarrassed as passengers, restricted by their seat belts, picked up items scattered at their feet.

There goes keeping a low profile, she thought as people passed the makeup down the line with understanding smiles.

"Thank you for flying LAN Airlines."

Susan looked out the window to discover a wet and gloomy Buenos Aires.

The passengers started to disembark. There was always a rush.

Susan waited.

She finally disembarked and made her way to a fully packed immigration hall. She followed the queue snaking its way towards the counter.

Susan was determined to remain calm.

Finally, after an hour, Susan Harvey handed her passport to a disinterested immigration officer. He swiped the passport, glanced at his computer screen, stamped the passport and waved her through.

Collecting her luggage she made her way through to customs.

She stood in the queue and watched as the overly officious security staff opened bags, rummaged through the contents and finally ordered passengers towards the exit.

Susan remained calm.

It was her turn. The customs officer unzipped her bag. Unzipped the side pockets. After a cursory inspection of clothing, shoes and toiletries, he pushed the bag to one side and asked for her holdall.

She stayed composed.

He took out the makeup bag and placed it on the counter. Next he placed the camera, mobile phone and wallet on the counter, next to the cedar box.

Jaspa's health and vaccination certificate was in her wallet.

If you are here on a tourist visa, why did you bring your cat?

She had rehearsed the answers, just in case.

He opened the cedar box and took out the contents. Opened her passport. Looked at her. Back at the passport. Stared at her.

I've worked in the same area, you moron.

He finally placed the articles into the bag and called for the next casualty.

Susan headed for the cargo counter when a man in a chauffeur's uniform approached her.

"Ms Harvey," he asked politely.

Susan acknowledge him with a slight nod.

"This way, please," he said, taking her luggage.

"I need to pick up my cat."

"That matter has been taken care of, Ms Harvey."

The rain had stopped and it was extremely humid as she stepped out of the main entrance of Ezeiza International Airport. She felt clammy as she followed the uniform towards a black limousine.

The chauffeur opened the door. Cold air gushed out like the blast of a wind instrument.

"Get in Susan," said a voice she knew.

Her spirits soared. She slid into the grey circular leather sofa ready to be embraced by her lover.

But she was met with a dark sinister glare.

"I told you to wait until I contacted you," he said.

"I had to leave," she said, looking into his eyes. He had to understand.

The limo had started to move and Susan glanced around at the luxurious interior. The wet bar area which was spread the full length of the interior housed two crystal decanters and a variety of crystal glasses. Above the bar was a full sound system together with a large television screen. To the right side of the sofa was the communication equipment.

Her eyes met his in the mirror above the bar area and she could see his anger mixed with lust.

He reached for the open bottle of champagne which was sitting in a bucket filled with ice inside a cavity on the counter and handed her a glass.

"To us," she said.

She downed the full glass and he refilled it.

"You know I'll do anything for you," she whispered, reaching for his hand and placing it on bare skin.

She lay back, her eyes scanning the velvet covered headliner with its tiny spotlights. She arched her back.

"I know you will, Susan," he said, his cold hands gripping her thighs.

She moved against him.

A loud beep came from the console.

He picked up the phone and spoke in Spanish.

"*Si. Mama.*"

Then he listened.

"*Si. Mama.*"

He hung up.

"My mother," he said.

Bewildered and confused, Susan posed her question. "I thought your mother was dead."

"No. She's alive and well."

"She's not the infamous Dona Alavarez?" she said almost as a joke.

"The one and only," he said grimly.

Susan was flabbergasted.

"Mama was worried that the police might be able to track you down."

"I've been very cautious," she said defensively.

"It may not be enough."

"I had to leave. The police were going to charge me with murder and blackmail."

He poured another glass of champagne. He fluttered his cold fingers around her inner thighs.

She was aching for him.

His fluttering turned to slow steady strokes.

She was ready for him.

Suddenly he grabbed hold of her hair and pulled her to the floor.

A slow sexy smile spread over her lips at the animalistic fantasies going through her mind.

"Don't worry Susan. The police will never find you."

The shot came like a clap of thunder. It shook the car.

The last thing Susan heard was the ringing of the phone.

"Our problem has disappeared, Mama."